"With *A Line in the Sand,* Al and JoAnna Lacy—a husband-and-wife writing team and Al who's a Western Writers Hall of Fame member—launch a new historical trilogy: The Kane Legacy. Readers who enjoy Westerns with family values will enjoy this lively introduction to the close-knit, gutsy Kanes."

—*Library Journal*

"The Place to Call Home series has been providing me with a great deal of reading enjoyment for the past few months. Each one of the heart-warming books will wrap itself around your heart. There is so much real emotion that can be felt in these delightful characters. Very highly recommended."

—MYSHELF.COM

"The Lacys' love of history and evangelism shines through. *The Land of Promise* beautifully illustrates the joys and sorrows of life for both the Indians and white settlers during the late-nineteenth-century land rush… A stirring, intriguing story filled with endearing characters."

—*Romantic Times BookClub Magazine*

"In *Bright Are the Stars,* the Lacys wove a strong Christian theme of God's saving grace and redemption throughout the story."

—ARMCHAIRINTERVIEWS.COM

"For those interested in history, *Cherokee Rose* is intimately intertwined with the history of the Cherokee people. We get a glimpse of the wise chiefs who made such a big difference in the lives of their people, the congressmen and presidents, as well as the soldiers, who played a part in this very black mark on the historical reality of our nation. This story is also one of God's love, faithfulness, and triumph."

—AUTHOR'S CHOICE REVIEWS

"In *The Land of Promise*, the Lacys detail the accounts of three settler families and the unspeakable torments endured by American Indians forced to give up their land to live on reservations in the late 1800s. Well-researched details and engaging characters make this a moving historical novel. The series will please fans of fast-paced, absorbing tales of the American West and may have crossover appeal for those who enjoy Larry McMurtry's works."

—*Library Journal*

# WEB OF
# DESTINY

# WEB OF DESTINY

THE
KANE LEGACY
BOOK TWO

# AL & JOANNA LACY

MULTNOMAH
BOOKS

WEB OF DESTINY
PUBLISHED BY MULTNOMAH BOOKS
12265 Oracle Boulevard, Suite 200
Colorado Springs, Colorado 80921
*A division of Random House Inc.*

ISBN: 978-1-59052-925-6

Library of Congress Cataloging-in-Publication Data
Lacy, Al.
    Web of destiny / Al and JoAnna Lacy. — 1st ed.
        p. cm. — (The Kane legacy ; bk. 2)
    ISBN 978-1-59052-925-6
    1. Texas—History—Revolution, 1835–1836—Fiction. I. Lacy, JoAnna. II. Title.
PS3562.A256W43 2008
813'.54—dc22

                                    2007037277

Printed in the United States of America
2008—First Edition

10 9 8 7 6 5 4 3 2 1

*This book is dedicated to Jennifer Barrow,*
*our new editor at Multnomah Books.*
*We love you, Jennifer, for your sweet spirit and congeniality.*
*You are a pleasure to work with.*
*3 John 2*

The series of fierce nineteenth-century battles between the armies of the United States and Mexico, which historians aptly call the Mexican-American War, are sometimes dated April 1846 to February 1848. However, the majority of historians who have written on the subject agree that this war actually stemmed from the Mexican army's surrounding the fighting Texans and their Tennessee friends at the Alamo in San Antonio, Texas, on February 23, 1836, and launching the fierce attack on March 6.

This attack, which was led by Mexico's president and chief military leader, Antonio López de Santa Anna, was in retaliation against the Texans for declaring themselves independent of the Mexican government.

In 1835, the people of Texas formed their own government and issued a declaration of independence from Mexico at a large meeting in Washington-on-the-Brazos in southeastern Texas. David G. Burnet was chosen as president of the new Republic of Texas, and General Sam Houston was appointed its military leader.

Thus, the majority of historians who have written of these events actually date the Mexican-American War from February 23, 1836, to February 2, 1848.

A bit of history: The land known as Mexico was conquered in the 1540s by Spain. By the 1730s, Spain had sent several expeditions into the land called Texas and claimed it for their own, since Mexico had claimed it before it was conquered by Spain. The city of San Antonio, Texas, which since 1758 had housed a military post and a Franciscan mission known as the Alamo, had become the administrative center.

Anglo-American colonization gained impetus in Texas when the United States government purchased the Louisiana Territory from France in 1803 and claimed title to all the land from the Sabine River as far west as the Rio Grande. All of Texas was then claimed by Anglo-Americans.

Mexico had remained in Spain's control until 1821, when the Mexican people rose up in determination to be free. They declared their independence from Spain and adopted a federal constitution modeled after that of the United States of America.

There was trouble between the Mexicans and the Spaniards because of this, but no blood was shed. The Spaniards withdrew peaceably when a Mexican revolt in 1833 placed Antonio López de Santa Anna in power. By military might, Santa Anna became the undisputed leader of Mexico.

In mid-1835, when the people of Texas declared themselves independent of Mexico and established their own republic, the government of Mexico was angry. The anger did not subside as time passed. On December 4, 1835, Mexican General Martín Perfecto de Cos brazenly led his 1,400 troops into San Antonio, Texas, and occupied the old Franciscan mission known as the Alamo.

The townspeople were frightened and sent riders to the nearest Texas army outpost to inform the leading officers that General Cos and his troops had taken over the land and buildings of the Alamo. The riders made it clear that the people of San Antonio were in grave danger.

On the morning of December 5, a well-armed band of some 300 Texan soldiers surrounded Cos and his troops in the Alamo.

Five days of battle ensued, and by December 10, 115 of Cos's men had been killed, and 185 had deserted him and run away. Cos and his

1,100 remaining troops threw down their weapons and surrendered to the 290 Texans who were still alive and strong.

When word of the rout reached General Antonio López de Santa Anna in Mexico City, he gathered his military leaders for a joint conference.

News of the conference reached Texas with reports that Santa Anna had declared that he would personally lead his Mexican troops on a punitive sweep across Texas. He would begin by punishing the people of San Antonio for backing the Texan troops in their attack on General Cos and his men.

At the time, Texas army headquarters under General Sam Houston were located at Washington-on-the-Brazos. Houston received the news of Santa Anna's threat and knew immediately that he would have to enlarge his army considerably to defeat Santa Anna's troops when they came to punish the people of San Antonio. Knowing the Mexican troops were going to San Antonio, Houston feared they would use the Alamo as a fort, as General Cos had.

Houston knew it would take Santa Anna better than two months to lead his army from Mexico City to San Antonio. He sent word by Texas newspapers and by word of mouth that he needed at least five thousand volunteers to join the army by March 1 so they could meet Santa Anna and his troops head-on when they arrived at San Antonio.

Time passed, and in mid-February 1836, Houston sent Lieutenant Colonel William Travis to go into Texas towns and challenge men to go with him to destroy the Alamo before Santa Anna and his troops got there. However, as Book 1 in The Kane Legacy, *A Line in the Sand,* related, Colonel Travis and the few men he could gather with him were forced to use the Alamo as a fort.

On February 23, 1836, in retaliation against the Texans for having declared themselves free from Mexico the previous year, Santa Anna and his troops surrounded the Texans who were fortified at the Alamo defending their freedom. On March 6, Santa Anna's army attacked the Alamo and killed every man behind its walls. The Mexican-American War, then, actually extended from February 23, 1836, until a peace treaty was signed between the two countries on February 2, 1848.

During the twelve-year period of 1836–1848, it was never the American government's desire to be at war with the Mexican government, but it seemed that the United States was caught in a web of destiny that forced them to fight Mexico, no matter how hard they tried to avoid it.

In the first book of The Kane Legacy, readers were introduced to the Kane family of Boston, Massachusetts, in early April 1834. Forty-nine-year-old Abram Kane, his wife, Kitty, and his four sons—Alex, twenty-eight; Abel, twenty-six; Adam, twenty-three; and Alan, twenty—were dock workers in Boston Harbor. The Kane brothers also had a sister, Angela, who was twenty-one. Kitty was quite ill with tuberculosis.

Born the son of Abner and Elizabeth O'Kane in Ireland on February 21, 1785, Abram was brought to Pawtucket, Rhode Island, in 1792. Neighbors in Pawtucket invited the O'Kanes to a Bible-believing church a short time later, and eight-year-old Abram found Jesus Christ as Saviour, as did his parents.

Within a year, Abram's paternal grandparents, Alexander and Maureen O'Kane moved from Ireland to Pawtucket and soon received Christ also. Abram was brought up in that solid church, and in his Christian home was taught the value of family living and hard work.

In 1793, since they were now living in the United States, the O'Kanes decided to change their last name to Kane.

In 1804, when Abram was nineteen, he married eighteen-year-old Kitty Foyle, who was also Irish and a fine, dedicated Christian who belonged to the same church in Pawtucket as the Kanes. The young couple moved to Boston shortly thereafter and found a good Bible-believing church there. Abram found employment as a dock worker in Boston Harbor. As Abram and Kitty's children came along, they gave them names that started with an *A*, which had been a tradition in the O'Kane family in Ireland for over a hundred years.

As their sons grew up, they joined their father as dock workers. In time, however, Adam and Alan decided they wanted to get into a business of their own. Alan had become well-acquainted with a wealthy Texas cattle rancher named William Childress, who often brought cattle hides to the East Coast to sell them. A Christian himself, he offered Alan and Adam jobs as ranch hands on his large ranch. The two brothers felt sure that if they took the jobs, one day they could have their own cattle ranch in Texas and do well.

Kitty Kane died in late April 1834. As time passed, Alan went to Texas first and was soon followed by Adam. On the trip that Alan took with William Childress, he and the rancher stayed with some close Christian friends who owned a large cotton plantation just outside New Orleans, Louisiana. Alan met their lovely daughter Julia and fell in love with her. Unaware of Alan's feelings for her, Julia Miller showed him kindness and spoke of their being very good friends. She even allowed him to call her Julie, which her close friends did. When Alan reached the big ranch in Texas and went to work, his thoughts were continuously on Julia.

Before Adam was able to make the trip to Texas, Childress died. Alan learned then that because he had saved the ranch owner's life a short time earlier at the risk of losing his own, Childress—who was a widower without children—had willed the ranch to him. Alan also came into a great deal of money from Childress's bank accounts.

Several months later, Adam made the trip to Texas. William Childress had told him earlier that the Millers would let him stay in their home in New Orleans while he waited for the boat that would carry him to Texas. When Adam and Julia were together those few days during his stay, they fell in love, but neither told the other. Adam went on to Texas, not knowing that his younger brother was also in love with Julia.

When Adam arrived at the ranch, he was surprised to learn of William Childress's death, of the ranch and money that had been willed to Alan , and that Alan had already legally made Adam half owner of all of it.

During the time since Alan had left Boston, much had been in the newspapers about serious trouble between the people of Texas and the government of Mexico, which was led by dictator Antonio López de Santa Anna. It seemed that war was inevitable.

Since the ranch now belonged to Alan and Adam Kane, they sent for their father, sister, and brothers, along with their brothers' wives, offering jobs and houses to Alex and Abel and homey places for Abram and Angela. The offer was gladly accepted by all.

As time passed, Alan decided that he must make plans to go to New Orleans to tell Julia that he now was wealthy and that he loved her and wanted to marry her. In the meantime, however, Adam—who did not know how Alan felt about Julia—took time off and went to New Orleans. There, Julia admitted that she was in love with him, and they were married.

When Adam came home to the ranch with Julia and announced that he and Julia were now married, the news hit Alan with a powerful jolt. He kept his love for Julia a secret, not wanting in any way to hurt Adam or his new bride.

Time passed and in early 1836, it was certain that Santa Anna and his Mexican army were coming to Texas to take it over. Alan and Adam learned of the need for volunteers to go with Colonel William Travis to San Antonio. Leaving their family at the ranch, they joined the other soldiers at the old Franciscan mission known as the Alamo, just outside of San Antonio. They ended up facing the fact that Santa Anna and thousands of his troops were already on their way. In late February, the Mexican troops had the Alamo surrounded, but they were waiting for more troops to arrive before they attacked.

Alan was sent by Colonel Travis to bear a message of their need of help to General Sam Houston, leader of the Texas army, who was situated on the Brazos River in east Texas. Even though Alan had to ride through the camped Mexican troops at night, risking his life to do so, he willingly went.

At dawn on March 6, 1836, the 182 men in the Alamo were attacked by thousands of Mexican soldiers, led by Santa Anna. By nine o'clock that morning, every man in the Alamo had been killed. One woman had been at the Alamo, Susanna Dickinson, wife of Captain Almeron Dickinson. She and her fifteen-month-old daughter were spared by Santa Anna and allowed to ride away on her husband's horse.

Susanna and her baby were some five miles outside of San Antonio, on their way to Gonzales, Texas, when she came upon a camp set up by citizens of San Antonio when they had fled their homes several days earlier, in the fear of the approaching Mexican troops. Moments later, Alan Kane came riding up on his way back to the Alamo. He was shocked to hear of the attack and that his brother Adam was dead, along with all the other men in the Alamo.

Susanna knew of the risk Alan had taken in order to ride through the Mexican troops at night, and in front of the crowd said she thought Alan's name ought to be changed to Alamo because of the risk he took to go for help. The people agreed. Alan told Susanna and the people that it would give him a special closeness with Adam.

When Alan arrived home at the ranch, he gave his family the sorrowful news of the deaths at the Alamo. He then explained why he had not been there and told them of Susanna Dickinson's suggestion that he now be called Alamo Kane. The family also agreed.

Alan "Alamo" Kane still had deep love in his heart for Julia, of which she had no idea. While spending some time alone that evening with the grieving, brokenhearted Julia, Alan was informed that she was expecting a baby, which would be born in late September or early October. Alan said he wished that somehow Adam could have known about the baby. Julia said that maybe in heaven the Lord had already told Adam that his little son or daughter was on the way. Alan agreed.

Then after Julia had reminded him that they were still good friends and that she still loved him, Alan went to his room in the ranch house and knelt in prayer. "Lord, You know I am still in love with Julie. The love she feels for me is a friendship love. Maybe…maybe someday, Lord, when she is over the jolt of losing Adam and becoming a widow who is expecting a baby, You could change that love in her heart toward me so it is like the love I have felt since I first met her. Maybe…maybe someday she could become Mrs. Alan—er—Mrs. *Alamo* Kane."

## 1

As the brilliant light of the Texas sun appeared on the eastern horizon on the morning of March 6, 1836, the Alamo was a tumultuous bedlam of barking rifles, roaring cannons, and shouting men. The acrid smell of burned gunpowder filled the smoky air.

Lifeless bodies of Mexican soldiers lay scattered outside the Alamo's battered stone walls. Others, still alive, lay on the ground in agony, their bodies torn by bullets and shrapnel. Inside the walls, many of the Alamo's defenders already lay dead and wounded as the battle went on.

While firing their cannons and rifles, the Texans atop the stone walls could see Generalissimo Antonio López de Santa Anna as he rode his white horse back and forth out of cannon range, shouting encouragement to his troops.

Along the walls, determined Mexican soldiers were raising ladders, leaning them against the walls and scrambling upward to gain entrance into the Alamo. Many were successful, and once inside they were met by gallant defenders wielding rifles, bayonets, revolvers, and bowie knives. Both Texans and Mexicans were going down, dead or wounded.

At other places along the walls, the stubborn men of the Alamo met the Mexicans with rifle butts, striking their heads and faces savagely, sending them to the ground outside the walls.

With the Alamo cannons firing into the swarms of charging Mexican infantrymen on all four sides, the Texas riflemen at the parapets on the walls had relatively easy targets to pick off with their rifles. But it seemed that no matter how many of the Mexicans fell, hundreds more took their places.

From where he stood atop one of the walls, Alan Kane could see Santa Anna's cavalrymen charging at a full gallop while firing their rifles at the men who controlled the cannons and occupied the parapets.

The Texans were taking their toll on the enemy, but fear touched Alan's heart as he saw thousands more Mexican troops running across the Texas plains toward them. A tight knot formed in his stomach. *The few men defending the Alamo don't have a chance.*

A cold shiver slithered down Alan's back as he ran his gaze over the dauntless fighting men of the Alamo and recognized most of them. He saw Captain Almeron Dickinson standing a few yards inside the west wall, where it was possible to scale the stones and drop down within the confines of the Alamo. Dickinson was blasting away with his revolver to defend his position.

Alan saw Colonel William Travis, sword in hand, standing on the south wall shouting orders to his men. Davy Crockett was on the ground near the north wall, firing his rifle at Mexicans who had made it over that wall.

Suddenly Alan's eyes focused on his brother Adam, who was atop the wall several yards from him, loading a cannon. Alan recalled that Adam had been trained to fire the big cannons. Alan tried to rush to his brother's aid, but his feet would not move. Adam was ramming gunpowder and a cannonball into the mouth of the cannon so he could fire it into the hordes of Mexican troops that were coming in waves across the prairie.

Alan blinked as he saw six or seven Mexicans scale the wall from ladders, aim their guns at Adam, and fire. Alan's eyes bulged with terror as the bullets ripped into Adam's body. Still, his feet would not move.

Adam fell to his knees clutching his midsection, which had taken most of the slugs. The Mexicans who had shot him laughed as one of them kicked him in the face and sent him rolling to the edge of the wall, where he lay flat on his back.

Alan saw Texans charging toward the Mexicans who had shot

Adam, firing their rifles. Three Mexicans were hit and peeled headfirst over the wall. The others jumped to the ground inside the wall, trying to get away. The Texans dashed past the fallen Adam Kane, intent on killing the Mexicans.

Alan's feet were finally able to move, and he ran across the top of the wall to his fallen brother, where he skidded to a halt. With the roar of the battle thundering in his ears, Alan looked down at Adam, who lay in a pool of blood. The sight tightened Alan's chest like cold steel bands.

Adam's droopy eyes widened when he saw his brother kneel beside him, realizing that somehow Alan had made it back to the Alamo after going to General Sam Houston for help, as ordered by Colonel William Travis.

Adam saw the terror on his brother's face. Alan was hardly able to speak as he gasped, "Adam, I don't want you to die! I—"

The touch of Adam's shaky hand on his arm cut off Alan's words.

Adam swallowed hard and said in a broken voice, "I *am* dying, little brother… But I will meet you in heaven." His eyes closed, and his head flopped to one side.

Alan's chest was heaving. "Oh, Ada-a-a-a-am-m-m!" he cried loudly and breathlessly. "No-o-o! Don't die! Ada-a-a-a-am-m-m! Don't die!"

Suddenly, Alan "Alamo" Kane found himself sitting up in his bed at the Diamond K ranch house, his own loud words echoing in his ears. Gasping for breath, he heard himself cry out at the top of his lungs, "No! Adam, no! I want you to live!"

Down the hall of the ranch house's second floor, Julia Kane raised up on her elbows in bed, rubbed her eyes, and looked toward the bedroom door. Alamo had invited Julia to stay in the big ranch house because it would still be too hard for her to return to the house where she and Adam had lived.

The loud cries from her brother-in-law's bedroom had awakened her. He was still crying out that he wanted Adam to live as Julia left her bed. By the dim light of dawn that was filtering through the curtains, Julia put on her robe, took a candle from the small bedside table, and felt around for a match.

Alan wiped his sweaty face with the bed sheet, dabbed at his tears, and looked toward the bedroom windows. He had not closed the curtains before going to bed the night before, and now he could see dawn lighting the sky.

He sniffed, rubbed his face and eyes again, and thought about how his own voice crying out had awakened him. Then it came to him that this was Thursday morning, March 10, four days after the battle at the Alamo, where every man had been killed—including his beloved brother Adam. He took a deep breath and shuddered in mortal agony. "I—I was having a nightmare! I—I was only dreaming. Oh, Adam… Oh, Adam!"

The effect of the horrible nightmare was still lingering on Alamo Kane as he wiped his face with the sheet again and breathed out the words, "Oh, dear Lord, it was as if I was there with Adam when he died. He—"

Alamo then recalled Adam's dying words in the nightmare: "I *am* dying, little brother… But I will meet you in heaven."

Tears burst from Alamo's eyes. "Yes! Dear Lord Jesus, Adam is with You right now in heaven. Thank You, Lord! Thank You for that time in our lives when Adam and I received You into our hearts as our Saviour. I *will* meet him in heaven!"

Suddenly there was a tap on Alamo's bedroom door, and he heard Julia call to him, "Alamo, are you all right?"

He pulled the covers up to his neck, choked slightly, and called, "Come in, Julie!"

The knob turned, and Julia opened the door. She took a couple of steps into the room, holding the lighted candle level with her chin. The flickering flame illuminated the tired lines in her face. Her long, dark brown hair was plaited into a single soft braid that hung over her shoulder. Sleep still misted her eyes as she peered toward the bed by the faint light of dawn that was coming through the windows and the yellow glare of the candle flame.

"I heard your screams from my room. Are you all right, Alamo?" As Julia spoke barely above a whisper, she took a few hesitant steps farther into the room.

"I'm all right, Julie," Alamo replied, reaching toward the lantern on the small table beside his bed. "Just a minute. I'll light the lantern, and you can blow out the candle."

He wiped his shaking hands down his face in an attempt to remove the tears that the nightmare had produced, then struck a match, lifted the glass chimney, and touched the flame to the wick. The glow of the lantern flame quickly brightened the room, leaving the far corners still shrouded in shadow. He put the chimney back in place.

Julia blew out the candle flame, then stepped up beside the bed. "I—I heard you crying out to Adam, telling him not to die, that you wanted him to live."

Alamo swallowed hard. "Julie, I was having a nightmare. I dreamed I was in the battle at the Alamo last Sunday. I saw all those men I knew getting killed. I saw Adam get shot by Mexican soldiers, and I knelt at his side. In my terror, I told him I didn't want him to die. He said to me, 'I *am* dying, little brother… But I will meet you in heaven.' Oh Julie, it was as if the Lord let me be there at the Alamo when my brother died. Of course, it was only a dream, but it was like I was really there!"

Julia bent down and touched his face tenderly. "Oh, Alamo. Adam will indeed meet you in heaven, but I hope you won't have any more nightmares about his death." Her heart was breaking at the anguish on her dear brother-in-law's features. Alamo's eyes were closed as he bit down on his lower lip and shook his head.

At the same time, Julia felt a presence at her side and turned to see Alamo's sister, Angela. She smiled and nodded.

Angela slipped her arm around Julia's waist and pulled her close. "Is he all right? I heard him crying out."

Alamo opened his eyes and looked up at lovely Angela. "I had a nightmare, Sis. I dreamed that I was at the Alamo. I—I watched Adam die." Tears filled his eyes. "He said he would meet me in heaven."

Angela reached down, closed her fingers around her brother's hand, and cradled it in her own. Julia touched his face again.

At that instant, Alamo Kane felt a soft shaft of peace pierce his heart. Running his teary gaze between the two young women, he said, "I'm so fortunate to have my family living here on the ranch. All of you have been such a blessing to me."

Angela gripped his hand tighter. "It is a blessing for all of us Kanes to be able to share our heartaches together and to depend on one another when we need help."

"That's for sure, honey," Julia said softly.

"Yes," nodded Alamo. "That's for sure."

Julia took a deep breath and let it out slowly. "When I was reading my Bible last night before going to sleep, the Lord brought some verses to my attention. They meant so much to me that I memorized them right then and there: Psalm 147:3–5. It says of our loving God, 'He healeth the broken in heart, and bindeth up their wounds. He telleth the number of the stars; he calleth them all by their names. Great is our Lord, and of great power: his understanding is infinite.'"

Alamo blinked at his tears. "Oh yes, Julie. Those verses are precious. We know that God feels our pain and is ever merciful to help us."

"Amen," said Angela. "His grace is always sufficient, and He will never leave us nor forsake us."

Tears were now in the eyes of all three heartbroken young people.

With his free hand, Alamo wiped tears from his cheeks with his palm and said, "I appreciate both of you coming to see about me. I think you should go back to your beds now and get some rest before it's time to get up for the day."

Both young women nodded. Angela kissed Alamo's hand, let go of it, and smiled at her brother. "I'm sorry about the nightmare, Alamo. I haven't had any nightmares since learning of Adam's violent death, but I have had a hard time getting a good night's sleep."

Julia looked down at her brother-in-law. "I'm still not sleeping soundly since you came home and told me that Adam had been killed." She then leaned over and planted a kiss on his forehead. "You stay here and get some rest yourself."

He smiled and nodded. "For a little while. I love you both. May God's peace and grace rest upon us all."

As the two young women left the room, Alamo put fingertips to the spot on his forehead where Julie had kissed him. He closed his eyes and held his fingertips there. "Lord, please one day, when the impact of Adam's death has eased for Julie...let her love me like I love her."

When Julia entered her room and slipped back between the covers, she burst into tears. "Oh, dear Lord, I miss Adam so much! Help me! Please help me!"

Sniffling, Julia let her thoughts go back to the time when Adam came to her parents' cotton plantation in Louisiana on his journey to join Alan in Texas...and how she and Adam had fallen in love.


Angela stepped into her room and closed the door behind her, leaning back against it. Her heart fluttered like the wings of a frantic bird. She could hardly breathe. The pulse in her throat, caused by her pounding heart, made her voice tighten as she closed her eyes. "Oh, Lord in heaven, please help Julia. She's trying so hard to keep control of herself. I could sense it the whole time we were in Alamo's room. Adam's death has hit her so hard."

Angela drew in a shuddering breath, walked to the bed, and sat down. "Lord, my heart goes out to Julia, as You well know. With her baby coming, I know she must be thinking a lot about the fact that this baby won't have a father."

She swallowed hard. "Dear Lord, I know Alamo has tried hard to camouflage his feelings for Julia, and he has done it well. I'm sure she has no idea how he really feels about her. But as his sister, I have seen enough in his eyes when they are together to read his thoughts. I may be wrong, Lord, but I don't think so. I believe he is in love with Julia. I—I am asking, heavenly Father, that You let it work out between them. Julia's baby is Alamo's nephew or niece, but it's going to need a father. How wonderful it would be if Julia could fall in love with Alamo after enough time has passed for her to adjust to Adam's absence and they could marry! Please, Lord. Make it happen."

Angela thumbed tears from her eyes and swallowed hard again. "And dear Lord, once again I ask You to work in *my* life. I'm twenty-three years old. Most women my age have been married three or four years by now. There are some fine young Christian men in our church. Some of them are employed right here on the ranch. But nothing has developed with one of them because it has not been Your will."

Angela sniffed. "I'm sure You have the young man You have chosen to be my husband somewhere. I don't mean to push You, Lord, but would You send him to me sometime soon? Please? You know that some of the married women on the ranch have been jokingly calling me an old maid, but it's beginning to get to me. Please, dear Father, send him soon."

Angela slid between the covers, closed her eyes, and prayed some more for Julia.

In Alamo's room, as his nerves began to settle down, his thoughts went once again to his brother's widow. He had fallen in love with Julia Miller when he first met her, which was some time before Adam had met her.

Alamo sat up, leaned against the headboard, and closed his eyes. His thoughts drifted back to the trip he had made by ship from Boston with William Childress in June 1834, on his way to work as a ranch hand at the Circle C Ranch in Texas. They had stayed a few days with Childress's Christian friends, the Justin Miller family, who owned a large cotton plantation just outside New Orleans.

Alan "Alamo" Kane sighed as he recalled the very moment he first laid eyes on beautiful Julia Miller and fell in love with her…

Alan and rancher William Childress had been riding in the backseat of a hired buggy from the New Orleans docks at sunset on June 28. The driver put his horse to a brisk walk and headed through the city.

As the steel-rimmed wheels rumbled over the cobblestone streets, William said, "I haven't really told you much about the Millers except that they're Christians and they're wealthy. They also have two beautiful daughters."

Alan met his gaze. "Oh really?"

"Mm-hmm. Sally is twenty and Julia is eighteen. Sally has a young man who belongs to their church that she's been dating steadily for some time, but even though many of the young men in the church have shown interest in Julia, the last I knew, she didn't have a steady boyfriend."

Alan nodded.

"Fine family, Alan. You'll like them."

Alan let his eyes roam to the lamplighters on each side of the street doing their job in the gathering dusk. "I'm sure I will, boss."

A bayou mist gathered among the moss-covered oak trees as the buggy rolled out of the city. The steel-rimmed wheels were comparatively quiet on the soft dirt road. It was totally dark as the buggy, its own lamps burning, had pulled up to the Miller mansion. A silver moon was rising in the east. Alan had a momentary feeling of unreality as he stepped from his side of the buggy while William stepped from the other. The mansion was exquisitely beautiful. The sound of countless crickets and fireflies flitting about only added to Alan's feeling of fantasy.

Moments later, Justin Miller welcomed his old friend William Childress in the vestibule, saying that his wife and daughters would be coming downstairs soon. William introduced Justin to Alan, explaining that he had met Alan in Boston and was taking him home to be one of his ranch hands. He quickly added that Alan was a fine Christian young man from a good Christian family. Mr. Miller shook Alan's hand and welcomed him warmly.

William looked Justin up and down and asked, "Ol' pal, why are you dressed up so fancy?"

"Well, *ol' pal*," Justin said, "we're attending a dinner this evening at the Dardanelle plantation. Sally and the Dardanelles' oldest son, Jeffrey, are formally announcing their engagement to the guests at dinner. Most of those guests are from our church in New Orleans, including the pastor and his wife."

William's eyes widened. "Oh! So Sally's going to marry that steady boyfriend of hers!"

Justin chuckled. "She sure is."

William and Justin talked about how quickly Sally and Julia had grown up. Then Justin said, "William, I'm sorry we have to be gone this evening. I hate to go off and leave you and Alan."

William gave him a warm look. "Hey, it's all right. We both understand. Alan and I will get a good night's sleep."

Presently, two lovely ladies approached the top of the stairs. At first Alan thought it was the Miller sisters, but as they moved down the stairs, he could see that one of them had to be the mother. He wondered if the younger one was Sally or Julia. Her dark brown hair was done in an upsweep, revealing a lovely, slender neck. She was strikingly beautiful. *The kind of woman a man dreams about,* Alan thought.

When the two ladies reached the bottom of the stairs, they were introduced to Alan, and he learned that the beautiful young woman was Sally. After they exchanged greetings, another young lady appeared at the top of the stairs and immediately caught Alan's attention. *This must be Julia.*

Alan swallowed hard at the sight of her and blinked. Julia's long, dark brown hair swirled around her head and lay softly on her elegant shoulders.

Alan watched her descend the spiral staircase with ease and grace like a dove descends from the blue. He thought, *Sally is beautiful, but Julia is* stunningly *beautiful!*

Julia's deep blue eyes fell on Alan as she neared the bottom of the staircase, and she gave him a warm smile. Alan felt his heart turn to flame. Somewhere deep within him, a drum seemed to thunder, vibrating his rib cage. Alan knew it. He had fallen in love!

William said, "Julia, I want you to meet Alan Kane."

Alan felt his knees turn to water as the stunning Julia Miller gave him her hand. "I'm pleased to meet you, Miss Julia."

William told Julia that he had met Alan some time ago in Boston and had hired him as a ranch hand. He was taking Alan to the Circle C. "Alan's going to work on the ranch and learn the cattle business. His brother Adam is coming down from Boston shortly to do the same. They plan to one day have a big ranch of their own in Texas."

Julia looked at Alan. "Your brother Adam?" she said with a giggle. "Is he as tall and handsome as you?"

Alan's face flushed. "He's…uh…he's exactly the same height as me, Miss Julia, but Adam is lots better looking."

She smiled. "I have a hard time believing that."

Alan's face flushed again.

"One's as good-looking as the other," said William. "And I want you to know that Alan is part of a fine Christian family, and he is dedicated to the Lord. He and I are going to church with all of you tomorrow."

Julia smiled at Alan. "I hope your new career as a cattle rancher works out well for you and your brother, Alan. I am glad to know that you have Jesus in your heart."

Yes, Alan Kane had fallen in love.

⌒

Now, sitting there in bed, Alan "Alamo" Kane remembered the day when his brother Adam made a return trip to New Orleans to visit the Millers a second time and brought Julia back with him to the ranch, announcing that they had gotten married.

The blow Alan had felt was powerful, but he hadn't let on. And since that day, he had never let Adam or Julia know that he was in love with Julia. She felt a friendship love for him, not knowing that he was head over heels in love with her and had been since the day he first met her.

Alamo's attention was drawn to the brightness now entering his room, and he looked toward the nearest window. The radiant morning sunlight was streaking across the sky.

He rose from his bed and was soon using his straight-edge razor at the mirror to plow through the shaving soap on his face. As he shaved, he thought of the baby in Julia's womb…his little nephew or niece. He told himself that since Adam had arrived in heaven, the Lord no doubt had told him that Julia was carrying his baby.

When he was finished shaving, Alamo splashed cool water on his face, used a towel to dry it, then put away the razor and shaving soap. His love for Julia still throbbing in his heart, Alamo looked upward and spoke almost the same words he had prayed the night before.

"Lord, You know I am still in love with Julie. The love she feels for me is a friendship love. Maybe someday, Lord, when she is over the jolt of losing Adam and becoming a widow who is expecting a baby, You could change that love in her heart so it is like the love I've felt for her since we first met. Maybe someday she could become Mrs. Alan—or as she would probably be called now—Mrs. *Alamo* Kane."

He picked up the comb before him, looked at himself in the mirror, then closed his eyes. "Lord, please keep my heart true to Julie if she's the one You have chosen for me."

Alamo combed his hair, dressed, and headed downstairs to eat breakfast with Julia and Angela.

## 2

When Alamo Kane entered the dining room, his sister and sister-in-law were seated at the table. His elderly cook and housekeeper, Daisy Haycock, was just pushing in a small cart bearing bowls and pans of hot food and a steaming coffeepot.

When Angela and Julia smiled at him, Alamo noticed that they both looked a little more rested than when they had been in his room at dawn. The smiles that greeted him appeared to be genuine and not forced.

"Good morning, little brother," said Angela. "Did you get some rest after we saw you in your room?"

Alamo nodded as he drew up to the table. "Yes, I did."

"Good!" chirped Julia. "I'm glad to hear that."

The tall, handsome young rancher bent down and kissed his sister's cheek, then moved to Julia and did the same. Only when his lips touched Julia's cheek, his heart did a secret *flip-flop*.

Daisy turned and looked at her boss with a smile. As per usual, he kissed her cheek also. She then ran her gaze from Alamo to the two young women. "You two were in Alamo's room earlier this morning?"

Angela nodded. "Yes. He had a nightmare about Adam's death at the Alamo and woke us both up crying out to Adam, telling him not to die."

Daisy's brow furrowed. "Oh, I'm so sorry, Alamo. Since my quarters are built onto the ranch house, I don't hear anything that goes on in here. If I'd heard you crying out, I sure would have come too."

Alamo smiled as he sat down at the head of the table. "It's all right, Daisy. I'm over it now. I'll be fine."

Daisy finished placing the hot food on the table, poured each of the Kanes a cup of coffee, then wheeled the cart toward the dining room door. "Hope you enjoy your breakfast. See you all later."

"Oh, we'll enjoy it, Daisy dear," Alamo said. "When it's *your* cooking, it is always enjoyed."

Daisy giggled as she moved through the door. "Flatterer!"

"It's not flattery, sweetie," said the boss of the Diamond K Ranch. "It's *fact!*"

Daisy could be heard giggling as she moved down the hall toward the kitchen.

Alamo reached toward the young women with both hands, and they each met his grasp. He felt a special tingle in the hand that Julie was touching. They bowed their heads, and he led them in prayer, thanking the Lord for the food and for sustaining them as they leaned on Him to help them adjust to Adam's death.

Alamo sipped coffee while Julia and Angela filled their plates and then his own. Not since his brother's violent death had he felt any kind of hunger, but this morning the aroma of ham, eggs, coffee, and biscuits was welcome. Looking up, he was aware that instead of just toying with their food, Angela and Julia were eating and enjoying it. He could tell that the Lord had answered the prayers he had offered for them. In his heart he said, *This is good for all of us, Lord. Thank You for Your comforting hand in our lives.*

While the three Kanes were devouring Daisy's fabulous cooking, Alamo looked at the young woman who unknowingly owned his heart. It took only seconds for her eyes to meet his. "Julie, have you written to your parents to let them know about Adam's death?"

Tears moistened her eyes. "Yes. Just yesterday. A couple of the ranch hands who were going to town in the afternoon took the letter and mailed it for me. I also told Mama and Papa that I'm expecting the baby. I told them that he or she will be born in late September or early October, as I told you. I hadn't written to Mama and Papa about the baby yet since I've only been sure of the pregnancy for just a few days."

Alamo nodded.

Julia dabbed a napkin at her tears. "I wish I could be there with my parents when they receive the bad news of Adam's death and the good news of the baby."

"I'm sure you'd be a real help to them over Adam," said Alamo. "And it would be such a blessing for you to be there when they learn that a baby is on the way."

"Yes," put in Angela. "I wish it could've happened that way."

Julia smiled at her. "Mm-hmm. I certainly wish I could see my parents. But like someone has put it, 'If wishes were horses, beggars would ride.'"

Alamo chuckled. "Wouldn't they though?" An idea tugged at Alamo's mind. *Maybe Julie's parents would like to come to the Diamond K for a visit. I'll have to think on this for a little while, then see how Julie might feel about it. It certainly would be quite difficult for her to make that long trip from here to New Orleans in her condition. But just maybe the Millers would come here.* He hid a smile behind his coffee cup as he picked up a small piece of biscuit.

Julia set her soft, deep blue eyes on her brother-in-law. "Alamo, there *is* a wish I have that really *could* come true."

Alamo swallowed the piece of biscuit he had just put in his mouth. "And what's that, Julie?"

"Well, it has been on my heart since you told us about escorting Susanna Dickinson and her baby to Gonzales. One day in the not-too-distant future, I'd like to go meet Susanna and talk to her. Since she is the last person still living to have seen Adam before he was killed, I'd like to talk to her about Adam's final days. Since there were relatively few men at the Alamo, I'm sure she was at least somewhat acquainted with him."

"No doubt." Alamo flashed her a smile. "To tell you the truth, I've been thinking about riding to Gonzales just to see how the dear lady and her little daughter are doing. I've had something on my mind that I'd like to do for them."

"What's that?"

"Well, I know that Susanna's friends, Arthur and Delia Washburn, took her and little Angelina into their home, and they mean well doing this for them. But these friends are in their late fifties and aren't wealthy. Having another family to house, feed, and provide for may eventually become difficult. What I've been considering is to offer to build a house for Susanna and little Angelina right here on the ranch. I would also provide for all their needs until Susanna should marry sometime in the future."

Angela's deep blue eyes widened, and a smile curved her mouth as she placed her fingertips to her lips and held them there a few seconds. "Oh, little brother, that's wonderful! You're so generous!"

He chuckled. "Well, Sis, after all, I owe it to Susanna that I am now *Alamo* Kane!"

Both young women giggled. Then Julia said, "I *love* that name! And I agree with Angela. You *are* so generous!"

Alamo's handsome features flushed. "I—I just want that dear lady and her baby taken care of. It may be that she'll marry again before I can get a house built, but I want to at least make the offer to her."

Angela gave him a soft look. "So when are you going to Gonzales to speak with her?"

"Right away. Julie and I can leave the ranch at dawn tomorrow morning and take a wagon to Gonzales. That all right with you, Julie?"

A bright smile lit up Julia's lovely features. "It sure is!"

Alamo nodded. "Good. Tomorrow is Friday. It will take us till late Saturday morning to get there. We'll stay in a hotel in one of the towns along the way tomorrow night. I'll get you a room at the hotel and another for myself."

Her heart overflowing with a welcome gush of delightful emotion, Julia said, "Oh, thank you, Alamo! I just know it will help me to learn about Adam's last days on earth from Mrs. Dickinson! Thank you so much!"

"I'm sure it will help you immensely, Julia," Angela said. "I'm glad Alamo is going to take you."

With breakfast over, the Diamond K's owner excused himself and left the house to see about work that needed to be done in one of the corrals. Both Angela and Julia carried dishes, bowls, pans, and silverware to the kitchen, saving Daisy the effort.

Having the trip to Gonzales to look forward to gave Julia a happy day. As she went about helping Daisy and Angela around the big ranch house, she told herself that having a talk with Susanna Dickinson about Adam would bring a measure of peace to her heart and some closure to this tragic event. While at her house later that morning, as she packed a small bag for the excursion, she even found herself humming a nameless tune.

~

On that same day, Thursday, March 10, 1836, while Julia Kane was humming her nameless tune at the Diamond K Ranch, General Sam Houston, the military commander of the Republic of Texas, was looking over his army on the west bank of the Sabine River in southeast Texas. Just across the river to the east was Louisiana.

Several days earlier, Houston had taken most of his Texas army with him from Washington-on-the-Brazos in hopes of getting volunteers from the nearby towns along the Sabine to join him. Colonel William Travis and his 181 men at the Alamo were facing an eventual attack by Mexican Generalissimo Antonio López de Santa Anna when all of his 6,500 troops arrived from Mexico.

Running his gaze over the 141 volunteers he had gained along the west bank of the Sabine, forty-three-year-old Sam Houston gave them a big smile. He removed his dark blue, wide-brimmed hat—which matched his uniform—and ran his hand over his receding hairline. "I very much appreciate all of you men volunteering to go with my soldiers and me to the Alamo to help Colonel Travis and his men fight off the Mexican army."

The volunteers smiled in return.

Houston gestured toward his men in blue. "I brought 577 troops here to the Sabine with me, and it is definitely encouraging to know that I now have 718 fighting men as we head for the Alamo."

One man among the volunteers, who looked to be in his early fifties, spoke up. "We're all loyal Texans, General Houston. We're glad to go with you to fight Santa Anna and his troops!" With that, he removed his hat and waved it vigorously.

The rest of the volunteers waved their hats in the same way, calling out encouraging words to General Houston and the troops who stood in a semicircle.

Clapping his own hat back on his head, the general said loudly, "All right, men! I'm ready to go to the Alamo and help Colonel Travis. He had sent a young man named Alan Kane to request help. Are *you* ready to go?"

Hats were once again being waved by soldiers and volunteers alike, while the men shouted back enthusiastically that they were indeed ready.

At that moment, one of Houston's captains pointed northward, up the bank of the river. "General! Look!"

Every eye turned to see what the captain was pointing to and caught sight of a group of riders coming toward them. Houston and his soldiers immediately recognized Major Fred Kitchell leading the group. Just behind Kitchell, riding three abreast, were the six uniformed men General Houston had left with Kitchell at the army post in Washington-on-the-Brazos. However, behind the uniformed men were a good number of riders in civilian clothes that Houston and his men did not recognize.

As Major Kitchell rode up and pulled rein, he smiled at Houston. "I'm glad, General, that you and your troops haven't already headed for the Alamo."

Houston grinned and took in the riders behind Kitchell, especially letting his eyes focus on those not in uniform. Then he looked back at Kitchell. "Major, if this is what it looks like, I'm *mighty* glad we haven't yet headed for the Alamo!"

"Well sir," responded Kitchell, "it definitely *is* what it looks like. In the past five days, I've had 58 men come to the post in Washington-on-the-Brazos and volunteer to go with you. They read in the *Washington Post* about what's going on at the Alamo and your need for more fighting men. They are eager to fight Santa Anna with you."

Houston smiled. "Fifty-eight, eh?"

"Yes sir."

Houston did some quick arithmetic. "Great! This will bring my force up to 776! I wish you and the 6 men I left at the post with you could go along too, Major. That would give me 783. But, as you know, I need you and those 6 to look after the post in Washington-on-the-Brazos."

"I understand, sir." Kitchell saluted. "We'll head on back now."

Houston saluted in return. "Okay. Good work, Major. See you when we get back."

"Yes, General. Please *do* come back." With that, Kitchell gestured to his 6 men, and they rode away.

Houston then spoke to his newest volunteers, thanking them for coming. The other men raised their voices, expressing their appreciation to the new volunteers also.

After making sure that every volunteer had his weapon—or weapons—and plenty of ammunition, General Houston led them northwestward toward San Antonio and the Alamo.

It was almost eleven o'clock on Saturday morning, March 12, when Alamo and Julia pulled onto the main street of Gonzales. Holding the reins, Alamo glanced at the lovely young widow. "The Washburns live on Elm Street. It's just two blocks off of Main at the next corner."

Julia smiled. "You're the driver, Mr. Kane."

Alamo chuckled. "Well, you're quite observant, ma'am."

"Why, thank you."

The young widow turned her face away as Alamo moved the horses up Main Street and rounded the corner eastward to Elm Street. As Alamo guided the two horses onto Elm, he pointed to a white frame house halfway down the block on the right. "That's the Washburn house down there. The one with the three cottonwoods in the front yard."

"Oh yes." Julia's voice quivered. "It's a pretty house." She reached over and placed a shaky hand on his arm.

Alamo looked at her, and his brow furrowed as he saw tears coursing down her pale cheeks. He immediately pulled rein and stopped the wagon. Placing his own hand over hers, he asked quietly, "Julie, what's wrong?"

Trying valiantly to stem the flow of tears, Julia gulped back a sob and in a faltering voice replied, "I—I can't say—exactly what's—wrong, Alamo. I—I want to talk to Mrs. Dickinson, but…I guess… I guess what's bothering me is that it's going—going to make it all so final. You know, hearing about Adam's last days. Do you understand?" Her clouded eyes searched Alamo's questioning features.

Alamo stared at his feet for several seconds, then looked up at her. "Yes, sweet Julie. I understand how you feel. Very much so. But for your own good, I think you need to go ahead and talk to her. Hopefully she'll have some things to tell you that will put your mind at rest."

Julia sniffed and used a hanky from her dress pocket to wipe the tears from her eyes and cheeks. She took a deep breath and looked at her brother-in-law. "Let's go."

Alamo smiled. "Good girl."

Moments later, Alamo turned the horses into the Washburn yard and drew rein, halting the wagon close to the front porch. He hopped off the wagon, tied the reins to a post that was there for just that purpose, and helped Julia down from the wagon seat. He took hold of her arm as they moved up to the porch and steadied her as they climbed the steps.

Alamo knocked on the door, and within seconds they could hear footsteps inside. The door opened, and when Delia Washburn saw the tall man with the sandy hair, she smiled. "Alamo Kane! How nice to see you!"

Alamo introduced Julia as his sister-in-law, reminding Delia that it was her husband—and his brother—who was killed at the Alamo. Delia took hold of Julia's hand, welcomed her, and told her how sorry she was for the loss of her husband. Julia smiled and thanked her. Then Delia invited them in.

"Mrs. Washburn," Alamo said, "Julia asked me to bring her so she could talk to Mrs. Dickinson. Is she here?"

"I certainly am, Mr. *Alamo* Kane," came the voice of Susanna Dickinson as she walked toward the foyer, carrying her little fifteen-month-old Angelina.

Alamo introduced Susanna to Julia, and the instant Susanna heard Julia's name, she wrapped her free arm around her, telling her how sorry she was that Adam had been killed at the Alamo.

Little Angelina looked at Julia with big brown eyes. Julia caressed the baby's cheek and wiped tears from her own cheeks as she thanked Susanna for her sympathy.

Alamo explained to Susanna that Julie had asked him to bring her to see Susanna for a very special reason. When Susanna asked Julia what it was, she wiped more tears. "Mrs. Dickinson, you were acquainted with my husband, I assume."

Susanna smiled and nodded. "Yes, I was. He was such a fine man."

Julia bit her lower lip. "Thank you, ma'am. He sure was. I just wanted to ask you about his last few days of life. Could you tell me anything that might make me feel good?"

Susanna smiled. "I sure can. Let's go sit down in the parlor."

Delia lifted a hand. "Ah…Julia, Alamo… May I feed you at lunchtime? It'll be noon in just a little more than half an hour."

"We'd be honored to have lunch with you," said Alamo.

"Yes, we sure would," Julia said.

"Arthur is in downtown Gonzales at the moment buying some things at the hardware store, Alamo," said Delia, "but he'll be home in time for lunch."

"Good. It'll be nice to see him again," said Alamo.

"And I'll be glad to meet him, Mrs. Washburn," Julia said.

"We heard so much about you from Alan—I mean, *Alamo,* dear," said Delia. "I know Arthur will be as glad to meet you as I am."

Julia warmed her with a smile. "I'm honored, ma'am."

Delia ran her gaze over the faces of Alamo, Julia, and Susanna. "You all make yourselves comfortable in the parlor, and I'll bring in some coffee."

"Thank you, ma'am," Alamo said. "Julia is carrying Adam's baby, which he didn't even know about. I'm sure she'll appreciate having a comfortable place to sit. Those ranch wagons leave a lot to be desired in the comfort department."

Delia and Susanna looked at each other, brows furrowed. "I'm happy to hear that you're expecting, Julia," Susanna said. "I'm just sorry that the baby won't get to know his or her father."

"Me too." Delia touched Julia's arm. "Any of the overstuffed chairs or the couch are quite comfortable. You go sit down with Alamo and Susanna, and I'll bring the coffee."

As Delia hurried toward the kitchen, Susanna led the way to the parlor. When they entered the room, Julia and Susanna sat down together on the overstuffed horsehair couch. Alamo asked if he could hold Angelina, and Susanna placed her in his arms. He then sat down on an overstuffed chair facing them. Angelina seemed to remember him and was quite satisfied on his lap.

Susanna turned toward Julia, and tears welled up in her eyes. "Sweetie, what I am about to tell you will make you feel good, I'm sure."

"You think so?"

Susanna nodded. "I had several opportunities to talk to Adam while we were at the Alamo, and from the moment we met until the last time we talked—the day before the big attack—Adam spoke so much about *you*."

Tears filmed Julia's eyes. "Really?"

"Really. He brought up several times what a wonderful wife you are and gave lots of reasons why he felt that way. He also talked about how beautiful you are, both outside and inside, and about how very much he loved you."

Tears were now coursing down Julia's cheeks.

After quoting some of Adam's exact words about Julia, Susanna explained that she and little Angelina had been staying in a small room in the Alamo missions building since arriving there with her husband. Upon mentioning Almeron, Susanna choked up and took a few minutes to get a grip on herself.

Julia patted her hand.

When her emotions were reasonably back under control, Susanna told Julia that on Sunday morning, March 6, when the Mexican troops attacked the Alamo, she and Angelina were in their room. She explained that the room had only one small window, which allowed her to see very little of the battle, though she heard the cannons roaring, the rifles and revolvers firing, and the men shouting.

As Susanna talked and Julia listened, they were unaware of Delia slipping into the room with coffee and cups on a tray. She quietly set the tray on a small table beside the couch and filled the cups with the steaming coffee. Suddenly both women saw her, and Susanna cut off her words. Delia handed each of them a cup, and they thanked her. She then handed Alamo a cup, and he also thanked her. Little Angelina looked up into Alamo's face and let him know with her eyes that she wanted what was in the cup.

"Let me have her, Alamo," Delia said. "I'll take her into the kitchen and get her some milk."

Susanna smiled. Delia picked the toddler up off of Alamo's lap and headed out the parlor door.

Susanna took a sip of the hot coffee. "Back to my story, Julia. Dead silence surrounded me around nine o'clock that morning. The Mexican soldiers were going through the buildings, and when some of them entered the missions building, they opened our door and found Angelina and me."

Susanna choked up and said with difficulty, "I learned quickly from one of the Mexicans, who could speak English, that every man in the Alamo had been killed. Including—including—my husband."

Julia wrapped her arms around Susanna, and they held each other as they wept. Alamo wanted to do something to comfort them, but he held back because the two young widows were obviously finding a measure of comfort in each other.

Delia then appeared, carrying Angelina, and told them that Arthur had just ridden into the yard, and lunch was ready. Alamo rose to his feet and offered a hand to each of the weeping widows. When he had helped them to their feet, smiles of shared sympathy graced their faces as they hugged each other again. They both then smiled at Alamo.

Julia turned to Almeron Dickinson's widow. "Thank you, Susanna, for sharing that horrific time with me. I know how painful it was for you. But maybe now we can both get on with our lives. Having Adam's child will be such a blessing to me. I'm sure your little Angelina will bring much joy to you as well."

3

At the same time the Washburns were having lunch with Susanna Dickinson and her guests, an array of people over on Main Street were watching a large number of riders coming into town from the east. Most were in uniforms of the Texas army, and some of the people called out to the leader, whom they recognized as General Sam Houston, to welcome him.

Houston signaled for his men to halt and explained to the gathering crowd that he and the 783 troops with him were on their way to the Alamo to help Colonel William Travis lead the battle against Santa Anna.

The general and his men were shocked to learn from some in the crowd that at dawn last Sunday, Santa Anna's army of about 6,500 had attacked the defenders of the Alamo and killed them all, except for a man named Louis Rose, who had run away from the Alamo the night before.

One of the men in the crowd stepped up. "Hello, General Houston. Remember me?"

Houston instantly recognized a man he had served with in the War of 1812. He smiled. "I sure do. You're Lamar Forbes. We fought that battle at Detroit together against the British in August of 1812."

"We sure did. I've read in the newspapers about how you've been such a help to the Cherokee Indians in the past few years and how not too long ago you became military leader of Texas. It sure is good to see you!"

"You too." Houston smiled down from his saddle. Then he shook his head. "It's awful to learn that there were no survivors at the Alamo."

"Well sir, there *were* two survivors."

Houston frowned. "These people over here just told me that every man at the Alamo was killed."

"Every *man,* yes sir. You no doubt know who Captain Almeron Dickinson was."

"Yes, of course. He was known as Colonel Travis's right-hand man."

Lamar nodded. "Well sir, the captain had his wife and little fifteen-month-old daughter there with him. Amazingly, that bloodthirsty Santa Anna let them live. He told Mrs. Dickinson to get on her husband's horse and ride away, which she did. The Dickinsons used to live here in Gonzales, and they were quite close to a family who happen to be our next-door neighbors. Their name is Washburn, and Mrs. Dickinson and her baby are now living with them."

General Houston said, "Lamar, I'd like to talk to Mrs. Dickinson, if possible."

"I'm sure she would talk to you, General. She is a very nice lady. I'll take you to the Washburn house now if you want, and I'll tell Arthur and Delia that you're interested in talking to their guest."

Houston smiled. "I'd really appreciate it."

"It's just a brief walk," said Lamar. "Only three blocks. You can leave your horse here if you want to."

The general swung his leg over the horse's back and dismounted. He tied the horse to a nearby hitching post and told his men to wait right there for him. He would be back shortly.

A few minutes later, as General Houston and Lamar Forbes walked onto the block where the Forbeses lived, Lamar pointed out his own house, then the one just past it. "That's the Washburn house."

When they came within a few yards of the house, they saw the ranch wagon with two horses hitched at the front porch. "Looks like the

Washburns have company," Lamar said. "I don't recognize the horses or the wagon."

Houston slowed his gait. "Maybe I shouldn't barge in."

Lamar grinned and shook his head. "It won't be a problem. Let's go."

Houston shrugged and followed Lamar up the porch steps. Lamar knocked on the door. "General, you'll like Susanna Dickinson. And Arthur and Delia Washburn too."

Houston smiled. "I have no doubt of that."

Footsteps could be heard inside, and then the door swung open. Arthur Washburn smiled at his neighbor. "Hi, Lamar. Who've you got with y—?" He gulped when he set eyes on the well-known commander of the Texas army. "G-General S-Sam Houston!"

Lamar chuckled. "General, shake hands with my neighbor, Arthur Washburn."

When the two men had shaken hands, Lamar said, "Arthur, General Houston and nearly eight hundred troops were riding through town a little while ago, and people on Main Street gathered around them in a hurry. The soldiers hadn't yet heard about the massacre at the Alamo last Sunday morning. When we told them about it, I also mentioned that Captain Dickinson's wife and baby had been allowed to leave the Alamo unharmed and that they came here and are staying with you. General Houston would like to talk to Mrs. Dickinson, if that could be arranged."

Arthur smiled at Houston. "Well, I'm sure she'd be happy to talk to you, General. We have a couple of guests who also came to see Mrs. Dickinson, but I'm sure they won't mind if she talks to you. The man is Alan Kane. He speaks quite well of you, sir."

Houston's eyebrows arched. "Alan Kane? I know him. He owns a ranch in southeast Texas. He's the one who courageously rode past the Mexican lines that surrounded the Alamo, risking his life to come to me for help. He must not have made it back to the Alamo after he left me down there on the Sabine River a couple of days before the big battle took place."

"That's him, sir. He has his sister-in-law with him. She was married to Adam Kane, who was killed at the Alamo."

"Oh yes," said Houston. "Alan told me that his brother Adam was with the men in the Alamo."

"I see. Well, Alan brought Julia here because she wanted to talk to Susanna, who is the last person still living to see her husband before he was killed."

Houston nodded. "I shouldn't bother them."

"It won't be a bother, General," said Arthur. "We just finished lunch, and we were sitting down in the parlor when you knocked on the door. Please come in."

When the general and Lamar stepped in, Arthur closed the door behind them and led them down the hall to the parlor.

He walked in ahead of them and said to the group, "Our neighbor Lamar Forbes here, has brought a very special guest to our house." He gestured toward the tall man in uniform stepping in beside him. "This is General Sam Houston."

Everyone stood up, amazement showing on their faces. Then Lamar explained that the general and his nearly eight hundred men were riding through Gonzales on their way to the Alamo to serve as reinforcements for Colonel William Travis and how they just learned of Sunday's battle at the Alamo—and of every man there being killed.

Alan Kane shook the general's hand and reminded him that when they had talked in the army camp on the Sabine River, he had told him about his brother Adam being at the Alamo.

"Yes, Alan," Houston said. "And Lamar told me that Mrs. Dickinson and her little daughter are now living here with the Washburns. When I learned that, I told Lamar I'd like to talk to Mrs. Dickinson if I could. He said he was sure she'd be willing to talk to me."

"I'm sure she will," said Alan. "Let me introduce you to her and to Julia Kane and Delia Washburn."

When the introductions had been made, General Houston expressed his sympathy to both Susanna and Julia for the loss of their husbands. He then thanked Delia and her husband for taking Susanna and her child into their home. His next move was to pat the cheek of little Angelina, who was in her mother's arms, and say how cute she was. Susanna smiled. "Of course I'll talk with you, General."

Houston returned the smile. "Thank you, ma'am."

Alan then explained to the general that on his way back to the Alamo after meeting with him at the Sabine River, he had run into Mrs. Dickinson on Sunday morning at a camp that some citizens of San Antonio had set up a few miles east of the town. The citizens had left when they saw the Mexican troops coming. Mrs. Dickinson had broken the news of the attack to him, telling him that her husband, Almeron, and Adam had been killed, along with all the other men in the fort.

Delia spoke up. "General Houston, would you like to speak to Susanna in private?"

Houston shook his head. "It doesn't have to be private, ma'am. I can talk to her right here."

"All right then," said Delia. "Let's all sit down."

Alan reached for Angelina. "Susanna, I'll hold the baby while you talk to General Houston."

Susanna nodded. "All right."

When everyone was seated and Alan had little Angelina on his lap, Susanna looked at Houston. "So, General, what is it you want to talk to me about?"

"I want to ask some questions about the attack, ma'am." With that, he began inquiring about particulars of the battle, especially how the Mexicans had approached the Alamo, how they got inside the walls, and about the hand-to-hand fighting that went on inside.

Susanna was able to answer a few of the questions, particularly about the hand-to-hand fighting, and how Davy Crockett and his men were very much involved. But she went on to explain that she couldn't answer most of his questions because she and Angelina were in a small room in the mission building when the attack was going on. She told him that through the one small window in her room she had seen the hand-to-hand fighting, especially involving Davy Crockett and his men.

"I understand, Mrs. Dickinson," Houston said. "I want to thank you for what you *have* been able to tell me."

The general then ran his gaze over the rest of the group. "I'm going to take my men to the Alamo. I feel we should bury the bodies of the Alamo defenders. I'm sure Santa Anna and his troops didn't bother to do that."

Susanna shook her head. "They didn't, General Houston. Santa Anna ordered his men to pile up the bodies outside the Alamo's front wall, pour oil on them, and set them on fire. The bodies were all burned."

Houston's eyes were instantly round and hot with anger. He sucked in his breath so hard it hollowed his cheeks. "That lowdown, vile Santa Anna! I'm gonna go after him! He'll pay for this! I'll have to build up my army some more, but this atrocity cannot be ignored!"

"I agree, General," said Alan Kane.

"Me too, Alamo!" said Arthur Washburn.

The general furrowed his brow as he looked at Washburn. "You called him 'Alamo.' Why?"

Susanna spoke up. "Let me explain, General." She then told the general that she had "changed" Alan's name to Alamo and why.

Houston's smile showed that he liked it. He then thanked Alamo for his bravery in riding through the lines of Mexican troops that had surrounded the Alamo to come to him for help.

Alamo shrugged humbly. "Colonel Travis needed *somebody* to do it, so he asked me, and I told him I'd go."

"Well, it took a lot of courage," Julia said. "I'm so proud of you."

Alamo's face flushed, while in his heart he was thrilled to hear Julie say she was proud of him.

General Houston said, "Alamo, if I remember right, the name of your ranch is the Diamond K."

Alamo nodded. "Yes sir."

"So how are things at the ranch?"

"The ranch is doing quite well, thank you, sir."

"Good." General Houston rose to his feet. "Well, ladies and gentlemen, I need to get back to my men. I'm going to take them to the Alamo, just to look the place over. Then we'll go back to the army post at Washington-on-the-Brazos. I hope I can build up my army real fast so I can somehow catch Santa Anna and bring him to justice."

Everyone in the group wished the general well and stood on the front porch, waving to him as he walked back to Main Street.

Lamar Forbes said, "Well, I'd better get on home. Nice to see you, Alamo. And it was a pleasure to meet you, Julia."

Alamo and Julia spoke kindly in return, and Lamar headed across the yard toward his house.

Alamo turned to Susanna. "I'd like to talk to you in private before Julie and I leave."

Susanna smiled. "Of course."

"You two can go back into the parlor," said Delia. "I'll take Julia and Angelina to my sewing room."

"And I'll get busy with some yard work," Arthur said.

Moments later, when Alamo and Susanna sat down together on the sofa in the parlor, he noticed that her face was still somewhat clouded with grief over her husband's death as she asked, "What did you want to talk to me about?"

After a brief hesitation as he searched for just the right words, Alamo said, "Susanna, I know how devastated you must be, losing your husband and having the full responsibility of your precious little daughter. Have you given any thought to your future?"

"Not really, Alamo. Right now my head is rather muddled."

"I can understand that." Alamo looked at his hands. "Susanna, I want to make you an offer. You can think about it and let me know if you want to take me up on it."

Susanna had her hands folded in her lap, her sad eyes fixed on Alamo. "I'm listening."

"I want to offer you and Angelina a place to live on my ranch. I'll be more than happy to build you a nice house on the Diamond K and take care of your needs for as long as you want to stay. I've talked to my family about it, and they would also like to see you and your baby come there to live."

Many emotions passed over Susanna's weary face.

"I don't want you to have to worry about your future or that of little Angelina," Alamo said.

Tears filled Susanna's eyes, and she seemed unable to speak.

Alamo frowned. "Have I upset you?"

Susanna blinked at the tears and shook her head. "Oh no. You haven't upset me. I'm just overwhelmed at your kindness and generosity."

As the tears started down her cheeks, Alamo pulled a clean white handkerchief from his hip pocket and placed it in her shaking hand.

She wiped at the tears. "My heart is so sore and raw right now. I have lost everything except my precious baby, and your outpouring of gracious goodwill is so welcome to me."

"I mean every word of it, Susanna. God has been good to me, and I promised Him that I would always share His bountiful blessings with others."

"Alamo," she said, her voice shaking, "I deeply appreciate this, more than I can tell you. I'm just going to need some time to think it over. The Washburns have been so generous, and I feel that I should stay here with them for a while yet."

Alamo smiled. "I understand. Just take your time, and let me know your decision when you're ready. Write me a letter, and send it to me at the Washington-on-the-Brazos post office. The offer will always be open to you."

"Thank you, my dear friend." She rose from the sofa.

Alamo jumped to his feet, took her hand, and helped her up. "I mean it, Susanna. You and Angelina are always welcome. For a day or a lifetime, this offer still holds."

"Thank you, and God bless you." She then rose up on her tiptoes and planted a tender kiss on his cheek.

Alamo and Susanna headed to the sewing room, and he told Julia they needed to get back to the ranch. He had plenty of work to oversee at the Diamond K.

Delia summoned Arthur from the yard, and Alamo and Julia spent a few more minutes with Susanna, Angelina, and the Washburns. Then they climbed aboard the wagon and headed back to the ranch.

Julia was eager to hear how it went with Susanna, and when Alamo told her, she smiled. "I think you'll get a yes when she's ready."

⌒

That afternoon, General Sam Houston and his men rode up to the battered, blood-streaked walls on the east side of the Alamo. The sight of the place was sickening, but the worst moment came when they drew up to the front gate and came upon the burned, blackened remains of the oil-soaked bodies stacked like cordwood some one hundred feet from the front wall.

A shudder of horror went through all 783 men and through General Houston as well.

Houston could hardly breathe as he told the men that they must somehow capture Santa Anna and make him pay for his evil crimes against the people of Texas. They all agreed. Some of the men were weeping, and others were nauseated as they rode away from the Alamo and headed southeast toward Washington-on-the-Brazos.

On Monday, March 14, at the Justin Miller plantation near New Orleans, the family butler, Garth, drove his buggy up to the wide front porch of the mansion, hopped out, and hurried inside. He found Justin and Myra Miller sitting in the parlor, and as he walked toward them, he said, "Mr. and Mrs. Miller, I bought today's edition of the *New Orleans Sentinel* when I was in town. It—it has some bad news on the front page."

The Millers both rose to their feet and frowned as Garth put the newspaper in Justin's hand. When they looked at the headline, they both gasped. In bold letters, the newspaper declared:

ALAMO BATTLE LEAVES ALL DEFENDERS DEAD

While they stared at the headline, Garth said in a choked voice, "I—I read the article. Every man in the Alamo was killed by Santa Anna's troops."

Myra burst into tears, gripped her husband's hand, and sobbed, "Oh, Justin! Adam and Alan were at the Alamo! They're both dead!"

As Justin began weeping himself and folded Myra in his arms, Garth said, "I'm so sorry to have to bring you this horrible news."

"Garth," Justin said, "it's not your fault. We *had* to know. There would be no sense in hiding it from us."

Garth then handed Justin a letter. "I picked up the mail, and this letter is all there was. I'll go now and let you two read it in private."

As Garth headed out the parlor door, the Millers both looked through their tears at the return address in the upper left-hand corner and saw that it was from their daughter Julia.

Myra gained control of her sobbing as Justin wiped his own tears and opened the envelope. He unfolded the letter. "It's dated March 9."

In the letter, Julia wrote of Adam being killed at the Alamo on March 6, then told them that Alan was still alive. She went on to explain that Alan had been sent to Washington-on-the-Brazos in late February by Colonel William Travis to take a message to General Sam Houston. Alan had not yet arrived back at the Alamo when the big attack came.

Once again, Myra began sobbing, and said in a choked voice, "Oh, Justin, how terrible this is for our Julia, to have her husband killed!"

Justin nodded, biting his lower lip. "Yes, darling. Terrible." He cleared his throat. "There is more news in the letter." Justin took Myra's hand. "Julia says she has just recently learned that she is expecting a baby, who should be born in late September or early October."

The news about the baby brought joy to the Millers in spite of the news that their son-in-law had been killed, and they embraced, both thanking the Lord for this blessing.

When their emotions had settled down, Justin said, "Honey, we need to go to Julia in this time of mourning over Adam's death and do all we can to comfort her."

"Oh yes, darling!" Myra said. "We're her parents. She needs us!"

"I'll ride to New Orleans right away and get reservations on the first ship heading for Galveston." He snapped his fingers. "And we need to send a letter to Sally and Jeffrey. Sally needs to know that her brother-in-law has been killed—and that she is going to be an aunt!"

"I'll write the letter quickly," said Myra, "and you can mail it when you're in town making reservations for our trip to Texas."

When Justin had ridden away on his horse, Myra hurried upstairs to their bedroom. Sitting down on her rocking chair, she let her emotions flow. "Oh, dear Lord," she said in a shaky voice, "our precious daughter has to be so distraught. Please give her Your own peace and grace, and comfort her with Your faithful love. And, Lord, please bless the little one within her womb. Thank You that Alan was spared, and please bless and care for him as well.

"And, heavenly Father, thank You that we indeed have the great Comforter, the blessed Holy Spirit. Thank You that You never leave us nor forsake us and that You will help us carry our burdens and give us rest in times like this."

After letting her tears run softly down her cheeks for a few minutes, Myra rose from the rocking chair, washed her face, and straightened her shoulders. She opened the closet and began selecting and folding garments, readying them to be packed.

"We're coming, sweet daughter," she said softly. "Your papa and mama are coming to do what we can to help you in your grief."

Late that afternoon, Justin returned home and told Myra that they had reservations on a ship to Galveston for the next morning at eight o'clock. He explained that the ship they would be on was brand-new, and because it had very large steam engines, it was quite fast. It would get them to Galveston early enough that they could take a boat upriver to Groce's Landing the same day. They would hire a wagon to take them to the Diamond K, and they'd be at the ranch by early afternoon next Saturday, March 19.

"Wonderful, darling!" said Myra. "I'm glad to hear that we can be there so soon! I'm going to go finish packing!"

## 4

Because of Generalissimo Antonio López de Santa Anna's brutal attack on March 6, ten days later the delegates of the Texas General Convention met in Washington-on-the-Brazos. They were determined to solidly and unmistakably establish their freedom from Mexico's control of the Texans and their land. Among the well-known delegates at the assemblage were General Sam Houston, David Burnet, Lorenzo de Zavala (a devoted Texas Mexican), Thomas Rusk, and forty-five other resolute delegates.

Before the meeting commenced, many of the delegates surrounded General Houston, anxious to hear what he had to say about the fall of the Alamo. David Burnet, who was chairman of the convention, was standing close-by. He quickly stepped up and said, "Gentlemen, I have already asked General Houston to give a detailed report to the convention concerning this terrible tragedy."

One man spoke up. "We're eager to hear it, Mr. Chairman!" The others joined in, letting Burnet know that they indeed were eager to hear General Houston's report.

When everyone had gathered in the auditorium of the convention building, Burnet stood before them on the platform and called the meeting to order. He spoke about what took place at the Alamo ten days earlier, then asked General Sam Houston to give his detailed report of the atrocities that Santa Anna and his army committed there.

Houston received a standing ovation when he stepped up to the podium. Once the delegates had seated themselves again, Houston began his report. He gave the details of the battle as best he could, then told the delegates about leading his 783 men to the Alamo on March 12 and what they felt when they found the burned, blackened, oil-soaked bodies of the Alamo men stacked like cordwood in front of the walls. The wrath General Houston felt toward Santa Anna was clearly communicated to his hearers, and they began to feel the same way.

"My friends," Houston said, "I want all of you to be aware that I had asked for assistance from the United States Army in battling Santa Anna and his thousands of troops—but was denied. The army officials I contacted made it clear that Texas must first establish a declaration of independence from Mexico before the United States government will offer any assistance."

Chairman Burnet, who was seated behind Houston, stepped up beside him and ran his gaze over the faces of the delegates. "Gentlemen, it is my opinion that this convention needs to immediately declare that the Texas government hereby resolves that its political connection with the Mexican nation has been forever ended and that the people of Texas do now constitute a free, sovereign, and independent republic."

Every delegate jumped to his feet, applauding and shouting out agreement.

Then and there, a declaration of independence was drafted and passed by a one hundred percent vote. A constitution was drafted, and again the vote was unanimous.

Chairman Burnet smiled at the delegates. "I'm pleased that we are all in total agreement on this issue. Now…something else that is very important. All of you know that the convention has recently been given authority by the people of Texas to elect a president of the Texas Republic."

Delegate Thomas Rusk jumped to his feet and shouted, "Chairman Burnet, some of us have been talking about this, and we want *you* as our president!"

The entire group was instantly on its feet, applauding and shouting their agreement.

Within the next hour, David Burnet had been elected president, and Lorenzo de Zavala, who was also very popular with the delegates, was elected vice president. Thomas Rusk was appointed secretary of war. Then, amid shouts of praise for his great work, General Sam Houston was reconfirmed as commander-in-chief of the army of the Republic of Texas.

The meeting was dismissed, and the happy delegates stood around for some time, congratulating the officers of the Texas Republic and discussing their joy over what had just happened.

As the days passed, word of the convention and its result was carried all over Texas by word of mouth and by the newspapers. People were very happy about the way the elections had gone and about the new Republic of Texas declaration of independence and constitution.

⌒

On Saturday, March 19, the sun was shining, but a blustery, cold wind was blowing out of the north. At the Diamond K Ranch, a bright fire burned cheerfully in the dining room fireplace as the Kane family sat down to eat lunch together.

Alamo had invited his brothers, Alex and Abel, and their wives, Libby and Vivian, to eat lunch with him and Abram, Angela, and Julia. He felt a deep need to keep all of his family close, and he sensed that with the recent death of Adam, everyone else needed it as well.

Daisy Haycock loved cooking for what she called "her family" and happily placed a steaming shepherd's pie on the table. The delectable aroma and golden crust on top set everyone's mouth to watering. Creamed peas and cinnamon applesauce accompanied the meal, as well as hot, fragrant coffee. Daisy had placed a chocolate cake on a small nearby table as well, which caught the eye of every person.

Abram led in prayer, then everyone dug in.

After a few minutes, Alamo swallowed and said to all, "This shepherd's pie is so tasty!"

Everyone nodded.

"It looks like we're all hungry for a change," Alamo said. "I know the sadness of Adam's death will never completely leave us, but knowing my brother, he would want us to go on with life and find happiness again."

Julia patted her abdomen and smiled. "Yes, he would, Alamo, and not a one of us, including his baby, would want to disappoint him."

"Amen to that, Julia," piped up Alex. "This whole family can find peace and comfort in knowing that Adam will always be with us in the blessed event of this child."

The conversation around the table then went to the baby in Julia's womb, and each person shared whether he or she thought it was a boy or a girl.

When lunch was finally over, they left the dishes for Daisy to take care of and headed toward the front of the house to sit for a while in the parlor. Just as everyone was sitting down, they heard pounding horse hooves and the rattle of a wagon pulling up outside.

Alamo said, "Go ahead and sit down, everybody. I'll see who it is."

He hurried to the big parlor window, and his eyes widened at what he saw. He had planned to talk to Julie about inviting her parents to come visit—and here they were! He turned and looked at the woman he secretly loved. "Julie! Your parents are here!"

Julia gasped. "Oh, Alamo, are you sure?" She ran to the window and began to shed happy tears as she saw her parents. "Oh, Alamo, it *is* them! How wonderful!"

Julia grabbed her shawl, and she and Alamo were first to dash out of the parlor into the hallway and head for the front door. The others followed, feeling joy for Julia.

Excitement filled the cold air as Alamo opened the front door of the ranch house with Julia at his side. Justin Miller was helping Myra from the hired wagon. When her feet touched the ground, Myra saw her daughter, burst into tears, and dashed toward the porch. Julia hurried through the doorway and met Myra as she reached the top step. Mother and daughter embraced, holding each other tightly and weeping.

Myra then held her daughter at arm's length and said, "Oh, Julia, I'm sorry about Adam's death. Your papa and I just had to come and be with you in this time of tragedy. We received your letter Monday and were able to board a ship on Tuesday."

Myra set her eyes on Alamo and reached a hand toward him. He took her hand and squeezed it. "I'm so glad you and Mr. Miller have come."

Myra smiled. "We're so glad we *could* come, Alan."

Julia glanced toward her father, who was at the wagon. He and the driver were unloading the luggage. She looked back at her mother. "You really made good time, Mama. How did you get here so fast?"

Myra explained about the new ship they were on from New Orleans to Galveston having large steam engines.

Julia hugged her mother again. "Well, I'm glad for that new ship!"

Myra hugged her back. "Me too!"

Justin paid the driver and hurried toward the porch, where he saw his wife and daughter clinging to each other and Alamo standing beside them. He bounded up the steps, spoke to Alamo, calling him "Alan," and shook his hand. Then he wrapped his arms around both daughter and mother. "Julia, sweetheart, I'm so sorry Adam was killed."

While Justin was speaking, the rest of the Kane family came out the front door. Amid the sorrow there was joy as Alamo introduced Justin and Myra to his family. They were warmly welcomed by Abram and Angela, as well as Alex, Libby, Abel, and Vivian.

Clinging to each other in the cold air, Julia and her parents talked about Adam's death, and Julia wiped away tears as she told them how much she missed him. The three of them agreed that Adam was much better off than they were, being in the presence of the Lord in heaven.

Alamo stepped off the porch, announcing that he would get the luggage. Justin followed him. "I appreciate this, Alan, but there are four pieces. I'll carry two of them."

"Hey!" came Alex's voice from the porch. "You fellas need help?"

"We're at your service!" called Abel.

Looking back as he and Justin walked toward the luggage, Alamo said, "Thanks, but there are only four pieces. We'll get them."

Moments later, when Justin and Alamo stepped up onto the porch carrying the luggage, Abram said, "Okay, everybody, let's all go inside."

Alamo set the luggage in the vestibule and told Justin to do the same, adding that they would take it to the guest room later.

Everyone followed Abram into the parlor. The Millers took off their coats, Julia laid her shawl aside, and they all sat down. Julia sat between her parents on the sofa, and they each took hold of one of her hands. Julia smiled. "Papa...Mama, are you hungry?"

Justin and Myra glanced at each other. "We can wait till suppertime to eat, dear," Myra said. "But a cup of hot tea sure would hit the spot. That wind out there is a cold one."

Angela rose from her chair, smiled at Myra, and headed toward the parlor door. "I'll go tell Daisy—she's our cook and housekeeper—to heat up some water and prepare tea right away."

Alex went to the fireplace and threw two fresh logs on the fire, then sat down again beside Libby. The group began to relax in the warmth of the fire, and Justin and Myra relaxed even more in the warmth of such a dear and precious family.

The conversation then went to the baby Julia was carrying, and the Millers spoke of how glad they were that they were going to be grandparents, adding that Sally and Jeffrey had no children yet.

Abram looked at his youngest son. "Alamo, is there anything Daisy needs to do in order to make a guest room ready for the Millers?"

Noting the name Abram had called Alan, Justin and Myra exchanged glances.

Alamo shook his head. "No, Papa. Since we get surprised by visitors now and then, she always has a couple of the guest rooms ready."

Justin blinked and ran his gaze to Abram. "Pardon me, sir, but why did you call Alan 'Alamo'?"

Julia spoke up. "Papa, it's his new nickname. Let me explain how he got it."

Justin and Myra both listened intently as Julia told them how and why Susanna Dickinson had given Alan the nickname Alamo. When they had heard the story, they both smiled. "I really like that," Myra said.

"Me too," Justin said. "That makes me mighty proud of you, Alan—er—I mean, Alamo."

The rest of the family laughed.

At that moment, Angela entered the parlor, carrying a tray with enough empty cups for everyone. Behind her was Daisy, carrying a large, steaming teapot. Angela introduced Justin and Myra to Daisy. They exchanged friendly greetings as Daisy poured cups of hot tea and Angela handed them out. When Daisy had headed back to the kitchen, leaving the teapot in case anyone wanted more, Alamo asked the Millers how long they were staying.

"We're booked to head back to New Orleans next Friday," Justin said.

"Oh, wonderful!" Julia said. "It will be so good to have you here that long!" Still sitting between her parents, she took a sip of tea and looked at her father, then her mother. "We'll take you to church with us in Washington-on-the-Brazos tomorrow!"

Justin nodded. "We figured you would. From what Adam told us about your pastor, we're looking forward to meeting him and hearing him preach."

The mention of Adam's name brought a sharp pain to Julia's heart, but she smiled. "Papa, I guarantee that you and Mama will love Pastor Merle Evans. And you'll love his preaching. He exalts the Lord Jesus in so many ways."

Some sixty miles due south of Gonzales, Texas, at the town of Goliad, was Fort Defiance. There Texas army Colonel James Fannin was stationed with some three hundred thirty soldiers.

At midmorning on Tuesday, March 22, Colonel Fannin and his men were gathered beside Coleto Creek, just north of Goliad. With the sound of gurgling water in their ears, Fannin talked with his men about the Alamo tragedy and shared how sorry he was that those brave men had been killed by the overwhelming numbers of Mexican troops.

One of the sergeants spoke up and commented on how cold-blooded and wicked Santa Anna was. Other men chimed in with their agreement.

Fannin, a muscular, square-jawed man in his late forties, rubbed his chin. "I agree, men. Santa Anna must have a block of ice where his heart should be."

Suddenly the soldiers heard pounding hooves and looked in the direction of Goliad. A lone rider was galloping along the road that lined the creek. All of them recognized Delmar Rogers, who owned the hardware store in town.

Rogers's face was pallid as he drew rein and halted his horse where Colonel Fannin stood. "Colonel, Mexican troops are coming this way from the west! I'd say there are about eight or nine hundred of them. Most of them are on foot. There might be about twenty on horseback. I figure they're coming to attack Fort Defiance!"

Colonel Fannin's features stiffened. "How close are they?"

"I'd say about four or five miles."

Fannin nodded. "Thank you for letting us know, Mr. Rogers. I suggest that you hurry and get back into town."

"Yes sir." Rogers wheeled his mount and galloped away.

Fannin ran his eyes over the three hundred thirty men. "We'll be much safer inside the old stone fort than here on the creek. Let's go!"

With the colonel in the lead, they ran hard toward Goliad, weapons in hand. As they drew near the fort, one of the men pointed his rifle toward the west and shouted, "Colonel Fannin! Here they come!"

Every man stiffened, gripping his weapon. The throng of Mexican troops was no more than fifty yards away, breaking through the thick forest that lay just to the west.

"Inside, men! Quick!"

On a large bay horse, riding in front of his troops, was the Mexican leader. He shouted loudly in English, "Stop! All of you! Surrender now!"

"Inside, men!" Fannin led them into the fort as Mexican rifles began roaring.

In unison, the officers cocked their revolvers, and the rest of the men cocked their rifles, the hammers clicking dryly. They closed the gate quickly, climbed up to the narrow platforms inside the front wall, and began firing back at the Mexicans.

Guns roared as the gallant Texans fought back against the overwhelming odds. The Mexicans began surrounding the other three walls while firing, forcing the comparatively small number of Texans to spread out along the walls to defend the fort.

As bullets flew, the Mexicans began taking their toll on the Texans.

Many of the people of Goliad looked on from a safe distance, their hearts heavy for the soldiers in the fort.

As the battle raged, a young Texan soldier who was blasting away at the enemy right next to Colonel James Fannin took a slug in the chest, cried out, and fell to his knees on the narrow platform along the inside of the wall. Fannin could not go to him. He was too busy firing at the Mexicans. As he reloaded his revolver, Fannin saw the young soldier bend forward until his forehead touched the bare planks. He stayed in that position for only a few seconds, then rolled onto his back and stared vacant-eyed at the sky.

Fannin swallowed hard, knowing that the soldier was dead, and opened fire once again on the charging Mexicans.

The battle went on, and as the sun reached its apex in the sky, seven Texans lay dead with some sixty wounded, including Colonel Fannin. Only a few Mexicans had been killed or wounded. Guns were still roaring, and finally Colonel Fannin, who lay on the ground with a bullet in his right leg, realized that they had no way of holding off the Mexican troops. He knew the Mexicans would stay until they had killed him and all of his men. He figured their only hope was surrender.

Fannin called to three of his officers as the battle continued and explained this to them. They agreed that the wise thing was to surrender, and they passed along the word to the men about what was happening.

Moments later, when the white flag of surrender was raised, the Mexicans moved into the fort and found the Texans holding their empty hands above their heads. The wounded Colonel Fannin lay on the ground with a leather belt around his leg, acting as a tourniquet. The other wounded men lay on the ground close to him.

The Mexican leader of the troops, who spoke English well, asked where their leader was. He was quickly directed to Colonel Fannin and told his name. He stood over the fallen Texan leader and in perfect English introduced himself as General José de Urrea. He then said, "I was glad to see the white flag raised, Colonel Fannin."

Fannin looked up at him. "We are too greatly outnumbered, General. Will we be treated as prisoners of war?"

Urrea nodded. "Yes, you will. I must hold all of you here and send word to Generalissimo Santa Anna, who is still in Texas, that you are being held as prisoners here at Goliad. When orders are brought from Santa Anna about where you are to be taken, my men and I will take you there."

Gritting his teeth because of the pain he was experiencing, Fannin said to the general, "I figured that Santa Anna and his troops had probably gone back to Mexico City after the men at the Alamo were killed."

"Most of the troops were sent back, Colonel," Urrea replied, "but Santa Anna and about fourteen hundred of them are camped many miles from here, in southeast Texas. It will take a few days for my riders to carry the message to the generalissimo and return with his orders."

Fannin swallowed hard. "And what do you think he will tell you to do with us?"

General Urrea spoke in a gentle voice. "I believe that Santa Anna may simply tell me to set you and your men free."

The Texas soldiers who were not wounded were standing around their colonel and the enemy general in a circle. Disbelief of General Urrea's words was written on their faces. Fannin saw it but hoped that somehow General Urrea was speaking the truth.

The general told his men that they would stay at the fort until the three riders he was going to send off to Generalissimo Santa Anna in the morning had returned. Urrea ordered his men to search the fort and confiscate every weapon belonging to the Texans.

At sunup the next morning, the general sent the three riders to bear his message to Santa Anna. Three days passed as the citizens of Goliad carefully observed the fort from a safe distance.

Then, late on Saturday afternoon, March 26, the riders returned, accompanied by one of Santa Anna's top generals and two other officers. All the soldiers, both Texan and Mexican, looked on as General Nepo Ruiz handed General Urrea a letter written by Generalissimo Antonio López de Santa Anna. When Urrea read the letter, the color drained from his face.

The Texans exchanged glances, wondering what was in the letter.

General Urrea cleared his throat nervously and said to the crowd, "I have no choice but to obey the command given me in this letter from our government leader."

There was a dead silence in the fort.

Urrea's voice shook. "Generalissimo Antonio López de Santa Anna has ordered that Colonel James Fannin and all of his men who are still alive are to be executed."

Anguish showed on the faces of the Texans.

General Urrea's voice still shook as he ran his dark gaze over their faces. "You understand that I must obey the generalissimo's orders. I have no choice. The execution will take place at sunrise tomorrow." With that, he turned and walked away.

Colonel Fannin could feel something acidic surging up in him like a giant ocean wave. Suddenly it stuck between his abdomen and his throat, remaining a lump of stabbing pain in his chest.

The Texan soldiers were not surprised to learn that Santa Anna wanted them executed. Facing certain death at the hands of the Mexicans, each man felt something drain from him, as if any warmth in his veins and flesh had been siphoned away, leaving his body oppressive and cold.

General Nepo Ruiz and the two officers stayed the night. They would observe the executions so they could report to Santa Anna that his orders had been carried out.

During the night, two of Fannin's lightly wounded men, Corporals David Graff and Thomas Wyatt, managed to crawl out of the fort unnoticed and hide in the woods a short distance away. The next morning at sunrise, which was Palm Sunday, the Texas soldiers were all shot to death by the Mexican soldiers, including Colonel James Fannin. The Mexicans hadn't bothered to count the number of wounded men they shot, thus didn't notice that two of the Texans were missing.

After the massacre, General Ruiz and the other two officers headed back to Santa Anna's camp to report that his orders had been carried out. General Urrea and his men left the bodies lying inside the walls of Fort Defiance and headed back to where they had been camped earlier.

⌒

On Tuesday morning, March 29, at the army post in Washington-on-the-Brazos, General Sam Houston was at his desk when his adjutant, Corporal Brad Mayfield, tapped on his door.

"Yes, Corporal," Houston called toward the door.

The door opened, and the young corporal stepped inside. "General, two men from the town of Goliad are here to see you."

"Do you know what they want?"

"No sir. One of them is John Higgins, Goliad's mayor, and the other one owns a hardware store there. His name is Delmar Rogers."

Houston frowned. "I wonder if it has something to do with Fort Defiance."

"I don't know, sir. They refused to tell me."

The general rose to his feet. "Well, bring them in."

Seconds later, the two men entered the office. Corporal Mayfield announced them to the general, stepped into the hall, and closed the door behind him. General Houston reached across his desk, shook the men's hands, and offered them chairs in front of the desk.

"What can I do for you, gentlemen?" Houston asked as he sat down in his desk chair.

"We're here to give you some very bad news, General," said Mayor John Higgins. "But as commander-in-chief of the army of the Republic of Texas, we know you'll want to hear it."

"Does this bad news have anything to do with Fort Defiance?"

"It does, sir," Delmar Rogers said. "It does."

General Houston listened intently as the two men related the brutal incident at Fort Defiance on Sunday. They explained that they had been told the details of the proposed executions by two of Colonel James Fannin's men, Corporals David Graff and Thomas Wyatt, who though wounded had managed to escape unnoticed the night before the executions. Higgins and Rogers quoted the two corporals, who had told them of the letter sent by Santa Anna ordering the executions. Then they related that people all over town heard the rifles firing inside the fort at sunrise on Sunday morning and that on Sunday afternoon they and other men of the town had gone to the fort and found every soldier inside the walls dead.

His face red with anger, Houston asked the two men if they knew where Santa Anna was. They answered that Graff and Wyatt had only heard that he was several miles away in southeast Texas, with fourteen hundred of his troops. The others had been sent back to Mexico City after the Alamo battle. They added that it had taken General José Urrea's riders three days to go to Santa Anna and return to Goliad.

The anger Houston was feeling also showed in his eyes. "That bloodthirsty Mexican dictator has plans to do more harm to the people of Texas, I am sure."

Higgins and Rogers agreed.

"I want to thank you gentlemen for bringing this news to me," General Houston said. "I am going to send riders out to see if they can locate the whereabouts of Santa Anna and his fourteen hundred troops. If we can locate them, I'm going to find a way to attack them."

"I hope you're successful, General." John Higgins rose to his feet.

"Me too." Delmar Rogers also stood.

Moments later, General Houston stood in front of his office building and watched the two men ride away.

Houston immediately sent fourteen of his cavalrymen out to ride to different areas of the southeastern part of Texas to see if they could find where Santa Anna and his troops had gone when they left San Antonio. They had orders to return as fast as possible if they learned where the Mexican general and his killers were camped.

## 5

As the news quickly spread through Texas by word of mouth and newspapers of the executions of Colonel James Fannin and his troops at Goliad, and of General Sam Houston having sent riders out to locate Santa Anna's soldiers, many more men came to Washington-on-the-Brazos and joined the Texas army. They declared to General Houston and his induction officers that they were eager to go to battle with the murderous Santa Anna and his troops.

On Sunday morning, April 3, five days after Houston had sent out fourteen of his cavalrymen to search for the Mexican army's camp, the general was on the porch of the small building that housed his office, talking to two young men who had just joined the Texas army. Suddenly a sergeant came running up to the porch. "General, twelve of the cavalrymen you sent out to find Santa Anna are riding in!"

Even as the sergeant was speaking, the general heard the sound of pounding hooves and looked up to see the dozen riders galloping toward him.

When they drew up, the first man to dismount was Captain Ted Peterson. He hopped onto the porch. "General Houston, we covered the areas you told us to, and none of us have seen any sign of Santa Anna and his troops."

The other cavalrymen were out of their saddles now and rushed up to the porch.

"Well," said the general, "Captain Hoverly and Lieutenant Benson haven't come back yet. Maybe they found the camp." He sighed. "If they return saying they haven't found the dirty killers either, I'll just have to send all of you out again to cover other territory. We've *got* to find those barbaric killers and make them pay for their vicious deeds."

Peterson nodded. "Yes sir."

"All we can do now," said Houston, "is wait till Hoverly and Benson return."

One of the riders said, "We're ready to go out again, sir, if we have to."

The rest nodded and spoke their agreement.

The next morning, Monday, April 4, General Sam Houston was in his office when he heard horses gallop up to the building and skid to a halt. Seconds later, he heard the door of the outer office open and the voice of Corporal Brad Mayfield say to the riders, "How'd it go?"

"We know where the bloody killer is!" came the joyful reply.

There were rapid footsteps in the outer office, and Houston was already headed for the door when he heard the corporal's knock. He jerked the door open and set eyes on Captain Dan Hoverly and Lieutenant Jim Benson, standing behind the corporal. "Did I hear you right? You found Santa Anna?"

"Yes sir!" Hoverly replied.

"Well, come in and tell me where he is!"

The general led them to a sofa, then sat down on a chair facing them. "Okay, let's hear it!"

"When we were in Galveston, General," said Captain Hoverly, "we learned from some loyal Texans there that Santa Anna and his fourteen hundred troops are camped about three miles west of town."

"Good!" Houston blurted, slamming his right fist into his left palm.

"Those Texans we talked to, sir," said Lieutenant Benson, "told us something else. Some Texas Mexicans passed by Santa Anna's camp and pretended to be devoted to Mexico. They found out that the bloody dictator had learned of the Texas General Convention meeting on March 16 and of the declaration of independence and the new constitution. Santa Anna was outraged at this news and vowed to punish the Texans."

Houston rubbed his jaw thoughtfully. "Mm-hmm. I can imagine he was mad, all right."

"Those loyal Texas Mexicans told the other Texans we talked with," Captain Hoverly said, "that in his anger, Santa Anna spoke of going to Washington-on-the-Brazos to attack the town and punish the Texas government leaders for what they've done. He said he is certain he has enough men with him to gain victory over the small Texas army at the post here."

The general clenched his fists and bared his teeth like a cornered wolf. "We've got to stop Santa Anna and his troops before they get here!"

Both men nodded.

Houston cleared his throat. "But even with the good number of men who have been coming here and joining the Texas army, I've got to round up more volunteers before we try it."

"Yes sir," Hoverly said.

"What can we do to help, General?" Benson asked.

Houston thought on the question for a few seconds. "I'm going to send you two back to the Galveston area. I want you to stay well hidden and watch for Santa Anna to begin moving his troops northward."

Both officers nodded.

"Here's what I want you to do. One of you is to ride back to me each day and let me know how it looks. In the meantime, I'll work at getting more volunteers."

"We'll keep you posted, General." Captain Hoverly rose to his feet.

"Yes, we will," Lieutenant Benson agreed, also standing.

Minutes later, General Sam Houston stood on the porch of his office building, with Corporal Mayfield at his side, and watched the two officers ride away.

⌒

Midmorning on Friday, April 15, at the Diamond K Ranch, Libby Kane had Vivian and Julia sitting with her on the back porch of her house. They were having tea together.

Libby's purpose for inviting her sisters-in-law there was to give comfort to Julia in the loss of her husband. It had been over a month since Adam had been killed at the Alamo, but Julia was still having a very difficult time. Both Vivian and Libby knew that part of Julia's struggle was that she was carrying Adam's child and was having a hard time facing the fact that her baby would have no father when he or she was born and was growing up.

It was a lovely day as the three women sipped their tea and ran their eyes over the land around them. The leaves on the cottonwood trees nearby were beginning to bud, and the crocuses had pushed their heads up through the sod around the houses that circled Alamo Kane's large ranch house, showing yellow, white, and purple blossoms. Birds of various plumage were nestling in the cottonwoods, merrily chirping their own happy songs. Puffy white clouds dotted the azure blue sky above.

Noting the sadness on Julia's countenance as she sipped her tea and stared off into the distance, Libby said, "My, what a glorious day! I'm sure glad spring finally got here."

"Me too," said Vivian.

Lost in thought, Julia did not hear or respond.

Trying again to do what she could to lift the young widow's spirits, Libby said, "Julia, when that sweet baby is born into the Kane family, he or she is going to get lots of love. Any plans you want to make for the baby's future, we'll all be right here to help."

"Yes, we will," put in Vivian.

"I appreciate that." Julia finally took in what her sisters-in-law were saying. "It's just so hard to think about my baby's future when my heart is torn in little pieces because of Adam's death."

Tears began to stream down Julia's wan cheeks. Libby went to Julia, bent over, and embraced her. Desirous to comfort Julia, Vivian did the same.

As both women embraced the weeping young widow, Libby said, "Honey, my heart goes out to you in your loss. I can't imagine how horrible it would be if Alex was taken from me in death."

"And I feel the same way if Abel were taken from me," said Vivian. "We love you so very much, Julia, and wish we could take the pain out of your heart."

Julia sniffed and ran her teary gaze from one to the other. "Thank you both."

Libby and Vivian released their hold on Julia. "This situation with Mexico is so horrible," Libby said. "Alex has often told me that if war breaks out between the United States and Mexico, he knows the Texas army will fight alongside the United States Army and that he will join up and fight."

Vivian's lower lip trembled. "Abel has said the same thing. If it happens, Libby, we could both lose our husbands too."

Libby put trembling fingers to her lips and nodded.

"I hope it never does happen." Julia looked up at them. "But I am so proud of Alex and Abel that they would be willing to fight. And—and—I am so proud of Adam, who was willing to go to the Alamo with Colonel Travis and his men."

Libby and Vivian nodded.

Julia wiped a tear from her cheek. "And then there's Alan, who so gallantly risked his life riding through the Mexican lines from the Alamo to get to General Houston and ask for help."

"Yes," Libby said. "God bless him."

Vivian's voice quavered. "If war with Mexico comes and Abel joins up with General Houston—as Houston is asking loyal Texans to do in the *Washington Post* articles—I will be very proud of him, even though I will be terribly frightened."

Libby nodded. "I feel exactly the same way."

Suddenly Julia burst into sobs. "It already happened to my Adam!" Her whole body shook as she wept.

Libby laid a hand on her shoulder. "Go ahead and cry, sweetie. It's what you need to do. God gave us tears to relieve our heartache. You've tried so hard to put on a brave front for all of us, but you don't need to. We understand. Adam was your husband, the light of your life. And that light was snuffed out only a few weeks ago. Let yourself grieve for him. In the long run, the Lord will see to it that your tears bring the healing you need."

Julia went on weeping. Libby kept her hand on Julia's shoulder, and Vivian laid her hand on the other shoulder and closed her eyes. "Dear Lord, have mercy on Julia, and bring healing quickly."

Within a few minutes, Julia's weeping faded away and only a few sniffles could be heard. Both sisters-in-law squeezed her shoulders, trying to show their love and compassion for her. Soon Julia took a lace-edged hanky from her sleeve and dried her tears.

Libby patted the young widow's shoulder and said softly, "Do you feel better now?"

Julia looked up at her with a weak smile. "Much better. Thank you for giving me permission to grieve for the man I love so much, though he's now in heaven. Now maybe I can begin to think more clearly and put my life and my baby's life back in perspective."

Vivian patted Julia's shoulder. "I'm sure you will have more lonely times, honey, but just remember that it's okay to cry. Sometimes God washes our eyes with tears so that we may truly see more clearly."

Julia looked down at her midsection and patted the small mound.

"You had a wonderful papa, and I will always make sure that you remember who he was and that you love him."

A glow came across her tear-washed face, and then a genuine smile curved her lips.

Libby and Vivian saw it and smiled at each other. Libby squeezed Julia's shoulder again. "Sweetie, you will never be alone in raising your child. There is plenty of family here who will help you any time you need it. This precious child is already loved by all of us."

"That's right," Vivian said.

Julia smiled at them. "Thank you so much. I'm a very fortunate girl to have such a special family. I think my parents will be coming for the baby's birth. That will be a good thing for them and for the baby and me."

Libby smiled. "You know your parents are always more than welcome here."

"Yes, and that makes me feel so good." Julia paused. Then with a grin on her lips, she said, "Papa and Mama have fallen in love with what they've seen of Texas, especially right here at the ranch. It wouldn't surprise me if when they have a grandchild here, they should decide to move here permanently. Do you think that would be okay?"

"Why, of course!" Libby said.

"Yes!" chimed in Vivian. "Texas is a big place. There's always room for two more grandparents!"

Julia actually giggled. "Great! I hope the Lord makes it possible for them to move here someday!"

While the conversation on Libby's back porch was going on, Alamo Kane and his brothers, Alex and Abel, were working together on a damaged hay wagon in one of the Diamond K's corrals when they looked up to see two uniformed riders galloping toward the ranch from the east. They watched as the riders came upon two of the ranch hands and drew rein. The ranch hands pointed toward the corral where the Kane brothers were working.

Seconds later, when the two Texas army soldiers rode up, Alamo recognized them, having met them at the army post in Washington-on-the-Brazos some time back. They were Sergeant Ross Hayes and Corporal Rick Lindall.

As the soldiers drew rein, Sergeant Hayes said, "Howdy, *Alamo*!"

"Yeah, howdy, *Alamo*!" Corporal Lindall echoed.

Alan smiled. "How did you two know about my new nickname?"

Lindall chuckled. "General Houston told us about it."

"Oh, he did, eh?"

"He's mighty proud of you," said Hayes.

Alamo's features crimsoned. "Well, I'm glad he is."

Alamo invited the soldiers to dismount, then introduced them to his brothers. When they had shaken hands, Sergeant Hayes asked all three Kane brothers if they were aware of the Texas General Convention meeting that had taken place on March 16. Alamo told them they had read about it in the *Washington Post* and that they were glad about the declaration of independence and the constitution.

The sergeant then asked if they had heard about what happened to Colonel James Fannin and his men at Goliad.

"We have," replied Alamo, anger coming into his sky blue eyes. "And we are plenty irate about it. My brothers and I have been talking among ourselves about General Houston's plea for volunteers to come to Washington-on-the-Brazos and sign up with the Texas army to help make Santa Anna and his troops pay for what they did at the Alamo and at Goliad."

Sergeant Hayes said levelly, "That's why we're here. Alamo, General Houston sent us to ask you if you would come and join up. The general has learned that Santa Anna and his fourteen hundred troops are camped near Galveston. He has reason to believe they are coming to Washington-

on-the-Brazos to attack the town and punish the Texas government leaders for what they did at the Texas General Convention meeting."

Alamo rubbed his angular chin. "Oh really?"

"Yes. General Houston and what troops he can gather will travel
toward Galveston soon to intercept Santa Anna and his troops and stop
them in their tracks. But at this point, Houston has only about a thousand men, and he needs all the volunteers he can get to go with him."

Alamo put down his tools. "I'll get my rifle and revolver, saddle up,
and go with you right now. As a loyal Texan, it's my duty to join the
fight to defeat Santa Anna and protect Texas from Mexican aggression,
especially my family and the ranch."

"Well, I'm telling you right now, Alamo," Alex said, "I feel the same
way. I'll go too."

"So will I!" said Abel.

"Sounds good to me, brothers!" Alamo replied.

"Do your brothers know how to handle guns, Alamo?" Sergeant
Hayes asked.

Alex and Abel looked at each other and grinned.

"They sure do, Sergeant," Alamo said. "I taught them how to use
both rifles and revolvers several months ago, and they have their own
guns. And I might add that even though they've never been in combat,
they are very good shots in target practice and in killing snakes and
hunting deer and jack rabbits."

Hayes smiled. "Good! This will make General Houston happy!"

"It sure will!" agreed Lindall.

Alamo turned to his brothers. "You need to go and tell Libby and
Vivian about this right now, and I need to talk to my foreman, Cort, so
he'll know he's in charge around here until I get back."

Sergeant Hayes grinned at Alamo. "So you don't have a wife yet?"

"No, I'm still not married."

"Any prospects?" Corporal Lindall asked.

"No." In his heart, Alamo wished he could know that Julie was his prospect, but he wasn't sure as yet what the Lord had in mind for the two of them.

The corporal grinned. "Well, don't worry, Alamo. That right young lady will come into your life one of these days. At least that's what my parents keep telling me."

Alamo nodded and laughed. "You two soldier boys can tie up your horses and come with us now. You can wait on the front porch of the ranch house while my brothers go talk with their wives and I do the same with my ranch foreman."

As they walked toward the big ranch house, Alex and Abel discussed the fact that Libby had invited Vivian and Julia for tea. When they reached the house and stepped up on the porch, Alamo pointed to the group of chairs and said to the soldiers, "Please sit down, gentlemen. We'll be back shortly."

Alex and Abel hurried away toward their houses. Hayes and Lindall smiled at Alamo and selected the chairs they wanted to occupy.

"Comfortable?" asked Alamo.

"Very," said the sergeant.

Alamo was about to turn and leave to hunt up his foreman when the front door of the house opened and Angela stepped out. She ran her gaze to the soldiers, then to Alamo, and asked, "What's going on, little brother? I saw you, Alex, and Abel escort these soldiers up to the porch."

Alamo introduced the soldiers to his sister and told Angela what was happening. He explained that Alex and Abel were on their way to tell their wives and that he was about to go talk to Cort Whitney.

Angela's heart went cold as she learned why General Houston's soldiers were there. She swallowed with difficulty as Alamo hurried away. Then she remembered her manners and said to Hayes and Lindall, "It will be a few minutes before my brothers come back. Can I get you each a cup of hot coffee?"

Both men had been standing since Angela stepped onto the porch. They both smiled and told her they'd love some coffee.

Angela entered the house and headed down the hall toward the kitchen. Her heart was pounding as she said in a low voice, "I've already lost one brother to Santa Anna. What will happen now to my remaining three brothers? Please, please, Lord, protect them, and bring them safely back to us."

## 6

The Diamond K Ranch foreman, Cort Whitney, was working with some of the ranch hands to repair the roof of a barn when he saw his boss walking toward them. He was on his knees at the peak of the roof with a hammer in hand as Alamo Kane drew near and called out, "Hello, Cort!"

The foreman rose to his feet with the hammer dangling in his right hand. "Howdy, boss! Is there something you need me to do for you?"

"I just need to talk to you for a moment," said Alamo. "Can you come down?"

"Of course." Cort placed the hammer on a stack of wooden shingles and made his way down the sloped roof toward a ladder that leaned against the edge near where Alamo was standing. When Cort touched ground, Alamo told him about the two soldiers General Houston had sent to ask if he would join him to battle Santa Anna's fourteen hundred troops. Alamo explained that Houston had solid reason to believe they would soon be coming to attack Washington-on-the-Brazos because Santa Anna was angry about the things that happened at the Texas General Convention meeting on March 16.

Cort nodded. "I imagine the big bull is pretty hot over that."

Alamo nodded. "He is. I mean, he's *really* mad. So General Houston plans to surprise the Mexicans and confront them with blazing guns before they get to Washington-on-the-Brazos."

"Could be a big battle, especially if Santa Anna's troops vastly outnumber General Houston's."

"Well, right now," said Alamo, "Houston has about a thousand men, but against fourteen hundred, they'll be well outnumbered. The general is trying to build his troops quickly. That's why the soldiers were sent here to see if I would join."

Cort grinned. "No question about you, boss. Houston knows you'll come."

"That he does. But he's going to get a nice surprise too."

"What's that?"

"Alex and Abel are going with me. They're ready to do battle with the Mexicans."

"Well, bless their hearts. Boss, I'll be praying for the three of you."

"I appreciate that, Cort. Thank you. Well, I needed to let you know that you're in charge, as usual, while I'm absent from the ranch."

"I'll handle it, as usual, boss."

"There's no doubt in my mind about that. Well, I need to be going. With the Lord's help, we'll be victorious, and we'll be back as soon as Santa Anna and his troops are defeated."

"That's the way I'll pray, boss, and I'll have all the Christians on this ranch praying the same way. I'll also let Pastor Evans know, if your father or the Kane women don't get to him first."

"Appreciate it, Cort. See you when we get back."

The boss walked away, and the foreman made his way up the ladder and returned to his work.

When Alamo arrived back at the big ranch house, he found his father there with Angela, Alex and Libby, Abel and Vivian, and Julia. They were in conversation with Sergeant Hayes and Corporal Lindall, and the four women were crying. As Alamo mounted the porch steps, the ladies looked up at him, wiping the tears from their cheeks.

Libby sniffled. "Alamo, Vivian and I fear for our husbands' lives, but we have assured them—and we assure you—that we stand behind them in their joining General Houston to stop that wicked Santa Anna and his troops."

"I appreciate that." Alamo hugged Libby.

"Alamo," Vivian said, "Libby and I know if Santa Anna isn't stopped, Mexico will once again take over Texas, and everything we Texans have will be lost."

The aging Abram spoke up. "You and Libby are right, Vivian." He then looked at his three sons. "I commend you boys for what you are about to do. I'm very proud of you."

"We women are all proud of you too." Julia's voice cracked.

"Yes, we are," put in Angela.

Alamo's line of sight was fixed on Julia, and his heart lurched in his chest as he saw her leave her chair and move hastily toward him. Tears streamed down her cheeks, and her arms were open wide. Wiping tears as she drew up to him, Julia wrapped her arms around his neck and held him tight.

Everyone in the family was looking on, wide-eyed, as Alamo folded Adam's weeping widow in his arms. There was dead silence on the porch. The two soldiers glanced at each other but said nothing. Julia had no idea how her closeness was affecting Alamo. It literally took his breath away.

After a few minutes, the weeping Julia found her voice and leaned back in Alamo's arms. "Oh, Alamo, I'll be praying for your safe return… and, of course, for Alex and Abel's safe return too."

Her hands were still clasped at the back of his neck. Alamo placed both of his palms on her face and wiped away her tears. "Thank you, Julie. Your prayers mean a lot to me."

As she released her hold on his neck and stepped aside, she smiled slightly. "When my baby is born, he or she will very much need Uncle Alamo."

Alamo managed a smile of his own, thinking that since the child's real father was in heaven, he would love to marry Julie, which would actually make it so that when the baby was old enough to talk, it would call him "Papa." He looked deeply into her eyes. "Well, Julie dear, Uncle Alamo plans to be here."

Alamo then turned to Sergeant Hayes and Corporal Lindall and said, "My brothers and I will go saddle our horses, get our guns, and put some shaving supplies and other things in our saddlebags. Then we'll be ready to leave."

Libby looked at her husband. "Alex, I'll come to the house and help you pack up what you need."

Alex smiled. "All right. That'll give us a few minutes together too."

Vivian set her eyes on Abel. Before she could speak, he said, "I'd love to have you come with me too." He took Vivian's hand and looked at the rest of the family. "We'll be back with our horses shortly."

"We sure will," Alamo said. "Let's go."

Moments later, Alex and Abel were leading their saddle horses in the direction of their houses, with their wives beside them. Alamo led his horse up to the porch of the big ranch house. Abram and the two soldiers observed as Alamo went into the house with Julia and Angela at his side. They reappeared several minutes later.

At that moment, Alex and Abel were seen leading their horses toward the big ranch house. As they drew up to the porch, it was obvious they were equipped with their weapons, stuffed saddlebags, and small clothing bags, which hung on their saddle horns.

As they stepped up on the porch, Abram looked at them curiously. "You boys bring your Bibles with you?"

"They're in our saddlebags, Papa," said Abel.

Abram stood and removed his hat. "I know you need to get going. Let's have prayer."

Those who were still sitting stood up, and the men removed their hats, including Sergeant Hayes and Corporal Lindall. Everyone bowed their heads as Abram led them in prayer, asking the Lord to protect his sons as they went into battle and to bring them home safely.

When Abram closed his prayer in Jesus's name, there were hugs and kisses as the Kane brothers showed love to their family members. While Alex and Abel kissed their wives good-bye, Alamo planted a kiss on

Julia's cheek, and she did the same in return. When her lips touched his cheek, Alamo's heart seemed to catch fire. But as before, he hid it.

Soon the Kane brothers and the two soldiers were mounted and put their horses in motion. There was much sadness in the small group of Kanes as they stood together and watched their loved ones ride away. They stood close, and when the riders reached the road, turned onto it, and were almost out of sight, they swung around in their saddles and waved. Everyone in the group waved back, tears filling their eyes. Seconds later the riders were out of sight.

As the group's tears continued to flow, Julia took her handkerchief out of her sleeve and mopped at the wetness on her cheeks. Clearing her throat, she looked around at the sad faces. "Okay, now, we've all cried enough for one day. We will certainly continue to pray for Alex, Abel, and Alamo. We'll pray hard for victory over the Mexican forces and for their safe return. We've put them into God's mighty hands, and we'll continue to pray for their safety. But life must go on here at the ranch, and going around with sad faces will only bring gloom to us."

"Amen, honey," said Abram. "We mustn't let this situation get us down."

Julia smiled at him, then ran her gaze to Angela. "How about we have Libby and Vivian eat supper with us here at the big house tonight?"

Angela nodded and smiled. "Sounds like a good idea to me, Julia."

"Me too!" said Abram. "Let's go tell Daisy so she can fix up a real feast for supper!"

Libby dabbed at her remaining tears. "We'll look forward to it. Now I've got to go do some housework."

"Me too," said Vivian, "but we'll both be back at suppertime!"

⌒

As the five riders headed across the Texas prairie toward Washington-on-the-Brazos side by side at a casual trot, Sergeant Ross Hayes looked at the Kane brothers. "I'm curious, fellas. How come you brought those Bibles with you?"

"Well, Sergeant," said Alamo, "we love God's written Word. It was through the Bible that we came to know the Lord Jesus Christ as our Saviour and have the positive assurance that whenever we die, we'll go to heaven and not to hell."

Corporal Rick Lindall looked at Alamo. "When I was a boy, I heard a preacher preach on hell, on its fire and torment, and it scared me. I've never gone to church since."

Alamo met his gaze. "But you believe what the Bible says about hell?"

"Well, ah…yes. The thought of it still scares me. What does a person have to do so he goes to heaven instead of hell?"

"Tell you what," Alamo said. "There's a creek about a half mile ahead. We need to stop and water our horses. How about when we stop, I take my Bible out and show you?"

"Sure. That'll be fine."

Soon they drew up to the creek, dismounted, and led their horses to the water. When the horses had taken their fill, Alamo said, "Okay, Rick, let's sit down on this fallen tree, and I'll show you what the Bible says about being saved."

Alex and Abel took the Bibles out of their saddlebags and sat down on the fallen tree beside their brother and the corporal. Though silent, Sergeant Hayes sat down with them.

"Let's start on the subject of heaven." Alamo opened his Bible and looked at his brothers. "I'm going to Luke 10."

The brothers quickly began flipping pages. Alex turned to Hayes. "You want to look on with me?"

The sergeant nodded. "Sure."

Alamo held his Bible so Corporal Lindall could look at the page. "The Lord Jesus here is talking to a group of men who have put their faith in Him for salvation. Look what He says to them in verse 20. He tells them to rejoice because their names are written in heaven. See that?"

Lindall nodded. "Yes sir."

"The Bible makes it clear, Rick, that only those whose names are written in heaven are going to heaven when they die."

"Makes sense."

Alex had his finger on the verse in his Bible. He looked at the sergeant. "See it?"

"Uh-huh."

"Make sense to *you?*"

"Yes."

"Okay, let's go to the famous Twenty-third Psalm, fellas."

When everyone was at the page, Alamo said, "David starts out here by saying the Lord is his shepherd. That means David is a saved man and will go to heaven when he dies."

"That's right," Abel said.

Alamo put his finger on verse 6. "Now look at what he says in the latter part of verse 6. 'I will dwell in the house of the LORD for ever.' The 'house of the LORD' is heaven. Anybody question that?"

Rick Lindall said, "No. Makes sense."

"Right," said Hayes.

"All right," Alamo continued. "Let's see what Jesus said about the house of the Lord in John 14."

When all three Bibles were open to John 14, Alamo said, "Again, the Lord Jesus is talking to saved, heaven-bound men. Look at verse 2. 'In my Father's house are many mansions: if it were not so, I would have told you. I go to prepare a place for you.' See? These are saved men, and Jesus makes it very clear that they have a place in heaven. Right, Rick?"

The corporal nodded. "Right."

"Now, look what Jesus says in verse 6. 'I am the way, the truth, and the life: no man cometh unto the Father, but by me.' Where is God the Father, Rick?"

"He's in heaven."

"Right. Please take note that Jesus Christ says of Himself that He is the one and only way to the Father. So He is the one and only way to heaven. Right?"

The corporal nodded. "Yes."

"So the way to heaven is not by doing religious deeds or good works. It is not through a church or a denominational system. It is through a *person,* and that person is the one who died on Calvary's cross, shed His precious blood, and raised Himself from the grave three days and three nights after He had been crucified. In John 10:18, before His crucifixion, Jesus said He had power to lay down His life, and He had power to take it again. So Jesus raised Himself from the dead, and He is the one and only way to heaven, right, Rick?"

"Right."

"So people who do not come to Him in repentance of their sin and don't put their faith in Him and Him alone to save them from their sins will die in their sins and spend eternity burning in hell."

The corporal licked his lips nervously. "Mr. Kane, how do I put my faith in Jesus? I don't want to go to hell."

For Sergeant Hayes's sake, Alex and Abel followed in their Bibles as Alamo took Corporal Rick Lindall to John 3 and showed him that Jesus said in verse 3, "Except a man be born again, he cannot see the kingdom of God." He explained that when we come into this world, we are God's *creation,* but not His children. Only God's children go to heaven when they die. To become children of God, they must repent of their sin, and believing that the Lord Jesus died on the cross for them so they could be saved, they must receive Him into their hearts as their own personal Saviour. He explained that repentance is a change of mind that results in a change of direction. The lost sinner must change his mind about his sin, turn from it and whatever religion or humanistic philosophy he is clinging to, put his faith in Jesus, and he will be saved.

Alamo showed Lindall that Ephesians 3:17 says Christ dwells in our *hearts* by faith...not the muscle that pumps the blood through our system, but the very center of the soul...the *heart* of the person. He also showed him John 1:12, which says of Jesus that to those who receive Him, He gives the power to become the sons of God.

Alamo then asked the corporal if he was willing to repent of his sin and receive Jesus into his heart as his Saviour.

"I sure am," said Rick. "How do I do that?"

Alamo turned to Romans 10:13 and pointed at the verse. "Read this verse to me."

Rick focused on it. " 'For whosoever shall call upon the name of the Lord shall be saved.' I just have to turn to Jesus in repentance, pray, and ask Him to forgive me of all my sins and to come into my heart and save me?"

"You've got it, my friend."

"Okay. I want to do that right now."

"So do I," spoke up the sergeant.

Smiles came alive on the faces of the Kane brothers. Alamo said, "All right. We'll kneel down right here, and I'll help both of you."

Alamo Kane had the joy and privilege of leading the two men to the Lord. When they had both called on the Lord Jesus Christ, acknowledging their lost condition to Him, and asked Him to come into their hearts, cleanse them of their sins, and save them, they wept with delight. Alamo prayed for them, that the Lord would help them in their new life and bless them.

The two new Christians both showed real peace as they mounted up, and the five of them once again headed for Washington-on-the-Brazos.

When the Kane brothers arrived at the army post at Washington-on-the-Brazos accompanied by the two soldiers, General Sam Houston was happy to see Alamo Kane and just as happy to meet his two brothers. He thanked all three for coming to join him.

Houston went on to update the Kane brothers and Sergeant Hayes and Corporal Lindall on the situation. He told them that one of his two scouts who had been observing Santa Anna's camp near Galveston just returned and reported that they saw a Mexican boat come up the creek next to their camp with supplies.

Alamo arched his eyebrows. "Supplies, eh? Well, General, since it was a Mexican boat, I'd say those supplies probably include ammunition, wouldn't you?"

Houston grinned. "I sure would, and I sure do! Which means Santa Anna has been waiting for these supplies, especially the ammunition, before making his attack on Washington-on-the-Brazos. It is only a matter of time now before the big bull leads his troops to town and to the army post for the attack."

"So how's it going, General, with your effort to build up the number of troops?"

Houston grinned again. "Good! Just an hour ago, over a hundred volunteers arrived to join us!"

"Great!" Alamo said.

The others smiled, showing they liked this good news too.

"Not only that," Houston said, "but a rider came in only minutes later to inform me that soldiers from a few Texas outposts are on their way! They'll arrive tomorrow."

"So how many will that give us, General?" asked Sergeant Hayes.

"Well, it looks like we may have as many troops as Santa Anna, maybe a few more."

The Kane brothers and the two soldiers were happy to hear this and said so.

Houston explained his plan further. "My scouts, Captain Dan Hoverly and Lieutenant Jim Benson, will keep me informed as to the whereabouts of Santa Anna and his troops, and as soon as the men from the outposts arrive tomorrow, I'll lead my troops south in a hurry and give the big bull a *big* surprise!"

"Good!" Alamo grinned. "This Santa Anna thing has gone on too long already."

His brothers and the two soldiers spoke their agreement.

"That's for sure," said the general. "After what Santa Anna and his Mexican army did to the men at the Alamo and at Goliad, I want to take them down. With the number of men like you Kane brothers who are volunteering to help fight them, I'm confident we can do it."

"Well, we're ready, sir!" said Sergeant Hayes.

"Yeah!" said Corporal Lindall.

Houston smiled and nodded. "If all my men have this attitude, we'll do it!"

"I can speak for my brothers and myself, sir," said Alamo. "We have this attitude!"

Alex and Abel grinned and nodded their assent.

"Good!" Houston turned to the sergeant and the corporal and said, "I want you fellas to take the Kane brothers to the bunkhouse and assign them their bunks."

Later, as Alamo, Alex, and Abel moved among the other men in the bunkhouse, they came upon two men who belonged to their church in Washington-on-the-Brazos. Mark Nichols and Herb Turner, along with their wives, had come to know the Lord Jesus Christ as their Saviour only a few months previously, under the ministry of the church. Mark's wife was part Mexican, and she had taught him Spanish so he could converse with her family, who now lived in southeast Texas.

Nichols and Turner told the Kane brothers that they were proud to serve in the army with them. Alamo, Alex, and Abel returned the compliment.

Alamo added that because of the prayers of Pastor Merle Evans and the people of their church, he felt strongly that they were going to be victorious over the Mexican forces.

The other four men emphatically agreed.

## 7

At the same time as the Kane brothers were getting settled at the Texas army post in Washington-on-the-Brazos, Generalissimo Antonio López de Santa Anna had his fourteen hundred men gather before him at the Mexican army camp near Galveston. He told them that with the arrival of the ammunition and other supplies, he was now prepared to march them to Washington-on-the-Brazos and wipe out General Sam Houston and his small army.

The Mexican soldiers waved their arms with excitement, shouting out that they were ready.

Santa Anna said they would leave at dawn the next morning. Then with a wicked smile on his lips, he said they would indeed slaughter Houston and all his men. Chuckling fiendishly, he added that they would also burn all the bodies just as they had at the Alamo.

There was loud cheering among the troops, who were eager to punish the Texans for declaring their independence from Mexico.

At midmorning the next day, Saturday, April 16, the mounted troops from other Texas outposts had joined together a few miles north of Washington-on-the-Brazos so they could all ride in at once. There were ninety-seven of them.

General Sam Houston was at his desk when there was a tap on the door, which he recognized as that of his adjutant, Corporal Mayfield. "Yes, Corporal?"

The door opened, and Corporal Mayfield said, "Sir, Sergeant Ross Hayes is here to see you."

Houston nodded. "Please send him in."

Mayfield motioned behind him, and the sergeant walked past the corporal to Houston's desk. "General, the outpost troops have arrived."

"Great!" Houston rose to his feet. He lifted his hat from the hook behind the desk and clamped it on his head. "Let's go!"

The general rushed past the sergeant, who followed on his heels. When they stepped outside, Houston saw that all his men were gathering around the new arrivals. Standing in front of the additional troops was Major Wes Daly, whom Houston knew well.

Daly hurried to Houston, and as they shook hands, the general ran his gaze over the men behind Daly, and said, "Looks like a good bunch. How many are there?"

"Ninety-seven of us, General."

A wide smile spread over Houston's face. He looked skyward, his lips moving while he did some arithmetic, then removed his hat and waved it joyfully. "Whoopee! That gives us a total of 1,486 men! Eighty-six more than Santa Anna has!"

The Kane brothers looked at each other, smiling, and Alamo said, "Praise the Lord!"

"Amen!" Alex and Abel chimed in.

As the Texas soldiers cheered, Houston saw his two scouts, Hoverly and Benson, ride up. Both of them ran their eyes over the large crowd of troops. Then Hoverly said loud enough for all to hear, "General Houston, Santa Anna and his troops were preparing themselves to march northward as darkness fell last night! No doubt they began the march at dawn this morning."

"You men hear that?" Houston shouted, looking around at his troops.

There was a collective affirmative reply.

"All right!" The general shook a fist. "Let's eat lunch and head south!"

Cheers were raised amid the men, and Houston told Sergeant Ross Hayes to ride into town and tell President Burnet what was happening.

Hayes galloped into town and was back in ten minutes.

Just after lunch, General Sam Houston led his mounted troops south through Washington-on-the-Brazos, intent on conquering Santa Anna and his Mexican soldiers.

From President David Burnet's office, word had spread quickly through town about General Houston and his men riding south to meet the Mexican troops. Nearly every resident of Washington-on-the-Brazos was on Main Street to watch them leave, and the crowd shouted words of encouragement as the soldiers rode past.

Included in the shouting crowd were President Burnet and his staff, looking on and calling out their own heartening words.

As the sun was setting on Saturday, April 16, General Sam Houston led his army up to the east bank of Spring Creek, some twenty miles south of Washington-on-the-Brazos. There, they set up camp. Among the 1,486 men who made up Houston's troops were 21 who were driving horse-drawn wagons. The wagons were loaded with food and ammunition.

While all the horses were fed and watered and the men who did the cooking lit fires, General Houston took four men aside who had expertly served him as scouts many times, including Captain Hoverly and Lieutenant Benson. The other two were Lieutenant Boyd Wyatt and Lieutenant Elwin Lang.

"I want you to head south after breakfast in the morning," Houston told them, "and keep your eyes on Santa Anna and his troops."

All four men nodded, the seriousness of the situation showing on their faces.

"The four of you are to switch off," Houston continued, "with two of you riding back to report to me each morning and two each evening. This way I'll know exactly where the Mexican troops are and what they're doing."

"That's the way we'll do it, General," said Captain Dan Hoverly.

The other three nodded, assuring Houston that they would carry out his orders exactly as stated.

Later, the Texas troops sat on the ground and ate their evening meal to the sound of the gurgling creek while talking about the upcoming battle they were going to have with Santa Anna and his army of fourteen hundred. The conversation showed that they were especially glad that the Texas army now outnumbered Santa Anna's soldiers. There was a strong optimism of victory among them.

As the men finished their meal, General Houston stood before them by the light of the campfires. "Men, I want every one of you to remember the vicious atrocities that Santa Anna and his 6,500 troops committed against our few men at the Alamo! Don't forget that they killed every one of them, and to add insult to this, they burned their bodies."

Houston was pleased to see that his words caused faces to twist in anger. "I also want to remind you that it was a message sent by the heartless, hate-filled Santa Anna to General José Urrea that brought about the cold-blooded execution of Colonel James Fannin and his men! When we come face to face with Santa Anna and his troops, I want you to remember the Alamo, and I want you to remember Goliad!"

The Texas troops jumped to their feet, angrily shaking their fists above their heads, and shouted in unison, *"Remember the Alamo! Remember Goliad!"*

⌒

At the Diamond K Ranch, late on that same day, the setting sun was casting a warm orange glow over the land. It had been a beautiful spring day, and Julia and Angela Kane were about to have supper together in the cozy kitchen of the big ranch house, along with Daisy Haycock, who had cooked the meal. Abram was spending a few days with some Christian friends who owned a large cattle ranch some five miles west of the Diamond K.

As the three women were sitting down at the table, Julia said, "This has been a lovely, albeit lonely, day." Her hand gently caressed the soft mound beneath her heart. "The days seem so long, but in spite of it, each day brings the birth of this precious baby closer."

"Yes." Daisy patted her hand. "I know the days grow long for you, dear, and I think it's getting close to the time for us to start making preparations for our newest little Kane family member. That should keep us busy in our spare time." Daisy hoped to ease Julia's grief over the loss of her husband and to put her mind on something she could happily anticipate.

Giving Daisy a warm smile, Julia said, "You're right. I need to concentrate on making preparations for this new little one's life. I can't just sit around moping all the time. It isn't good for my baby or for me."

"That's true, dear." Daisy smiled. "Life is for the living, and this wee mite you're carrying deserves everything you and the rest of us can do for him or her."

"That's for sure," agreed Julia.

"I think it's my turn to pray." Angela reached for the women's hands.

They bowed their heads, and when Angela had thanked the Lord for the food, Daisy said, "All right now, girls. Let's eat. I want both of you to enjoy this meal. I cooked it with love, and I want you to eat it, not just push it around on your plates. Your baby needs nourishment, Julia. So do you. And you too, Angela. So please eat up and enjoy. All three of us have work to do keeping this ranch house in order and the upcoming garden prospering."

"You are so right, Daisy," Angela said. "Alamo left us in charge of these things, and we don't want him to come home and find things undone."

Julia took a short breath and let it out. "I know this much. Adam would not want us to be sorrowful all the time because of his death. We know that busy hands will help ease the pain of our loss." A genuine smile lit up her features.

"You're right, sweetie," said Angela.

"You sure are." Daisy paused and looked at Julia. "Honey, do you plan to go back to living at your house, or are you going to stay here in the big ranch house with Angela?"

Julia looked at Angela. "We've talked about it, Daisy. Ultimately I will go back to my house here on the ranch. But right now, even when I go into it for various items during the daytime, I get the shivers just remembering happy times I had with Adam when he was alive and we were living there." Tears welled up in Julia's eyes. She choked up and said in a tight voice, "Oh…here I go, crying again."

While Julia wiped her tears with her napkin, Daisy said, "Oh, Julia, I'm sorry for bringing up your house. I—I'm just interested in what your plans are."

Julia pushed her chair back, rose to her feet, went to silver-haired Daisy, and hugged her. "Daisy, dear, I very much appreciate your interest in how things go in my life. You don't have to apologize for asking about me living in my house again."

Daisy kissed Julia's cheek. "Thank you, sweetie. Now go eat your supper."

As Julia, Angela, and Daisy were finishing their meal, the conversation went to the Kane brothers, who were with the Texas army somewhere in southeast Texas. They discussed the cold-heartedness of Santa Anna and what he had done to the men at the Alamo. Julia broke down for a moment as she thought about how Adam had been killed there. She soon collected her emotions and apologized for the outburst.

Angela reached across the corner of the table and tenderly patted Julia's arm. "Honey, Daisy and I understand."

"For sure," Daisy said.

They then discussed the horrible execution of Colonel James Fannin and his men at Goliad. The three women agreed that Santa Anna was a wicked, brutal man. They each spoke their hopes that when General Houston and his army met up with Santa Anna and his Mexican army, the Texans would be victorious.

Later that night, when Daisy had gone to her apartment connected to the ranch house and Angela and Julia had gone to their rooms, all was quiet except for the sounds of a couple owls in the trees outside.

Julia lay in her bed in the darkness, and the sound of the owls hooting gave her a lonely feeling. She missed Adam so much…

After weeping for several minutes, Julia choked back her sobs. "Oh, dear Lord, please give me peace and rest."

She rolled over, trying to go to sleep, but her mind went to Alamo, Alex, and Abel, who were making ready to fight Santa Anna's troops—or for all she knew had already fought the battle. More tears came. Her heart pounded as she said, "Lord, You know if they have fought the battle. Please…please, if it has been fought and they're still alive, bring them home safely."

Her thoughts settled on Alamo. She pondered how close they had been as friends ever since they met and found at that moment that she missed him very, very much. In her heart, she hoped he was still alive and would be coming home soon. Alamo was still on her mind when she finally dropped off to sleep.

Sometime deep in the night, Angela Kane awakened. She blinked against the darkness. *What woke me up?*

Then she heard the muffled sound of Julia's voice coming from her room down the hall. She sounded anguished. Angela sat up and rubbed her eyes. "That's it. That's the sound that woke me up."

She threw back the covers, rose from her bed, and lit the lantern on the small table beside the bed. The muffled sounds of Julia's voice were still in the air as Angela pulled on her robe from the chair beside her, picked up the lantern, and hurried down the hall. When she approached Julia's door, she could hear sobbing. Angela tapped on the door, opened it, and stepped in. By the light of her lantern, she saw Julia sitting up in bed, holding her hands to her face.

As she saw Angela coming toward the bed, Julia made a choking sound and struggled to gain her composure.

"Honey, what's the matter?" Angela asked as she drew up, her brow furrowed.

Julia tried to answer but could not speak.

Angela set the lantern on a nearby table and took hold of her hand. "Did you dream about Adam, sweetie? Is that why you're crying?"

Julia shook her head, choked up again. She took a deep breath and found her voice. It was hoarse, but she spoke. "I—I've had many dreams about Adam since he was killed, Angela, but this time I was dreaming about Alamo."

"Alamo?"

"Yes. I dreamed he was killed fighting the Mexicans with General Houston, wherever they are right now. Angela, I went to sleep thinking of him. With his life in danger, I—I suddenly realized how very much he means to me."

Angela didn't know what to say. She prayed in her heart for wisdom from the Lord.

"Angela, Alan—ah—Alamo and I have been close friends since the day we first met, but we have grown even closer since Adam was killed. Alamo has been so especially kind and good to me."

Those last few words came out in a squeak, and Julia burst into tears. "Oh, Angela, when I dreamed that Alamo was killed, it was horrible! I—"

"It was only a dream, Julia!" Angela leaned over and wrapped her arms around her. "It doesn't mean that Alamo was really killed!"

Julia wept more, and Angela kept repeating that it was only a dream.

After a few minutes, Julia's weeping eased. Angela took hold of Julia's arms. "Here, honey, let me get you more comfortable."

She helped Julia into a sitting position on the bed and propped pillows behind her back.

Julia sniffed and made a tiny smile. "Thank you."

Angela smiled back and patted her cheek. She sat down beside her on the bed. "You're more than welcome."

Julia took hold of Angela's hand and told her more of Alamo's kindness and compassion toward her since Adam was killed and how very much it had helped her. As Julia went on, Angela began to get the feeling that what Julia felt toward Alamo was more than just friendship. She reminded herself of the times she was sure she had seen in Alamo's eyes and facial expressions that he was in love with Julia. Angela wanted to question Julia about her feelings for Alamo, but she refrained, thinking that it might be too soon to ask whether Julia might be falling in love with him.

When Julia had gone on about Alamo for several minutes, Angela could see that the tension was easing out of the young widow and expectant mother. She squeezed the hand that was holding hers then let go of it. "Honey, I'm going to go to the kitchen and heat up some milk for you. It will soothe you and even help you get back to sleep. You really do need your rest, for your sake and for the sake of this precious little one you're carrying."

Julia watched Angela hurry from the room, then sank back against the soft pillows as tears filmed her eyes. She pulled up a corner of the sheet and dabbed at the tears, saying in a half whisper, "Oh, Lord, I'm so blessed to be here close to Adam's family. I know this baby will never lack for anything, especially love. Thank You, Lord, that You always supply what is needed *when* it is needed."

Julia stayed in that comfortable position and thanked the Lord over and over for His manifold blessings to her.

Soon Angela returned, carrying a big cup of warm milk. It didn't take Julia long to drink it down.

Angela had prayer with Julia, then gently tucked her in, kissed her cheek, and carried her lantern with her as she left the room. As she walked toward her own room, Angela thought about it and was convinced that there were special feelings in Julia's heart toward Alamo.

When she entered her room and closed the door, she removed her robe, put out the lantern, and crawled back into bed. Angela tucked the covers up under her chin. "Lord, I just have the feeling that You are going to make things happen between Alamo and Julia. How wonderful for both of them! Yes, and for that precious baby too!"

Angela Kane took a deep breath and let it out slowly. "And dear Lord, this 'old maid' is sure looking forward to the day when You bring the man into her life that You have chosen to be her husband."

## 8

The next morning, at the spot on the bank of Spring Creek where the Texas army was camped, General Sam Houston sent his scouts—Captain Dan Hoverly, Lieutenant Jim Benson, Lieutenant Boyd Wyatt, and Lieutenant Elwin Lang—off to keep watch on the Mexican troops.

Each day, as the Texas troops moved continually southward, the scouts returned two at a time, morning and evening, to report the location of Santa Anna and his troops as they moved northward.

Late in the afternoon on Tuesday, April 19, Houston and his men came upon Groce's Landing on the winding Brazos River. General Houston had explained to the troops that morning that they would camp that night at Groce's Landing, which was owned by Jared Groce, whom he knew well. He told them that Jared had a large plantation there along the river and that he would welcome them to pitch camp for that night on his land.

When they arrived, Jared indeed gladly invited Houston and his men to camp there and gave them more food for their wagons, including some beef from his herd of cattle.

Houston thanked him for the hospitality and gave orders for his men to make camp and cook the beef.

Jared smiled. "General Houston, I have a real nice surprise for you."

He had the attention of all the nearby troops as Houston smiled and said, "Well, what's that, my friend?"

"A few days ago, a boat that regularly travels up and down the river drew up to the dock here at the landing. The boat's captain told me that some citizens of Cincinnati, Ohio, who are concerned about our potential war with Mexico had shipped two cannons to you, along with a number of cannonballs and a good supply of gunpowder. I told the captain that I figured based on the news I had heard about Santa Anna and his troops coming from Galveston toward Washington-on-the-Brazos, I'd have the pleasure of seeing the Texas army passing by on their way to confront them. When I did I would make sure you received the cannons, cannonballs, and gunpowder."

The general smiled and looked at his crowd of men. "Did all of you hear that?"

The men nodded. "We can use those cannons, Mr. Groce!" called out one of the men.

"We sure can, Jared," Houston said.

"Well, come on, General." Groce headed toward a large shed. "I have them right in here, along with the cannonballs and gunpowder."

When Groce opened the double doors of the shed, Houston spotted the two large cannons, which were mounted on wheels, and called for several of the men to go in and wheel the cannons out of the shed. Groce then pointed out the large stack of wooden boxes, explaining that the gunpowder and cannonballs were inside.

When the cannons had been brought out so all the men could get a good look at them, there were comments about how surprised Santa Anna and his troops would be when the big guns opened up on them.

General Houston eyed the wooden boxes of gunpowder and cannonballs. "Jared, our wagons are already loaded with ammunition and food, including what food you gave us. I don't know how we'll transport the cannonballs and the gunpowder."

Groce smiled. "I'll donate one of my wagons, General. It'll hold all the cannonballs and gunpowder. But I don't have any spare horses."

"That's all right," said the general. "We can hook your wagon up behind one of our other wagons."

While the men were loading up the wagon, Groce said, "General, when my wife saw these two cannons and that they look exactly alike, she named them the Twin Sisters."

Houston chuckled. "Twin Sisters, eh? I like that." He turned to some of the men. "You men take the cannons—the Twin Sisters—and attach them to the back sides of two of the ammunition wagons."

By the time the general's orders had been carried out, the army cooks were cooking supper. The large number of troops got in line for food, holding plates and cups, and soon were sitting on the ground around campfires, eating. They were especially enjoying the beefsteaks Jared Groce had given them.

The Kane brothers were sitting by one of the campfires, talking about how the beefsteaks made them lonely for their ranch, when they saw two riders galloping into camp. They instantly recognized Captain Dan Hoverly and Lieutenant Jim Benson.

The men gathered around as the two scouts dismounted where General Houston was now standing. "General," Captain Hoverly said loudly, so all the men could hear him, "Santa Anna has led his troops on a swerve eastward."

Houston frowned and gusted, "Eastward? Why do you suppose they're doing that?"

Still speaking loudly, Hoverly replied, "We figure it's because Santa Anna wants to attack Washington-on-the-Brazos from the east rather than the south for some reason. For sure, he's still planning on attacking the town and the army facility there."

"He *has* to be," boomed Houston.

"Absolutely, General," Jim Benson said loudly. "The way they're heading, we figure they're about a day's march south of the juncture at Buffalo Bayou and the San Jacinto River."

Houston nodded solemnly and ran his gaze over his men. Lifting his voice, he asked, "Did you all hear what Captain Hoverly and Lieutenant Benson just said?"

Heads nodded, even on the outside edge of the large group.

"All right," the general said loudly, "we'll move fast tomorrow and be ready to intercept the big bull and his troops. We can make it to the juncture of Buffalo Bayou and the San Jacinto from here in little more than half a day. We'll be ready for them when they show up."

"Yes, we will, General!" shouted out one of the sergeants. "Remember the Alamo! Remember Goliad!"

The whole crowd of fighting men joined in, shouting excitedly, "Remember the Alamo! Remember Goliad!"

After the Texas troops had enjoyed their beefsteaks and all that went with them, Alamo, Alex, and Abel Kane were still sitting by their campfire. They were talking about the battle that lay ahead, which they now knew would happen at the juncture of Buffalo Bayou and the San Jacinto River.

As the conversation went on, they soon saw two men in the shadows walking toward them. When they moved into the light of the fire, the Kane brothers recognized Sergeant Ross Hayes and Corporal Rick Lindall.

"Well, howdy, fellas," Alamo said. "You like that beef Mr. Groce gave us?"

Ross licked his lips. "Sure did."

"Yeah!" said Rick. "Good stuff!"

Ross hunkered down and looked at Alamo by the light of the flickering fire. "Rick and I just wanted to come and thank you for leading us to the Lord last Friday."

Rick was now crouched beside Ross. "Alamo, we know men will be killed on both sides when the battle takes place. Ross and I have been talking about it, and we want to assure you that if either of us should be among those killed, we have peace in our hearts knowing that we will be in heaven."

"Praise the Lord!" said Abel. "The three of us have the same peace!"

"Amen!" Alex said.

Alamo smiled broadly. "Hallelujah! We sure do! Isn't it wonderful to have peace about going into eternity?"

Ross blinked at the excess moisture welling up in his eyes. "It sure is!"

"Yes!" Rick said. "Only Jesus can give that kind of peace!"

⌒

At dawn on Wednesday, April 20, the Texans began their trek in the direction of Buffalo Bayou and the San Jacinto River to intercept the Mexican troops. At midmorning, Lieutenants Boyd Wyatt and Elwin Lang came galloping up to General Houston and skidded to a halt. Riding in the lead of the troops, the general signaled everyone to stop.

"General," said Wyatt, "we know that Captain Hoverly and Lieutenant Benson gave you the information about Santa Anna's eastward turn, so we knew where to find you."

Houston nodded. "You have news?"

"Yes sir," Wyatt said. "Santa Anna and his troops didn't leave the spot where they camped last night until about an hour ago. At their normal pace, this should bring them within three or four miles west of the juncture of Buffalo Bayou and the San Jacinto River by sundown."

"Good," said Houston. "We'll be there long before that. Probably between one and two o'clock this afternoon."

The general turned his horse around, faced the company of men on horseback and in wagons, and told them what his scouts had just reported.

When the Texas troops heard the general's words, one of the sergeants called out loudly, "We're ready to fight those Mexicans, General Houston!"

Instantly more loud voices called out their agreement with what the sergeant had just said.

Houston turned to the scouts. "Make sure Captain Hoverly and Lieutenant Benson understand that I want them at the juncture just before sundown so they can let me know exactly where Santa Anna and his troops have camped for the night."

"We'll make sure they understand that, General," Boyd Wyatt said.

Houston smiled. "Thank you."

"Our pleasure, sir," said Elwin Lang.

They both saluted the general and galloped away.

Houston and his men kept moving at a steady pace, and just before two o'clock that afternoon, they reached the juncture of Buffalo Bayou and the San Jacinto River.

Immediately they began making preparations for the battle that would take place the next day, including loading the Twin Sisters and making them ready. As his men worked, General Houston rode among them and told them that as soon as his scouts arrived before sundown to let him know exactly where the enemy had made camp, he would make plans for exactly what time to pull away from this spot in the morning and launch the attack.

Again the Texas troops let him know in no uncertain terms that they were ready to do battle with the Mexicans.

～

As General Sam Houston and his troops were preparing for the battle to come, at the Diamond K Ranch, foreman Cort Whitney and two ranch hands arrived from Washington-on-the-Brazos, where they had purchased new tools to replace some that had either broken or become worn out.

Pulling the wagon up in front of the big ranch house, Cort handed the reins to the man next to him. "You boys go on over to the toolshed and unload the tools. I'll take this letter to Julia."

When Cort touched ground, the wagon moved on. He took the envelope from his shirt pocket, mounted the steps of the front porch, and knocked on the door. A few seconds passed, and then the door opened. Angela Kane smiled. "Hello, Cort. Find all the tools you needed at the hardware store?"

"Sure did," he replied, returning her smile. "Is Julia here?"

"Mm-hmm."

He raised the envelope. "I picked up the mail at the post office. This letter is from Julia's parents."

"Oh, that'll make her happy. I'll let you give it to her."

Angela turned and called out, "Julia! Julia! Come to the front door!"

Within a few seconds, Julia could be seen coming along the hallway from the rear of the house. She smiled when she saw the Diamond K foreman at the door, and as she drew nearer, she looked at Angela. "Does Cort want to hire me to herd the cattle?"

Angela laughed. "Not yet, honey. But he's got something for you."

Cort extended the envelope to her. "I picked up the mail while I was in town. It's for you, from your parents."

Julia smiled as she took it from him. "Thank you, Cort."

He grinned. "You're welcome, ma'am. And if you ever want to become a hired hand, let me know."

She shook her head. "I was just funning you. When my baby is born, I'll have plenty of work to keep me busy."

Cort gave her an admiring look. "Julia, I appreciate the way you work a little humor into your day. You've only been a widow for a little over six weeks, yet your spirits seem to be lifting marvelously."

"It's the Lord's doing, Cort," she replied softly. "I couldn't do it without Him."

"That's a real good testimony, little lady."

"Well, not *all* my moments are this good yet, Cort, but the Lord is helping me because my family is praying for me, as are the Christians here on the ranch and the people at our church."

"Well, praise the Lord," said Cort. "I've got to go now, and I'm sure you're eager to read the letter."

As Cort walked away, Angela closed the door, and Julia quickly opened the envelope. When she unfolded the letter, she saw instantly that it had been penned by her mother. Her heart quickened as she began reading her mother's words.

Angela could tell Julia was pleased with what she was reading and waited in silence until she finished.

Julia's eyes sparkled. "Oh, Angela! Mama says here how much she and Papa enjoyed being with me at the Diamond K and getting to meet the rest of the Kanes and all the ranch people. She says that she and Papa really love Texas, and—and—"

"And *what,* honey?"

Julia swallowed hard. "Oh, Angela! Do you remember me telling you after Papa and Mama were here that something they said just before they left made me think they might come back to be here when the baby is born?"

"Yes… Are they coming?"

"They want to. I'm supposed to find out if it would be all right if they come."

"Well, honey, since the boss man of the Diamond K isn't here right now, I can speak for him. I'm sure Alamo would absolutely approve of you telling them that they are welcome to come! We loved having your parents here before, and now it's even more important that they be here!"

Joy was well-written on Julia's features.

Angela hugged her good, then eased back, holding both shoulders in her hands. "I know it will mean a lot to you to have your mama here when you give birth."

"Oh yes! Sometimes I have a tingle of fear when I think of delivering my baby without—without Adam here. But with Mama at my side, it will relieve my mind so much!"

"All right then. It's settled. You write your parents immediately, and tell them that they are *more* than welcome to come."

Tears filmed Julia's eyes. "Oh, I will, Angela. I'll go to my room right now and respond to Mama's letter. I appreciate how welcome my parents are here at the ranch."

Angela grinned. "Why not? They're *family*! Besides, it's a pleasure to have them here. God has blessed us Kanes so abundantly, and this home is ready to receive any who need it. Besides, I became very fond of your parents when they were here. I wish they would just pack up and move here to this part of Texas! It would be great having them close-by."

"Yes, it would!" Julia said. "Since I don't have Adam, it would be wonderful to have their help in raising this child."

Angela chuckled. "Well, your little one will also have a grandfather and aunts and uncles to help raise him or her. This baby will be very blessed."

"Very blessed, indeed," Julia replied quietly, her eyes shining.

⟋⟍

At the juncture of Buffalo Bayou and the San Jacinto River, where General Sam Houston and his men were camped, scouts Hoverly and Benson rode in at sundown and dismounted at the spot on the riverbank where the general was in conversation with a few of his officers.

The setting sun was shining beautifully off the surface of the gurgling San Jacinto as Captain Dan Hoverly said, "General Houston, Santa Anna and his troops are camped on the north bank of the San Jacinto River a little less than three miles away, around a slight bend in the river. They can't see this camp at all from where they are."

Excitement showed in Houston's eyes. "Good! I'll call all the men together and tell them right now!"

When the Texas troops were gathered before their leader, he told them the location of the Mexicans as reported by the scouts. "Now that Santa Anna and his soldiers are this close," Houston said loud enough for all to hear, "we will attack their camp at dawn!"

Excitement showed amongst the men as they displayed their eagerness to launch the attack, and conversations were soon going on about the coming battle.

The general turned to Hoverly and Benson. "You two can stay here in the camp, now. There is no need for you to do any more scouting. Lieutenants Wyatt and Lang will be returning at dusk as usual."

Both men nodded. "That's the plan, sir," said Hoverly. "One other thing we need to tell you about is the bridge just a short distance from where the Mexicans are camped."

"Bridge?"

"Yes sir. Like where we are now, the river is about sixty yards wide at that spot, and the bridge spans the river this direction, about thirty yards from where the Mexicans are camped. We need to take out that bridge with the cannons so no Mexicans can use it to escape."

"All right," said Houston. "I'll tell my experienced cannon men that when the attack is launched, they are to aim at that bridge and destroy it."

"That's it, sir," said Benson. "We knew you'd see the need for that."

General Houston immediately went to his cannon men and gave his orders concerning the bridge. He then passed the word on to all the other men so they would know what was happening.

While the cooks were preparing supper, the rest of the troops worked to get everything ready for the attack they would launch at dawn the next morning. Soon they were all eating their evening meal.

The men had just finished eating at dusk when the other two scouts came riding in. They dismounted and approached General Houston, who was seated on the ground by a small fire. He rose to his feet as Lieutenants Wyatt and Lang drew up. All the other men stood up and gathered close to hear what the scouts would say to their leader.

By the firelight, the general could see the concern written on their faces. "Something wrong?"

"Yes sir," said Lieutenant Lang. "Santa Anna must've had scouts out. He must know we're camped here."

Houston's brow furrowed. "What do you mean?"

"We saw the Mexicans stacking up breastworks of trunks, baggage, and other equipment from which to fire at us when we attack, General," said Lieutenant Wyatt. "No question about it. They're building a makeshift fort."

Houston nodded. "Hmm. Santa Anna's plan then is for his troops to fortify themselves and catch us out in the open as a surprise."

He looked around at his troops. "Well, the surprise is going to be on Santa Anna. We won't attack at dawn, as he most surely expects. We'll wait until midafternoon and catch them off guard. Mexicans like to have their siestas at midafternoon. We'll take advantage of that fact and attack while a great number of them are snoring."

The men in the crowd spoke up, agreeing with General Houston that this was a good tactic. Houston smiled at all of them and waved. They applauded him.

The general then turned to his four scouts, who were standing together. "Men, I'll send all four of you out in the morning to see what is going on at the Mexican camp."

Hoverly, Benson, Wyatt, and Lang nodded their assent.

As darkness fell and the stars appeared in the sky, Alamo Kane and his brothers were sitting at a campfire with Sergeant Hayes and Corporal Lindall. Alamo had his Bible in hand. Both Hayes and Lindall talked about the joy they had knowing that they had Jesus in their hearts. Alamo opened his Bible and read more Scripture about heaven, which gave them more joy.

Later, when all but the men on guard duty were bedded down on the ground, many men had trouble sleeping soundly. In his bedroll, Alamo Kane thought of Julie, and the love he felt for her warmed his heart. He prayed that Julie and the baby would both do fine when the baby was born.

## 9

Dawn came on April 21, 1836, with a clear sky overhead. The majority of the Texas troops began climbing out of their bedrolls in the early morning light and saw that the soldiers who were also the cooks already had their cook fires going.

By the time the men were eating breakfast, daylight was spreading from the eastern horizon, a soft brightness coming up from the undulating prairie around them. A faint tinge of rose lighted the translucent sky.

Sergeant Ross Hayes and Corporal Rick Lindall were eating with the Kane brothers. They were all enjoying hot coffee, bacon, hot cakes, and cornmeal mush. Sitting close-by were General Sam Houston's four scouts.

Ross Hayes glanced toward the scouts. "How soon are you heading out to check on Santa Anna's camp?"

"Right away," replied Dan Hoverly. "As soon as we finish breakfast. General Houston wants us to get there early enough to see if they're staying put."

"I would think they'd stay put since they stacked up those breastworks," said Lindall.

Boyd drained his coffee cup and said, "The general talked to us last night as we were slipping into our bedrolls. He said he just wants to be sure those breastworks weren't put there simply to fool us. You know— launch a surprise attack on us instead."

"That's wise," Lindall said.

Jim Benson grinned. "The general is a wise man."

"That's for sure." Lindall nodded.

A few seconds later, the four scouts finished breakfast and set out on foot to get a good look at the Mexican camp. In the Texas camp, the troops made ready for the attack, trying to keep their nerves settled.

At midmorning, the scouts returned. General Houston was in a discussion with some of the men and saw them coming into the camp. He removed his hat and waved it to get their attention. One of the scouts saw him immediately and told the others. They made a beeline for their esteemed leader, and as they drew up, Houston asked, "Well, what's happening?"

Captain Hoverly said, "They're still at the same spot, sir. Santa Anna has his Mexican flags on long poles, flapping in the breeze over the camp. Many of the soldiers are grouped up behind the breastworks. He and his troops appear to be ready for our attack."

Houston nodded. "Right now maybe, but I know those Mexicans. A good many of them will be taking their siestas when we actually do attack."

Hoverly licked his lips. "You're the one who knows, General. We all trust your knowledge of the Mexicans."

Other men within hearing distance spoke up their agreement with Hoverly's statement.

Lunchtime finally came, and the Texans, knowing that they would soon be in the battle, ate very little.

To General Houston and his men, the time seemed to drag by, but finally, as the sun dropped nearly halfway down the afternoon sky, the general mounted his horse and led his troops, who were on foot, across the prairie toward the Mexican camp.

They drew up in the thick woods and hid behind trees, where they could not be seen, and looked over the Mexican camp. Indeed, the majority of Mexican soldiers were lying on the ground, enjoying their customary siestas.

General Houston had dismounted and was standing behind a tree, peering at the encampment. Alamo was behind a tree just to the general's left. Keeping his voice low, he said, "General Houston, you certainly were right. I don't think Santa Anna is expecting us to show up now. He probably thinks it'll be tomorrow at dawn."

Houston nodded. "Exactly, Alamo. It's time for us to attack."

General Houston mounted his horse, took out his pocket watch and focused on it. Then he put it back in his pocket and said to those close-by, "It's exactly three thirty. Let's go!"

As the two cannons were wheeled forward several yards to the general's left, the entire Texas army broke into a run as the general trotted his horse toward the Mexican camp.

Seconds later, as the Texan soldiers rushed out of the woods, rifles blazing, the stunned Mexicans who had not slept began firing back. All over the camp, sleeping soldiers were awakened and groggily attempted to make ready for battle.

As General Houston had directed his cannon men, the Twin Sisters were hauled to a spot where the bridge across the San Jacinto River was a clear target. The cannons first belched their charges of iron slugs into the enemy barricades with loud roars, quickly taking their toll on the surprised Mexicans. Many were already down, bullets and shrapnel ripping into their bodies.

As the Texans drew closer, their rifles blasting away at Santa Anna's troops, the twin cannons were aimed at the bridge General Houston had ordered destroyed. The cannonballs effectively caused the bridge to collapse, much of it falling into the river.

The Twin Sisters once again opened fire on the breastworks and other barricades the Mexicans had put up.

Generalissimo Antonio López de Santa Anna was seen riding his white horse back and forth among his men, shouting loudly as if in absolute panic. The brass epaulets and brass on his fancy uniform reflected the brilliant sunlight. General Houston saw him and told himself that it appeared Santa Anna hadn't had lookouts posted. Indeed, the

Mexican leader had believed that the Texans wouldn't attack until the next morning.

As the Texans charged closer to the Mexican lines, their rifles blazed away practically point-blank at the surprised and panic-stricken Mexicans. The Texan soldiers shouted repeatedly, "Remember the Alamo! Remember Goliad!"

The Twin Sisters thundered loudly, shooting cannonballs that exploded when they hit solid subjects, sending deadly shrapnel into the Mexicans.

Running hard and fast, the Texas troops stormed over the already shattered breastworks, sending bullets ripping into the Mexicans who manned the artillery, dropping them like flies. When the Texans' rifles had been emptied, they joined in hand-to-hand combat with the Mexicans, slashing right and left with their bayonets.

Though a few Texans were going down in the battle, the surprised and outnumbered Mexicans were falling by scores under the impact of the deadly assault.

In the midst of the savage action, the Texans continued to shout, "Remember the Alamo! Remember Goliad!"

Above the roar of the battle, many of the Mexicans shook their heads and cried out, "Me no Alamo! Me no Goliad!"

At one place in the Mexican camp, Sergeant Hayes and Corporal Lindall were fighting two Mexican soldiers with their bayonets. Just as they were putting their combatants down with their bloodstained bayonets, a Mexican soldier appeared from behind an ammunition wagon, his eyes bulging with hatred, and aimed his rifle at Sergeant Hayes's face. The rifle spit fire, and Hayes went down with a hole in his forehead.

Corporal Lindall swung his rifle on the Mexican's chest and fired. The Mexican collapsed with a slug in his heart.

Some forty yards away, General Sam Houston was moving about swiftly on his horse, repeatedly firing his revolver at the Mexicans, reloading, and firing again. Suddenly a Mexican bullet struck his right ankle. He let out a yelp and fell from the saddle.

One of his officers, Major Dan Hockley, saw him fall. He zigzagged his way amid flying bullets and knelt down beside the general. Houston was gritting his teeth in pain, his eyes locked on the major.

Hockley saw the bloody boot on the general's right foot. "Just lie still, General! I'll look at your wound."

He removed Houston's boot and found that the slug had sliced skin and chipped a small piece of bone from the backside of his ankle but hadn't lodged in his foot or boot. He told the general so, then hurriedly used the scarf from his own hip pocket to bandage the ankle, leaving on the general's torn stocking.

At that moment, some distance away, as bullets were flying and bayonets were swishing in combat, Santa Anna's number-one officer, General Manuel Castrillon, fell dead when a number of bullets ripped into him. When several Mexican soldiers saw him go down, they turned toward the Texans' line, threw their guns down, raised their empty hands above their heads, and cried out, "*¡Rendición! ¡Rendición!*"

Many of the Texans looked on, wide-eyed. "Anybody know what that word means?" someone yelled.

Another Texan who knew Spanish said loudly, "Yes! *Rendición* is Spanish for 'surrender'! They're surrendering!"

In another area, a number of the Mexican soldiers were looking for Santa Anna, wanting him to tell them what they should do since the Texans were taking control of the battle. When they could not locate their leader, they left the camp area and began running in wild terror over the prairie, into the boggy marshes or along the bank of the San Jacinto River. They soon saw that the Texans were following them, guns blazing.

Most of them stopped, threw down their guns, and lifted their hands over their heads. "¡Me no Alamo! ¡Me no Goliad! ¡Rendición! ¡Rendición!"

Others kept running. Some were cut down by the Texans' bullets. When the Texans saw that some were now out of range for their rifles, they let them go.

General Houston, who was on the ground leaning against a tree with Major Dan Hockley standing over him, noted that the firing had stopped. "What's going on, Major?"

At that instant, several officers came running toward him. "Looks to me like the battle is over, General," Hockley said.

Houston blinked and focused on the coming officers. When they drew up seconds later, they told him that a number of the Mexicans had fled and gotten away. A larger number had surrendered and were now captive, and still others lay on the ground, wounded or dead.

The general lifted a hand to Major Hockley. "Help me stand up, will you?"

Hockley lifted Houston and helped him lean against the tree, his weight on his left leg. The boot for his right foot lay on the ground.

The general took out his pocket watch, looked at it and then at the surrounding officers. "Well, men, the battle lasted eighteen minutes. Though I'm sure some of our men have been killed and others wounded, we are the victors."

As the officers showed their pleasure at the news, they noticed the general's bandaged foot. Major Hockley quickly explained that a bullet had chipped off a small piece of bone from the general's ankle, adding that it did not appear to be serious. The bleeding had already stopped.

Houston quickly assigned some of his officers to put all the Mexicans who had surrendered in one place, along with the wounded ones, and see that they were guarded carefully. He sent others to check on the wounded Texans and get a count of how many had been killed.

The officers hurried away to carry out the orders, and Major Hockley helped the general to sit down on the ground once again.

Untouched in the battle, Alex and Abel Kane were among the Texans assigned to check on their dead and wounded. Alamo Kane, also unhurt, was handling the captured and wounded Mexicans. As he moved over the blood-splattered area, he passed by Mark Nichols, who was bending over some of the dead enemy. Just then Alamo came upon a young Mexican soldier who lay on the ground, seriously wounded. The young man looked up at him with distrust, clenching his teeth in pain.

Alamo knelt down beside him and quickly saw that cannonball shrapnel was buried deeply in his chest, part of which had to be very near his heart. His uniform coat was torn and soaked with blood. Alamo felt sure he was dying. He ran his eyes to Mark Nichols, who was now looking his way. Motioning, Alamo said, "Mark, I need your help."

Mark headed toward him, and as he drew up, Alamo said, "This young man is dying. Since you know Spanish, would you translate for me so I can try to lead him to the Lord?"

"Of course," said Mark.

At the same moment, Alex and Abel Kane were moving among the dead bodies of Mexicans nearby, searching for fallen Texans. The two brothers overheard Alamo and came over to him and Mark.

Alamo glanced at his brothers.

"We'll be standing right here praying, little brother," Alex said.

While Alex and Abel prayed in their hearts, Mark knelt beside Alamo. When he saw the shrapnel in the Mexican soldier's chest, he knew the man was dying.

Speaking softly in Spanish, Mark told the wounded Mexican soldier that he was mortally wounded. The soldier nodded, saying he knew it too.

Mark told Alamo what he had said to the soldier and what the soldier had said in return.

Alamo nodded. "Tell him I want to talk to him about where he is going to go when he dies…that I want to talk to him about Jesus Christ."

When Mark told the soldier in Spanish what Alamo had said, the wounded man nodded.

Then Alamo said, "Ask him if he believes that Jesus is the virgin-born Son of God, that He died for sinners on the cross of Calvary, and that He rose from the dead."

When Mark questioned him in Spanish as directed by Alamo, the dying soldier replied weakly. "*Sí. Sí. Sí.*"

"Ask him if he knows he's going to heaven," Alamo said.

Mark asked the question in Spanish, and the soldier replied weakly. Mark turned to Alamo. "He said he hopes so. He has tried to live good."

Knowing he had little time, Alamo began briefly quoting Scriptures on hell, heaven, repentance, and salvation. As Mark translated them, the frightened young soldier listened intently.

Once Alamo had made salvation's plan clear to the dying soldier, who now admitted to Mark that he was a guilty sinner before God, Alamo asked if he was willing to repent of his sin and ask Jesus to come into his heart and save him. Hearing Alamo's words in Spanish from Mark, the Mexican nodded his head, saying he wanted to be saved. Alamo's face lit up when Mark told him the soldier's reply.

With Mark doing the translating, Alamo had the joy of leading the dying young soldier as he called on the Lord Jesus to save him.

As Alamo, Mark, Alex, and Abel rejoiced at the Mexican soldier's salvation, they saw his eyes roll back in their sockets. He gasped, smiled faintly, and took his last breath.

"Praise God!" said Mark. "He's in heaven now!"

Two Texas soldiers who had been observing the scene from a few yards away stepped up. The taller one lashed out at Alamo and Mark angrily. "You traitors! You shouldn't have shown kindness to an enemy soldier!"

"Yeah!" said the shorter one. "What'd you do that for?"

Alamo met their hot eyes and said in a steady voice, "These three men and I are Christians. Our greatest desire is to bring lost people to the Lord Jesus Christ for salvation."

The short soldier snapped, "This Mexican was your enemy! You shouldn't have been kind to him!"

Alamo said, "Jesus told His followers, 'Love your enemies, do good to them which hate you.'"

The two soldiers looked at him blankly.

"The young Mexican is now in heaven because he put his faith in the Lord Jesus Christ to cleanse his sins and save his soul," Alamo said. "Let me ask you something. Where would you two be right now if you had been killed in this battle we just fought? Heaven or hell?"

Both men gave him a dirty look, glanced at each other, then quickly turned and walked away muttering.

Alamo shook his head sadly as he watched them go. Then he turned to Mark. "Thank you for your help. I couldn't have done it without you."

Mark smiled. "It was my pleasure. Well, I need to get back to my assignment."

"Us too," said Alex. "Praise the Lord. Another soul snatched from Satan's grasp."

"Amen," said Abel.

Alamo watched Mark walk away in one direction and his brothers in the opposite direction. He was about to move on himself when he saw Corporal Rick Lindall hurrying toward him.

As Rick drew up, Alamo could see tears in his eyes. "Rick, what's wrong?"

The corporal took a short breath and cleared his throat. "Ross was killed in the battle, Alamo."

"Oh no!"

Rick nodded sadly. "The two of us were fighting side by side. I—I won't go into the details right now, but Ross took a slug in the forehead.

It killed him instantly. I wanted to be the one to tell you, Alamo, because you led us both to the Lord. I'm so thankful to know that he's now with the Lord in heaven."

Though saddened by Ross's death, Alamo and Rick rejoiced together, knowing that their friend was now in the presence of the Saviour.

At the same time, some distance across the piece of land that had been the Mexican camp, close to the spot where the Mexican prisoners were being held, General Houston was lying under an oak tree while Major Hockley was tightening the makeshift bandage on his wounded right ankle.

Houston had called for four of his officers. He looked up at them with pain-filled eyes. "I need to know as soon as possible how many of our men have been killed or wounded, and I also need to know the same count on the Mexicans, as well as those we are now holding as prisoners. When you come up with that count, we'll know how many of the fourteen hundred escaped."

One of the officers said, "General, I know Spanish well, and I heard the Mexican prisoners discussing the fact that Santa Anna had vanished during the battle."

Houston's eyebrows arched. "Vanished, you say?"

"Yes sir. Do you suppose he turned tail and ran away with those other Mexicans?"

The general shook his head. "I don't know, but maybe the big bull did turn chicken and run away."

Major Hockley, who had just finished with Houston's bandage, stood up and pointed past the spot where the prisoners were being held. "General, look. One of our soldiers is bringing a Mexican soldier this way. The Mex's uniform is ripped up and bloody. It's a wonder he can walk. Our man has the Mexican's hands bound behind his back and is holding a revolver to the back of his head."

As the others looked that direction, General Houston sat up and fixed his eyes on the Texan and his captive. "That uniform is torn and bloody, all right. *Humpf.* Well, our man will just add him to the rest of the prisoners."

The general and those with him watched, expecting the Texan to guide the prisoner into the crowd of other prisoners. But the Texas soldier kept his prisoner headed toward the spot where General Houston was sitting.

As the Texan ushered the Mexican soldier past the crowd of prisoners, they began to cry out, *"¡El presidente! ¡El presidente!"*

Houston said to the men around him, "Why are they calling that Mexican *el presidente?* That's not Santa Anna."

As they came closer, Houston and his men recognized Sergeant Jess Sylvester as the soldier who had the Mexican in hand.

Major Hockley gasped. "General Houston! I've seen Santa Anna up close before. That *is* Santa Anna!"

The eyes of every man in the group bulged, and their mouths went dry. They stood in shock as Sergeant Sylvester ushered the president and military leader of Mexico up to General Sam Houston, who was now on his feet.

## 10

Sergeant Jess Sylvester kept the muzzle of his revolver pressed firmly against the back of the forty-two-year-old Santa Anna's head as he brought him to a halt and said in a crusty voice, "This man facing you is General Sam Houston."

Santa Anna, who was taller than the average Mexican man, was clad in the blue uniform of a common soldier. The coat was torn and blood-soaked on the left side. The pant legs were obviously too short, as were the sleeves. Though uncomfortable with the gun held to his head, he said in broken English, "I am Generaleesseemo Antonio López de Santa Anna, a preesoner of war at your deesposition."

Texan soldiers and captive Mexican soldiers looked on as General Houston scowled at Santa Anna and focused on the common soldier's tattered and bloody uniform. Ignoring Santa Anna's words, he looked at Sergeant Sylvester. "How'd you catch him?"

"I happened to be making my way through the woods over there to the east after all the firing stopped, sir, and I saw what I thought was a wounded Mexican soldier attempting to escape from the battlefield. I was in some brush when I spotted him heading straight toward me and saw the blood on his uniform. I stayed down and pulled my gun. I've seen Santa Anna up close before so when he came closer, I recognized him. I stepped out of the brush pointing the gun at him and told him to stop, which he did."

"Good for you," Houston said.

Santa Anna ran his dark eyes back and forth, showing his discomfort at the gun still held against the back of his head.

"So what about this uniform he's wearing?" Houston asked.

"I made him lie facedown on the ground while I tied his hands behind his back. Then I stood him up, put my gun to his head, and asked him why he was wearing the uniform of a common Mexican soldier. I discovered quickly that he had taken the uniform off a dead soldier, discarded his own, and put on this one to disguise himself in an effort to escape."

By this time, a large crowd of Texas soldiers had gathered at the scene and were glaring with hatred at the bloodthirsty Mexican leader.

Santa Anna was already trembling because of the sergeant's gun still pressed to the back of his head, but the trembling grew worse as he saw the hatred in the Texans' eyes. He looked at them as though he expected them to rip him to pieces and cringed with fright. His dark-skinned features blanched at the thought of being the victim of their rage.

Santa Anna met the general's harsh gaze, and fear showed in his eyes as he spoke in a shaky voice. "Gen'ral Houston," he said. "I am asking for treatment due a preesoner of war. I plead for mercy."

A slow scarlet wave flowed over Houston's face, which was rigid, like rudely chiseled stone. Scowling at Santa Anna, he retorted, "What claim have you to mercy? You certainly showed no mercy at the Alamo, nor when you sent orders for all the Texas soldiers to be executed at Goliad!"

Santa Anna ran his tongue over his lips and avoided the general's bitter eyes.

Because Houston was aware that Santa Anna's knowledge of English was somewhat limited, he turned to Mark Nichols. "Mark, I've got to talk to Santa Anna. I need you to interpret for me."

Mark stepped up to the general. "I'll be glad to, sir."

Houston set his eyes on Jess Sylvester, who still held the gun muzzle against the back of Santa Anna's head. "You can ease up now, Sergeant. I'm going to sit down with the generalissimo under that tree over there."

Jess nodded and withdrew the revolver from Santa Anna's head, though he kept it in his hand. "I'll be standing close-by, General." He flicked Santa Anna a quick look.

The Mexican leader avoided the glance.

Houston nodded. "Fine, Sergeant."

The general motioned for Santa Anna to follow him, and Mark Nichols moved alongside the Mexican leader as they walked to the large oak tree behind the limping Houston.

Houston looked at Santa Anna and gestured toward the ground. "We'll sit down right here."

Mark translated for Houston, but Santa Anna had already understood and was easing himself down, though uncomfortably with his hands still tied behind his back. Seconds later, the two of them were sitting on the ground, only a couple feet apart, facing each other with Mark seated beside the general. The crowd of Texans remained there and stood silently as General Houston began conversation with Santa Anna.

With Mark there doing the interpreting, Houston and Santa Anna talked for nearly an hour, but no matter how hard Houston angrily pressed the Mexican president and military leader about the way he had led his army to shed the blood of Texans, there was no apology from Santa Anna for the attack on the defenders of the Alamo or for his order for the men at Goliad to be executed.

Finally Houston rose to his feet, limping on his wounded leg, looked to a nearby captain, and pointed to an oak tree a few feet away. "Captain Fleming, I want you to leave this bloody killer's hands tied behind him and bind him to that tree over there."

Santa Anna had picked up enough from Houston's words to know what he was being called. The look on his swarthy face showed the hatred he held for General Houston and all the other Texans.

Houston saw it. His eyes narrowed to dark slits, and he bared his teeth. His voice was a burning hiss as he said, "You're not a bit sorry for killing those gallant men at the Alamo, are you?"

"Alamo?" Santa Anna echoed, then blinked and shook his head, showing that he did not fully understand.

Houston turned to Mark, who was still close-by. "Tell him what I just asked him."

Mark gave it to the generalissimo in Spanish. The only word Houston could understand was *Alamo*.

Santa Anna met Houston's angry look, but said nothing.

Houston's eyes flashed hot with wrath. "You're not sorry for ordering those men at Goliad to be executed either, are you?"

"Goliad?" Santa Anna breathed, blinking and shaking his head again, indicating once more that he did not understand.

The general turned and looked at Mark, who showed his own anger and told Santa Anna in Spanish what the general had just said.

Santa Anna met Houston's wrathful eyes, but said nothing.

"You're a dirty, heartless killer!" Sam Houston boomed.

Mark repeated it quickly in Spanish, and it was evident by the fire that flashed in Santa Anna's eyes that the words impaled his mind. He bit down on his lower lip, started to speak, then closed his mouth and looked at the ground.

Houston turned to Captain Fleming. "Tie him to the tree!"

Fleming called for help from some of the nearby soldiers, asking one of them to go get a length of rope and a bandanna. Less than ten minutes later, a gagged and mute Santa Anna was bound to the tree. General Sam Houston gave him a cold look then walked away, as did most of the soldiers. Those who remained had been assigned by the general to stand guard close to Santa Anna.

Santa Anna spent the night tied to the tree while he and all the other Mexican prisoners were guarded in shifts by the Texans.

The Kane brothers were put on the first shift, which lasted until midnight. When Alamo, Alex, and Abel found a grassy spot for sleeping, they lay down by the light of a half moon and stared up at the twinkling stars.

"Beautiful night," said Abel.

Alex sighed. "Sure is."

At that moment, the quietness of the night was split by the cry of a coyote. It rose strange and mournful for a few seconds, then faded away.

"He sounds lonely," Alamo said.

"Yeah," Alex said. "Like me. I miss Libby something terrible."

Abel sighed. "And I miss Vivian the same way."

There was a moment of silence; then Alex said, "Alamo, I wish you had a wife to miss when you're away from home."

Alamo didn't comment.

"I wish he had a wife too," Abel said, "but the Lord just hasn't brought that right young lady into his life yet."

There was more silence. Then Alamo said, "Thanks, big brothers. Just pray for me on the subject, will you?"

"Sure," said Alex.

"Of course," Abel said. "Well, we'd better get to sleep, boys. Morning will be here before we know it."

Soon, Alex and Abel were breathing steadily, and Alamo knew they were asleep. He had been thinking of Julie, and his mind went quickly back to her. He pictured her lovely face and her captivating smile. "Lord," he whispered, "I know it's only been seven weeks since Adam was killed. Of course Julie is still in a state of mourning. That's only natural. Even though I'm expecting You to turn her heart my way, as I've been praying, I know it's going to take some time for her to get over Adam's death to the point that You can begin working to cause her to fall in love with me. Even though it's hard because I love her so much, Lord, I'll be patient. It'll be worth it when You make it happen."

❧

Before breakfast the next morning, General Houston gathered a dozen of his officers around him and told them he wanted them to make a recount of how many Texans had been killed in the battle. He knew that thirty had been wounded, because they were being cared for by some of the men. But not all the dead bodies of the Texans had been located.

He also had to verify the number of Mexicans killed and wounded, and then they would know the number that escaped. He explained that they would have to take the wounded Mexicans to Washington-on-the-Brazos so they could be treated by the doctors in town.

The officers understood that it was only right that they treat their wounded enemies with compassion and spoke their agreement with the general.

Houston then told them that they would have to use the horses and wagons left behind by the Mexicans to carry all their wounded to Washington-on-the-Brazos. The wounded Texans and the bodies of their dead would be carried in the Texan wagons.

The officers gathered some of the soldiers to help them in making the count. By late afternoon, the numbers had been calculated and reported to General Houston. The general then brought all his men together and gave them the figures, explaining that they would have to use every possible wagon to haul all the wounded men and the bodies of the dead Texans to Washington-on-the-Brazos. They would load up first thing in the morning and head for home.

Though it nettled him to do it, General Houston allowed Santa Anna some time away from the tree to which he had been tied so he could move about a little. He did so under heavy guard. That evening he was tied to the tree again and spent the night that way, as he had done the night before.

Shortly after dawn the next morning, Houston led his army out of the Mexican campground toward Washington-on-the-Brazos. The bodies of the dead Mexican soldiers were left where they had fallen in the battle, but the bodies of the dead Texans, as well as the wounded Texans, were placed in the Texas army wagons. The wounded Mexicans were placed in the wagons belonging to the Mexican army, which were driven by Texan soldiers.

The Twin Sisters were attached to the rear of two of the Texas wagons.

Corporal Rick Lindall and the three Kane brothers walked behind the wagon that carried the body of Sergeant Ross Hayes.

The Mexican prisoners who were unharmed from the battle were made to walk while guarded by the Texans. This included Generalissimo Antonio López de Santa Anna, whose hands were still tied behind his back. He walked with his face twisted in a scowl. His deep hatred for the Texans was obvious to all.

When they arrived at Washington-on-the-Brazos just after sunrise a few days later, the prisoners were placed in a fenced area just outside of town, which was normally used to hold cattle. General Houston made sure they were heavily guarded.

The wounded Texans were taken to the town's doctors for care, and the wounded Mexicans were taken to the army post there and kept in an enclosed area, where the town doctors would care for them as they could.

At the Washington-on-the-Brazos jail, town marshal Shelby Mayfield was sitting at his desk, doing some paperwork, when he heard footsteps at the door. He looked up to see General Houston enter with two Texas army soldiers walking beside a Mexican soldier whose uniform was torn and blood-soaked.

The marshal stood up. "Well, General, I'm glad to see you back. Looks like you've got yourself a prisoner from the battle."

"We have lots more Mexican prisoners, Marshal," said Houston, "and we've got them penned up just outside of town. But I want this one locked up in one of your cells."

Mayfield looked at the Mexican and frowned. "He do something really bad, General?"

Houston nodded. "Yeah. He led his Mexican troops to slaughter those relatively few men who were defending the Alamo, and he gave the order for General José Urrea to execute Colonel James Fannin and his men at Goliad."

The marshal's eyes widened in shock. "You mean—"

Houston nodded. "Yes. This is Santa Anna."

The Mexican leader's dark eyes locked on the lawman.

A paleness like frost formed on Marshal Mayfield's cheeks. Through gritted teeth, he said, "I'll be glad to lock him up, General. I'll just throw the key away." His words seemed to change shape after he had spoken them, then froze in place like icicles.

Santa Anna gave him a wicked look.

"Well, you can keep him here until I talk to President Burnet and he gives the order on what to do with him."

"Wish he'd just let *me* choose what to do with him," Mayfield said frigidly.

Santa Anna scowled at him.

Mayfield then looked at the uniform Santa Anna was wearing. "General, how come he's in that ordinary soldier's uniform?"

"He took it off one of his dead soldiers and put it on in an effort to escape after the battle we fought on the banks of the San Jacinto River on Thursday. But one of my men caught him."

"Good for him!" said the marshal. "Well, let's get him in a cell."

Moments later, in the jail's cellblock, when Marshal Mayfield swung a cell door open and the two soldiers ushered Santa Anna inside, the marshal looked at Houston. "You want I should leave his hands tied behind his back?"

Houston grinned. "I'd like to say yes, but you can untie him."

The marshal looked at the two soldiers. "Go ahead."

When the rope was removed, the soldiers shoved Santa Anna down onto one of the bunks and stepped out of the cell. Mayfield locked the barred door and led the general and soldiers out of the cellblock. As he watched them go, Santa Anna's dark eyes were filled with a fiery hatred.

When the four men returned to the office, General Houston said, "I'm going to see President Burnet. Just keep the generalissimo locked up. We'll see what's next."

Texas president David Burnet happened to be in the outer office talking to his secretary when he saw General Sam Houston come through the door. He hurried to him, hand extended. "General! Good to see you! How'd the battle go?"

As they shook hands, Houston said, "I'll tell you all about it right now if you have time."

When the two men had sat down on overstuffed chairs in the president's office, facing each other, General Houston told President Burnet the whole story of the San Jacinto battle. When Burnet heard that Santa Anna had been captured and was now in a cell in the Washington-on-the-Brazos jail, he clapped his hands together.

"We'll just leave him in the jail until you say differently, Mr. President," Houston said.

Burnet nodded. "Fine. For the moment, he can just stay there. Tell me now about the casualties among our men."

"I'll give you the statistics on the Mexicans first if that's all right."

"Certainly."

The general then reported to him that 630 Mexican soldiers had been killed and their bodies had been left where they lay on the battlefield. He went on to tell him that 208 Mexicans had been wounded and were now at the army post, waiting for the town's doctors to care for their wounds.

Burnet nodded. "That's the way it should be."

Houston reported that 347 Mexican soldiers were being held as prisoners at the cattle pens just outside of town under heavy guard and that during the battle, 215 Mexican soldiers had run away and escaped.

Burnet adjusted himself on his chair. "I have a feeling you're going to give me much smaller casualty numbers on our men."

Houston made a thin smile. "Yes sir. Nine of our soldiers were killed, and some of my men are burying them right now at the town cemetery. Their relatives in many parts of Texas are being mailed letters by one of my officers."

Burnet shook his head. "I'm sorry for the 9 who were killed, but that's a lot better than 630."

"Yes sir," Houston said. "Our number of wounded, Mr. President, is 30. They are at the offices of the town doctors right now."

Burnet smiled. "Well, that's a whole lot better than 208."

Houston nodded. "That's for sure. As soon as our 9 men are all buried, I'm going to gather all the surviving volunteers who fought in the battle, express my deep appreciation for their help, and let them go home."

Burnet leaned forward, meeting Houston's gaze. "I'm all for that, General. I would also like to express my appreciation to them. Will you let me know when the gathering is going to happen?"

"I'd be glad to," replied Houston. "It'll be a couple of hours or so." He rose to his feet. "Well, Mr. President, I need to be going. Lots to do yet."

Burnet extended his hand again, and as they gripped each other, he said, "You did a great job, General. I'm sure glad you head up the Texas army."

"Thank you, Mr. President." Houston gave the president's hand an extra squeeze. "I wish I could say the San Jacinto battle was the last of our trouble with Mexico, but even without Santa Anna, there are still plenty of Mexican military, government leaders, and civilians who hate us Texans. I'm afraid we may not be through fighting them yet."

Burnet stroked his chin. "You're probably right, General. Well, I'll let you go now."

As they walked toward the office door together, Burnet said, "I'll be waiting to hear about your gathering the volunteers."

"You'll hear shortly, I assure you."

Two hours later, General Sam Houston and President David Burnet stood before the volunteers at the army post in Washington-on-the-Brazos and expressed their appreciation as planned. Houston had allowed the president to speak first, then made his own speech. When he had finished and was about to bid them good-bye, Alamo Kane raised his hand.

The general smiled. "Yes, Alamo?"

"Sir, I want to tell you and President Burnet that my brothers here and I feel that it was an honor to fight the San Jacinto battle for Texas alongside the soldiers. And we want you to know that if we are ever needed again, we will do the same thing."

Alex Kane removed his hat and waved it. "That's right!"

Waving his hat also, Abel Kane said, "Yes. That's right!"

The combined voices of nearly all the volunteers expressed mutual feelings. Both the president and the general smiled and waved at them warmly.

Moments later, the Kane brothers mounted up and rode away, eager to see their loved ones at home.

## 11

It was almost noon on Thursday, April 28, when two of the young Diamond K ranch hands, Randy Allison and Dean Grantham, arrived back at the ranch on their horses. They had begun the thirty-mile ride to Washington-on-the-Brazos early that morning to do some business at one of the town's banks and get back home by noon.

When they neared the barns, corrals, bunkhouse, and ranch houses, they saw Cort Whitney leaving one of the corrals and heading for the bunkhouse.

"Let's go!" Dean prodded his horse into a fast trot. "We need to tell Mr. Whitney!"

"Yes!" Randy did the same with his horse.

"Mr. Whitney!" Dean called out. "Mr. Whitney!"

When Cort heard his name, he stopped and turned to see the two ranch hands riding toward him.

When they drew up, he said, "Everything go all right at the bank for you?"

"Just fine." Randy slid from his saddle. "We need to tell you something!"

Dean also dismounted quickly.

Whitney stepped up closer as both young men stood side by side, facing him. "What is it you need to tell me?"

Randy said excitedly, "We learned from some folks in town that General Sam Houston and his army fought Santa Anna and the Mexican troops on the bank of the San Jacinto River last Thursday! Our soldiers told them all about it!"

"Yeah!" put in Dean. "And the Texans won the battle!"

"Good!" exclaimed the foreman.

"A great number of Mexicans were killed," Dean said. "Over six hundred of them! And quite a bunch were wounded!"

"How about our men?" Whitney inquired.

"Only a small number of them were killed, sir," Randy replied. "Only nine. Thirty of our men were wounded. Over two hundred Mexicans were wounded."

"Many Mexican soldiers are being held as prisoners of war in that fenced area just outside town where cattle are kept at times," Dean said. "And the wounded Texans are being taken care of by the doctors in town. The doctors are going to take care of the wounded Mexicans too."

"The nine dead Texans were buried in the town cemetery, Mr. Whitney," said Randy.

Dean's eyes bulged. "And guess what!"

"What?" Whitney asked.

"One of our soldiers captured Santa Anna!"

Whitney's head bobbed. "Really?"

"Yes sir!" said Dean. "Marshal Shelby Mayfield's got him locked up in the town jail!"

"Wow! That's great!" said Whitney. "Ahh…did you fellas see the Kane brothers?"

Both young men shook their heads. "No, we didn't," said Randy.

"Did you hear if they are all right?"

"No sir," replied Dean. "We weren't able to learn anything from the citizens about Mr. Alamo and his brothers. You see, when the people were telling us about the battle, all the Texan fighting men were gathered in a meeting with President Burnet and General Houston at the army post, and no one else was allowed to go near the place."

"I see," said the foreman. "Well, I want you to go with me to the Kane family right now and tell them what you just told me."

"Sure, Mr. Whitney," said Randy. "We'll go by Alex's and Abel's houses and tell Libby and Vivian we want them to come with us to the big house so you two can tell everyone your news all at the same time."

"Let's go," said Dean.

Moments later, the Kane family members were gathered on the front porch of the big ranch house, and they listened intently as Randy Allison and Dean Grantham told them the news they had just shared with the foreman.

Angela looked at both of them questioningly. "What about my brothers? Are they all right?"

"We don't know, Miss Angela," Randy replied. "All the soldiers were gathered with President Burnet and General Houston at the army post, as we told Mr. Whitney, and no one else was allowed to go near the place. We had no idea how long the meeting would last. Dean and I have work to do, so we decided we should come on home."

Abram Kane's brow furrowed. "I've got to know about my sons. One, two, or all three could have been killed in the battle."

Libby broke into tears. "There must be a way we can find out! I can't stand not knowing about Alex and, of course, Abel and Alamo!"

Vivian, Julia, and Angela spoke their agreement, wiping their own tears.

Abram blinked at the excess moisture in his eyes and looked at the foreman. "Cort, we've *got* to know about them. Will you take Randy and Dean and ride to town right now? Whether the meeting is over or not, tell the soldiers at the gate of the army post that you need to talk to General Houston immediately and find out if Alamo, Alex, and Abel are still alive."

"I sure will," said Cort. "Let's go, fellas."

At that instant, Julia's attention was drawn toward the front gate of the ranch, where she saw three riders just turning off the road. A smile spread over her face as she wiped tears from her eyes. "Cort, there will be no need to do that!" She pointed toward the gate. "Look! All three of them are here!"

Every eye was immediately fixed on Alamo, Alex, and Abel as they trotted their horses toward the big ranch house. Other ranch hands who were near the gate saw them, waved, and called out their welcome.

Cort, Randy, and Dean looked on as the excited group quickly left the porch and ran to meet the three riders who were fast approaching them. The trio pulled rein, swiftly left their saddles, and were met with open arms.

Libby and Vivian dashed into the arms of their husbands, happy tears flowing.

Angela and Julia rushed to Alamo, and he circled an arm around each, holding them tight.

Angela raised up on her tiptoes and placed a kiss on his cheek. "Randy and Dean were in town earlier, big brother. They just got back and told all of us about the battle at the San Jacinto River, but they weren't able to find out about the three of you! Oh, I'm so glad you're all okay!"

"Yes! Me too!" Julia rose up on her tiptoes to plant a kiss on Alamo's other cheek. This kiss made his heart feel like it was suddenly on fire.

"I hope you three never have to go fight in a battle again," said Angela.

"Me too, Sis," Alamo said, but deep inside his mind, he feared that more battles might lie in the future for him and his brothers.

Abram waited patiently while the women embraced his sons. Then he hugged each of them. Having heard Angela tell Alamo that news of the war had been brought to them by Randy and Dean, he passed it on to Alex and Abel. He then looked around at the happy group. "I know we're all glad that Alamo, Alex, and Abel are alive and well. Let's bow our heads right now and thank the Lord for keeping His mighty hand on them."

A hearty "amen" came from the four women, and it was repeated when Abram closed his prayer of thanks a few minutes later.

By this time, a number of ranch hands and some of their wives had been drawn to the scene at the big ranch house, and Cort, Randy, and Dean told them of the battle at the San Jacinto River. They explained how no one knew if the Kane brothers were dead or alive until they came riding in a short time ago. Some of the ranch hands then hurried away to give the news to other Diamond K people, and in a short time quite a crowd had gathered.

Seeing their interest, the Kane brothers stood before them and gave them the details of the battle, including the numbers of men killed and wounded on both sides and the fact that Santa Anna was General Sam Houston's prisoner in the town jail.

The Diamond K people rejoiced in the Texas army's victory and that their boss and his two brothers were unscathed.

Also present by then was cook and housekeeper Daisy Haycock. As the ranch hands and their families began moving away, Daisy stepped up to the Kane brothers and said, "I'm going to prepare a special dinner this evening for the whole Kane family to celebrate your safe return home."

Abel grinned. "Sounds good to me, Miss Daisy. I'm sure tired of that army food."

Daisy smiled. "Well, supper will be at the usual time. This will give you boys opportunity to put your horses away, store your gear, and ah…ah…from the scent I'm picking up, I'm thinking that a nice hot bath for each of you would be in order."

Alex lowered his head and sniffed himself. He grinned at her. "Why, Miss Daisy, whatever are you talking about?"

Alamo sniffed himself and looked at her innocently. "Us boys don't stink."

"Yeah," Abel said. "We don't stink."

Daisy giggled. "You'll have plenty of time this afternoon to bathe, even if you don't think you stink. See you at supper."

Everyone laughed as Daisy turned and headed for the kitchen.

The married couples headed for their own houses, and Alamo ascended the stairs to his room.

That evening, the fresh-smelling Kane brothers and the rest of the family sat down at the dining room table as Daisy looked on. The tempting aromas of a glorious feast greeted them.

As the family bowed their heads, Abram led them in a fervent prayer of thanksgiving for God's protection of his sons in the battle and for the food they were about to eat. More tears were shed, but these were happy ones.

The next day, Friday, April 29, Alamo and his brothers joined in with Cort Whitney and the ranch hands in work that needed to be done.

❧

On that same Friday, April 29, there was a meeting of the Texas General Convention in Washington-on-the-Brazos, which had been set up the day before by Texas president David Burnet. Calling such meetings was simple since the majority of the delegates lived in town, and what few lived in the country close-by could be advised of the meetings easily by messengers on horseback.

The delegates gathered in the auditorium of the convention building, with reporters present from the *Washington Post* and other relatively nearby Texas newspapers.

Standing on the platform before the delegates, President Burnet called the meeting to order and then invited General Houston to come and tell them about the San Jacinto battle.

Houston stepped to the podium and gave a detailed report, including how many casualties there had been on each side, the number of Mexican soldiers being held as prisoners, and the number that had escaped. When the general announced that they had Santa Anna in custody at the town jail, the delegates were surprised as well as happy. So were the newspaper reporters. Everyone was stunned when Houston told them that the battle had lasted only eighteen minutes.

When General Houston was finished with his report and had returned to his seat toward the rear of the platform, President Burnet told the delegates and the general that he had sent a letter in late March to United States president Andrew Jackson, advising him of the declaration of independence and constitution drafted by the Texas General Convention on March 16.

Burnet said, "Gentlemen, just yesterday I received a letter from President Jackson in which he stated his joy over the Texas Republic's complete separation from Mexican rule. He said in the letter that he will sanction military help from the United States Army if we Texans need it."

"Wonderful!" called out General Houston.

As Burnet turned to look back at him and smile, a chorus of voices from the delegates called out their pleasure in hearing the news.

When the pleasant outburst faded, the smiling President Burnet said, "Gentlemen, tomorrow I am sending a letter to President Jackson to let him know that General Houston and the Texas army are holding Generalissimo Antonio López de Santa Anna in our town jail. I'm interested to see what his reaction will be."

The delegates stood to their feet, calling out General Houston's name and applauding.

---

A few weeks passed, and late one morning at the Diamond K Ranch, foreman Cort Whitney gathered a few of the ranch hands together and told them to climb on their horses, ride all over the ranch and tell all personnel and their families that Alamo Kane wanted them to come to the ranch house promptly at three o'clock that afternoon. Alamo had just returned from Washington-on-the-Brazos with the morning edition of the *Washington Post* and wanted to share some news about Santa Anna.

At precisely three o'clock that afternoon, Alamo stood before his Diamond K people, including his family, holding the folded newspaper in hand. Lifting it up before the curious faces, Alamo said, "This is the May 24 issue of the *Washington Post*. Since today is May 24, this is fresh news. The story is here on the front page.

"I want to remind you that General Sam Houston and the Texas army are still holding Santa Anna in the Washington-on-the-Brazos jail, under the guard of Marshal Shelby Mayfield and his deputies."

Shouts of joy filled the air.

When the shouting had abated, Alamo said, "It tells in here that on April 30, Texas president David Burnet sent a letter to United States president Andrew Jackson, advising him that in the San Jacinto battle, his army had captured Generalissimo Antonio López de Santa Anna and that they had him in a cell in the Washington-on-the-Brazos jail. Now President Burnet has a letter from President Jackson requesting that Santa Anna be brought to Washington, D.C., as soon as possible. He wants to meet with the Mexican leader."

Alamo could see a quizzical look on most faces in the crowd. "This article announces that President Burnet and General Houston are personally taking Santa Anna to Washington, along with four Texas army soldiers, who will accompany them to ward off any attempts of escape by Santa Anna or any Mexicans who might somehow get on the train with the intention of freeing their leader. They are already on their way to Washington, D.C."

Abel Kane, who was near his younger brother in the crowd, spoke up. "Alamo…"

Meeting his gaze, Alamo said, "Yes, Abel?"

"Why do you suppose President Jackson wants to meet with Santa Anna?"

"Good question, my brother," said Alamo. "I have no idea."

The Diamond K people began talking to each other about it, sharing their curiosity as to why President Jackson wanted to meet with Santa Anna.

In Washington, D.C., on Friday, May 27, President Andrew Jackson was at his desk in his office in the White House, reading over some notes from a recent meeting of Congress, when there was a tap on his door. He recognized the rhythm of the tap and called out, "Come in, Mr. Vice President!"

The door came open, and vice president Martin Van Buren stepped in. "Mr. President, General Sam Houston and Texas president David Burnet are here with Generalissimo Antonio López de Santa Anna. They also have four Texas soldiers with them who have come along as guards."

Jackson rose to his feet. "They made good time. Bring them in."

Van Buren made a half turn. "You may come in." He stepped aside to allow them room to pass through the doorway.

President Jackson was already acquainted with General Houston, and he had seen newspaper photographs of President Burnet. He watched them enter with the dark-skinned Santa Anna between them, making note that the Mexican's hands were cuffed behind him and that he wore a tattered and bloodstained Mexican army coat along with matching trousers.

On their heels were the four soldiers of the Texas army in uniform.

Jackson rounded his desk and, ignoring the prisoner for the moment, welcomed General Houston, saying it was good to see him again.

"It's good to see you also, Mr. President," Houston said as they shook hands.

Houston introduced President Burnet to President Jackson. The two presidents shook hands and greeted each other warmly.

General Houston then introduced the four soldiers to President Jackson, and he shook hands with them.

Jackson turned his attention to the obviously puzzled Mexican leader and, figuring that Santa Anna knew no English, used hand motions to guide him to a chair directly in front of his desk.

When Santa Anna was less than comfortably seated because of his hands being cuffed behind his back, Martin Van Buren said, "Mr. President, I'll go and get Diego Mendoza now."

Jackson ran his gaze between Houston and Burnet. "Diego Mendoza is a Mexican American friend of one of my men on the White House staff and has agreed to come and interpret. He has stayed here since yesterday so he would be on hand when you gentlemen arrived."

"I see," said Houston. "That will help a great deal."

"I figured it would."

Just as the other men were getting seated in a semicircle in front of his desk, Van Buren came in with Diego Mendoza at his side.

After Mendoza had been introduced to Houston, Burnet, and the soldiers, he moved up to the empty chair next to Santa Anna, where he knew he would be sitting, introduced himself in Spanish, and explained why he was there. Santa Anna surprised everyone by speaking to Mendoza in broken English, but then admitted in Spanish that he did not know English well enough to carry on a conversation.

Mendoza then sat down in the chair next to Santa Anna, and Martin Van Buren sat down in a chair reserved for him beside Jackson's desk.

Easing onto his desk chair and placing his elbows on the desktop, the United States president began talking to Santa Anna through the interpreter, discussing what Santa Anna had done in leading his troops to attack the men at the Alamo, killing them all. He followed this with the orders Santa Anna had given that every man at the fort in Goliad was to be executed.

His dark face flushing, Santa Anna told him through the interpreter simply that war was war, and military leaders have to do what they feel is best to win.

When Mendoza had translated Santa Anna's words into English, General Houston's lips curled up in a baleful snarl. Eying the Mexican leader heatedly, he snapped, "What you did at the Alamo and ordered to be done at Goliad was cold-blooded murder!"

Diego Mendoza translated Houston's words to Santa Anna, who saw instantly that they fit the obvious anger he was displaying.

Santa Anna avoided Houston's blazing eyes and turned to President Jackson. His voice soft, through the interpreter he told Jackson that he wanted no more war with the people of Texas, nor did he want any war with the people of the United States.

As they were hearing it in English, Houston and Jackson looked at each other dubiously.

Jackson pressed Santa Anna hard on the issue, and the Mexican leader's response when translated convinced Jackson that Santa Anna was sincere in what he was saying.

Jackson told Houston and Burnet how he felt, then said, "Gentlemen, I believe we should release Santa Anna and allow him to return to Mexico. If we do, it is my opinion that the people of Mexico will see it as a gesture of friendship on the part of the people of Texas and the United States and will be convinced that we want to live in peace with them."

"I agree, Mr. President," said David Burnet. "I think it's the best thing to do."

General Houston appeared to have a fierce struggle going on inside him, as he thought of the slaughter of the men at the Alamo and at Goliad, but he saw President Jackson's point, and not wanting any more war with Mexico, he said, "I understand what you are saying, President Jackson... And you too, President Burnet. I agree. Let's show the people of Mexico that we want peace."

Jackson smiled and looked at Diego Mendoza. "Tell him we are going to release him and allow him to go back to Mexico. And make sure he understands that this is a gesture of kindness on our part, to show the people of Mexico that we want peace with them."

Relief showed on Santa Anna's dark features as the interpreter made this known to him.

Jackson then said to Houston and Burnet, with the four Texas soldiers and Diego Mendoza listening, "I'll have a large unit of the United States Army take Santa Anna back to Mexico City."

Houston and Burnet thanked Jackson and left the Mexican leader with him.

The next morning, after spending a night in a Washington, D.C., hotel, Houston, Burnet, and the four soldiers boarded a train and headed back to Texas.

## 12

On Wednesday afternoon, June 1, Alamo Kane and Cort Whitney returned to the Diamond K Ranch from Washington-on-the-Brazos. While Alamo rounded up the members of his family and gathered them on the front porch of the big ranch house, Cort obtained the help of several ranch hands to round up all the other Diamond K people and assemble them out front.

When everyone was there, Alamo stood at the top of the porch steps, holding that day's edition of the *Washington Post.* "I want to read the front page story to all of you," he said.

"Cort and I read it in town this morning, and we want all of you to hear the news."

Everyone listened intently as Alamo read to them about the interview president Andrew Jackson, Texas president David Burnet, and General Sam Houston had had with Generalissimo Antonio López de Santa Anna in Washington, D.C., on May 27.

When Alamo had read the entire story aloud, they appeared stunned at learning that Santa Anna had been released from custody and was being escorted back to Mexico City by a large unit of the United States Army.

Abel Kane spoke up. "Alamo, how could both presidents and General Houston possibly believe Santa Anna when he said he wants no more war with the people of Texas? He hates us with a purple passion!"

Many voices rose in agreement with Abel.

Alamo took a deep breath and let it out slowly. "President Jackson persuaded President Burnet and General Houston into backing him on letting Santa Anna go because he felt that the generalissimo was telling the truth about not wanting any more war with us. President Jackson feels that this gesture will assure the people of Mexico that we want to have peace with them."

Abram said, "Son, this scares me. I don't trust Santa Anna."

"I don't trust him either, Papa," Alamo replied. "I have absolutely no doubt that that cold-hearted killer will take over the Mexican government again as dictator. And when he does, there will be war between Mexico and Texas—and between Mexico and the United States."

Fear showed on the faces of the Diamond K people as they spoke their agreement with Alamo.

On the porch, Julia turned to the family members. "I've been afraid that something like this would happen! Why is President Jackson so willing to believe Santa Anna? The man is a killer and a liar!"

"He's a bad one, all right," Alamo said, "but President Jackson wants so much to see an end to the bloodshed like what happened at the Alamo and at Goliad and now at the San Jacinto River."

"I appreciate President Jackson's desire for no more bloodshed," Abram said. "But I sure hope he keeps a close eye on that evil man and his activities!"

The Diamond K people nodded their agreement.

A troubled look passed over Alamo's face. "All we can do is pray for our government leaders, that they will do right in this situation. Well, I'll let all of you go now. Time to get back to whatever you were doing before I interrupted you."

On Friday, June 24, word spread through newspapers across the United States and Texas that Santa Anna had resumed his dictatorship in Mexico. Many Texans interviewed by reporters felt certain that they had not heard the last from the vicious dictator despite his assurances to President Andrew Jackson that he wanted to remain at peace with the people of Texas and the people of the United States.

～

On Monday, June 27, in the president's office at the White House in Washington, D.C., President Jackson and Vice President Van Buren discussed what the Texans had been quoted in the newspapers as saying about their distrust of Mexico's dictator, Generalissimo Antonio López de Santa Anna.

Jackson rubbed his chin. "I sure hope the Texans are wrong."

Van Buren nodded. "I hope so too, because if they are proven right and Santa Anna leads in the shedding of more American blood, the people of this country are going to blame *you,* Mr. President, for letting Santa Anna go when General Sam Houston had him in custody."

Jackson sighed. "Martin, I still feel that I did the right thing in releasing Santa Anna in an attempt to show the people of Mexico that the people of the United States and of the Republic of Texas do not want war with them. I—I only hope that Santa Anna will keep his word."

The vice president laid a gentle hand on the president's arm. "We've just got to believe that Santa Anna was being honest with you."

Andrew Jackson's face was a bit pale as he nodded and bit his lower lip. "Yes, Martin, we've got to believe that."

～

On Tuesday, June 28, Alamo Kane and his sister were making ready to take Julia to Washington-on-the-Brazos for a routine appointment with her physician, Dr. Dennis Dewitt.

As Alamo was helping Angela into the wagon in front of the big ranch house, she said, "Little brother, Julia needs some more maternity dresses. The ones she is wearing were given to her by some of the older women on the ranch, but they're really worn out."

Alamo helped her settle on the seat. "Oh? I hadn't noticed that they're worn out."

Angela giggled. "That's just like a man. Especially one who owns a ranch. Everything must be pointed out to him before he notices it, unless it has to do with barns, corrals, hay fields, pastures, cattle, or horses."

Alamo chuckled. "Well, Sis, I guess that just proves that I'm a typical male rancher. Nothing wrong with that as far as I can see."

She giggled again. "Oh, you're very typical, my dear brother. *Very* typical!"

Alamo laughed as he circled around the rear of the wagon and climbed up onto the seat. He took the reins in hand. "Sis, I assume you're wanting to take Julie to that dressmaker, Lisa Akins, while we're in town and get her some new maternity dresses made."

"That's what I had in mind. We'll let her pick out the fabrics she wants and choose how many dresses to have Lisa make."

He put the horses into motion. "Fine with me. Let's do it. I'll pay for as many dresses as she wants."

Angela smiled at her handsome brother. "That's very kind of you."

"Well, it's my pleasure to look out for Julie, Sis. Tell you what. Let's not tell her what we're doing. Let's wait till after she sees Dr. Dewitt; then we'll just drive over to Lisa Akins's shop and announce to Julie that she's going to be fitted for some new maternity dresses."

Angela smiled. "Yes! Let's do it that way!"

"You do remember that while Julie's with the doctor, I'm going to President Burnet's office to see him for a few minutes?"

"Yes." Angela nodded. "I remember."

As the wagon rolled toward Julia's house, where she was now staying on a regular basis, Angela thought, *My precious brother is in love with Julia, for sure. He keeps it a secret, but I can read it in his eyes when he talks about her or when he's with her. Lord, when her time of mourning Adam's death finally passes, I sure would love to see You work things out between them.*

Angela leaned toward Alamo and planted a kiss on his cheek.

He looked at her and grinned. "What was that for?"

"Oh, just that I love you, little brother."

"I love you too, big sis."

Seconds later, they pulled up in front of Julia's house, where she was waiting for them on the porch. Alamo hopped out of the wagon and helped her onto the seat next to Angela. Then he hurried back around the rear of the wagon, climbed onto the seat, and put the wagon in motion.

On the thirty-mile trip to Washington-on-the-Brazos, Angela and Julia mostly talked about the baby's arrival, and as they drew near town, Angela talked about how she would help Julia with the baby in whatever way she needed. Alamo could tell that this made Julie very happy.

When they reached the doctor's office, Alamo helped the women down from the wagon and guided them inside to the waiting room. He explained to Julie where he was going, then hurried outside and made his way down the street toward President Burnet's office.

As he walked hastily in that direction, Alamo remembered his first meeting with the Texas president. President Burnet, having learned from General Houston of his act of courage regarding the Alamo and that he fought bravely in the battle at San Jacinto, had made it a point in late April to meet Alamo when he was in town visiting the general. When Burnet came to Houston's office that day, he had commended Alamo for his honorable deeds. They had become friends, and Alamo had stopped by the president's office a couple of times since just to say hello.

Alamo found President Burnet at his desk and spent a few minutes with him. He then hurried back to Dr. Dewitt's and was happy to learn that the doctor had said Julia and the baby were doing just fine. As the Kane wagon pulled away from the doctor's office, Alamo steered the horses in the opposite direction than he would if they were headed for the ranch. Julia turned and looked at him curiously. "Where are we going?"

Alamo looked past Julie to his sister. "How about *you* tell her, Sis?"

Angela smiled, then took hold of Julia's hand. "I told my brother about the worn-out maternity dresses you've been wearing, and he decided that after you had seen Dr. Dewitt, we would take you to the dressmaker here in town who has made several dresses for me. Her name is Lisa Akins."

Julia's eyes widened. "I—I've seen her shop on Main Street, but—but I don't mind wearing these old dresses."

Alamo shook his head. "No, Julie. I'm paying for them. I want you to tell Lisa how many dresses you'd like and pick out the fabric for each one."

"Alamo," Julia said, "I appreciate your willingness to pay for them, but I have the money. Since you and Angela are taking me there, I'll order some, but I want to pay for them. There's no need for you to do so!"

"I know Adam left you money, Julie, and of course you own his portion of the ranch, but I'm doing this for you. You hang on to your money so you'll have plenty to take care of my brother's child. I will provide whatever is needed beyond that."

Julia went deeply into thought for a few minutes. Alamo could detect the emotions she was experiencing as she pondered his offer on the dresses. Sighing deeply, she smiled up at him and said softly, "Thank you, Alamo. You are so kind and generous, and I very much appreciate it. I will comply with your wishes and let you buy the dresses for me."

Alamo nudged her with his elbow. "Good!"

"I'm honored that you've allowed me to own Adam's portion of the ranch. I know absolutely nothing about ranching, but I sure would love to learn."

"Great!" Alamo said. "In the coming months, I'll take some time to teach you everything you need to know."

"All right," Julia said. "I will try to be a quick learner. And if my baby is a son, I want him to learn ranching as well. Thank you, Alamo.

You always seem to know just how to encourage me." She surprised him by raising up and kissing his cheek.

Angela smiled to herself as she noted the pleasant look that swept over her brother's countenance.

At that moment, Alamo pulled the horses to a halt in front of the dressmaker's shop. When he left the wagon seat and headed around the rear of the wagon, he carefully touched his right cheek where Julie had planted the kiss.

An hour later, Alamo, Angela, and Julia came out of the dressmaker's shop. Alamo was pleased that after Julie had been measured, she had chosen to have Lisa Akins make her four maternity dresses and picked out four different fabrics and patterns that pleased her. Lisa told her the dresses would be ready the following Saturday.

When they arrived back at the Diamond K, Angela told Julia that she needed to talk to her and asked if she had some time right then. Julia invited Angela to her house, saying she'd love to spend some more time with her. Alamo helped the ladies out of the wagon, told them he would see them later, then climbed back onto the wagon seat and drove toward the nearest barn.

When the two women had sat down on the sofa together, Angela said, "Sweetie, I've had this on my mind for a couple weeks now. I want to come and stay here at the house with you until the baby is born. I'll sleep in one of the spare rooms so if anything should go wrong these last few months of your pregnancy, I'd be here to help you."

Julia's brow furrowed. "Angela, dear, it's very sweet of you to make this offer, but are you sure you want to do this?"

"Of course, I'm sure. I just can't let you stay here alone at night any longer. Either I move in here, or you move back into the big house until the baby is born."

Julia smiled. "Well, when you put it that way, all I can say is, welcome to my home! It's much easier for me to be here."

"Fine!" Angela clapped her hands with joy. "If it's all right, I'll start staying here with you tonight."

"Okay!" Julia said. "That will be great. I'll make sure the larger spare bedroom is all freshened up for you." Julia reached over and touched Angela's hand. Emotion quivered her voice as she said, "Thank you for caring and for being so willing to stay with me. It would be very scary to go into labor and have no way to reach any of the family."

Julia then brought up what it meant to her for Alamo to buy her the maternity dresses. Angela bragged on her brother's generosity, saying that the Lord was blessing him for being such a generous person. She went on to talk about how the Diamond K was flourishing under Alamo's leadership. The cattle herds were growing larger, and meat and hide sales were at an all-time high.

Angela then told Julia that she had best go home and prepare some of her things so she could spend the night with her as planned.

Julia walked her to the door and watched her head toward the big ranch house. When she passed from sight, Julia closed her eyes. *Thank You, Lord, for letting me be part of this loving, considerate family. I—I miss Adam so much, but I'm so very grateful that he left me with such sweet people.*

Julia headed for the larger spare bedroom, wiping tears from her eyes. When she entered the room, she made sure that everything was in order for her guest. She opened the windows, just to freshen up the room, and a cool breeze wafted in, ruffling the sheer curtains.

She smiled. "This is such a pleasant room. I'm sure Angela will have comfortable nights sleeping here."

❧

On Saturday afternoon, July 2, Alamo rode up in front of Julia's house with a package in one hand. He found her sitting on the front porch.

She smiled. "I assume those are my dresses."

He dismounted. "Yes'm. And they're really pretty." He stepped up on the porch, handed her the package, and sat down beside her.

Julia quickly opened the package and took out the four maternity dresses. "Oh yes! They're beautiful! Lisa did a wonderful job on them! Thank you so much for riding into town to get them for me."

"My pleasure." He smiled warmly at her.

Julia looked around at the open ranch land. "Oh, Alamo, it's such a lovely day. I just needed to be outdoors and breathe in this fresh country air."

"It *is* a beautiful day," Alamo responded, secretly reveling in the beauty of the young lady next to him.

Julia rose to her feet. "Can you stay for a while?"

Alamo nodded. "I have a little time right now."

"Good! I just made some lemonade and cookies. I'll be right back!"

The tall rancher grinned. "Lemonade and cookies sound good."

Julia entered the house, and Alamo sighed as he relaxed into the wicker chair.

Moments later, Julia returned, carrying a tray with two full glasses and a plate of oatmeal cookies. "I know you like oatmeal cookies." She handed him a glass of lemonade and set the plate of cookies on the small table beside him.

As Julia sat down, Alamo picked up a cookie and took a bite. "Mmm-mmm! These are good!" He then took a sip of the lemonade and smiled at her. "Good lemonade too! So refreshing on such a hot day!"

While they nibbled on cookies and sipped lemonade, Alamo talked joyfully about the baby's birth. Julia was pleased that he was so excited about his new little nephew or niece. She was still unaware that he had been praying that one day he could marry her and that when the child was old enough to talk this young one would call him papa instead of uncle.

"I'm really happy your parents will be coming as the time for your delivery draws closer," Alamo said. "I know it will be a blessing to you to have them here when the baby is born."

Julia smiled. "Indeed it will. You know, Alamo, when they were here before, they fell in love with this part of Texas. And I've told you how their letters have been full of praise for this ranch and its surroundings."

Alamo nodded.

"It wouldn't surprise me at all if at some point in time, they decide to move here."

"Oh, that would be great! Then we could be sure of keeping you here." Alamo had been a bit concerned that Julie might want to move back to the plantation once her baby was born.

Julia met his gaze. "Alamo, I have no intentions of ever leaving this ranch. This is home to me, and I want to raise my child here, close to his or her father's family."

Alamo smiled. "I'm glad to hear that, Julie. I can't even imagine this place without you."

"I'm so glad you feel that way."

*If you only knew all that I feel,* he thought.

Then she said, "Thank you for always making me feel so welcome and so protected."

He looked into her eyes. "I will always see that you feel welcome and that you are protected."

After Alamo and Julia had spent nearly an hour together, he took a final sip of lemonade. "Well, sweet lady, I must be going. I've got some work to do on one of the corrals. Thanks for the cookies and lemonade."

"You're very welcome," she replied sweetly.

Julia followed Alamo down the porch steps and walked to his horse with him. The bay gelding set his eyes on her and whinnied, bobbing his head. She smiled and reached up to stroke his long face. "Hello, big boy. You are one magnificent horsey."

Alamo chuckled as the gelding whinnied again. "He likes you, Julie."

"I like *him* too." She looked longingly at Alamo. "I sure miss being in the saddle. I'm looking forward to being able to ride once the baby is born."

"Oh, Julie, I can't wait until the day we can go riding together again."

"Me too." She patted his hand. "Thank you for going after those dresses for me."

Even the touch of Julie's hand sent a warm sensation up Alamo's arm. He swung into the saddle and looked down at her. "You're very welcome. It was a pleasure to do it for you. Well, I'll see you in the morning if not before. I'm really looking forward to church services tomorrow, especially Pastor Evans's morning sermon."

Julia smiled up at him. "I'm looking forward to that sermon too. Pastor Evans always does extra good when he preaches on the cross of Calvary."

## 13

When Julia Kane awakened on Sunday morning, she was experiencing some mild discomfort in her midsection, and her lower back was aching. She opened her eyes and rolled from her back to her right side. Looking through the facing window, she saw night's darkness gradually changing from pitch black to a pale obscurity.

As early as it was, Julia knew that it was the pain that had awakened her.

"Just goes with pregnancy," she told herself in a whisper. "I'll stay in bed till sunrise; then I'll get up and get breakfast started."

Later, when Julia and Angela were eating breakfast together in the kitchen, Angela looked across the table at her. "Honey, you look a little pale. Are you all right?"

Julia swallowed her mouthful of scrambled eggs. "I woke up this morning with some cramps in my midsection, and my back is aching. I suppose it just goes with carrying a baby when you get this far along. I'll be all right, I'm sure."

"I sure hope so," said Angela. "I'll do the dishes. You go put on one of your new maternity dresses and get ready for church. When you're all fixed up, just go into the parlor, sit down, and rest. There's still plenty of time for me to get the dishes done and be ready for Alamo when he comes in the wagon to take us to town."

Julia smiled at her sister-in-law. "You're so sweet. I sure went off to sleep easily last night knowing you were here in the house with me."

Angela smiled back. "I'll be here till you have that baby—and even longer if you want me to."

"This world would be a better place to live in if it had more people like you, Angela. I sure do love you."

Angela reached over and squeezed her hand. "I love you too, sweetie. Now finish your breakfast so you can get ready and have some time to rest before Alamo gets here."

Angela and Julia rode to the church in Washington-on-the-Brazos with Alamo, while Abram and Daisy Haycock rode in a buggy with the Kane couples. Those ranch hands and their families who were Christians followed in their own wagons, and the single Christian ranch hands rode their horses.

As the congregation had expected, in his morning sermon, the aging Pastor Merle Evans thrilled them with powerful truths about the amazing, stunning, and wonderful things the Saviour did and experienced when He was hanging on the cross before He died. When the invitation was given, two adults and three teenagers walked the aisle to receive the Lord Jesus as Saviour.

Julia was sitting between Angela and Alamo, who was seated on the aisle. The rest of the Kane family and Daisy Haycock were seated on the same pew. Just after Pastor Evans dismissed the service and Alamo stood up, Julia was rising from the pew when a powerful pain gripped her midsection. She gasped and clutched her abdomen as a moan escaped her lips.

Angela touched her arm. "What is it?"

Alamo leaned over, eyes wide. "What's wrong, Julie?"

"I'm not sure," Julia said through clenched teeth. "I've been feeling a little uncomfortable since I woke up this morning. It's way too early for the baby to come, but—" Just then another spasm of pain gripped her.

As she bent over, she gasped again and moaned.

By this time, the others were on their feet and were looking on with concern.

"Now just stay calm, honey." Angela patted her arm. "We'll get Dr. Dewitt."

"I'll run down the street and get him!" Alex said.

Libby shook her head. "That might take too long. It would be best if someone carried her to the doctor, especially since his office is right next door to his house."

"I'll carry her," Alamo said. "It's only a little over two blocks."

He swiftly swept Julia up in his arms, and as she groaned in pain, he charged out of a side door in the church sanctuary and ran down the street. Church people were looking on, and the Kane family, Daisy, and Pastor Evans were trailing behind him.

An hour later, Dr. Dennis Dewitt came out of the back room in his office into the waiting room. Everyone rose to their feet, waiting to hear what the doctor would tell them.

"No need to worry, folks," said the middle-aged physician. "Just a little false labor. She's fine now, but I told her she needs to get more rest and not be as active as she has been. I also suggested that she go back and stay in the big ranch house so she'll have family close-by." He looked at Angela. "She told me that just last night, Angela, you began staying with her and that you will do this until the baby is born."

Angela nodded. "That's right, Doctor."

"Good for you, Angela," said the pastor.

Dr. Dewitt turned around. "I'll be right back with Julia."

Two minutes later, the doctor appeared, leading Julia on his arm. Alamo stepped up quickly. "I'll take her, Doctor."

Julia ran her eyes over the group. "I'm sorry I upset you."

"No need to apologize, Julie," Alamo said. "We all care about you and the baby and want to be sure you're well taken care of."

She smiled up at him. "Thank you."

"Now, let's get you home," Alamo said. "I think it would be best if you stay at the ranch house the rest of the day and tonight. Tomorrow you can decide whether you'd rather go on back to your house and have Angela stay with you, even in the daytime for a few days if you wish."

"I sure will," put in Angela.

Julia smiled at her. "Thank you." She then looked up into Alamo's eyes. "And thank you, Alamo." Turning to the others, she thanked them for coming to the doctor's office too.

"We love you, honey," Abram said.

"We sure do!" said Vivian.

"That's for sure!" chimed in Abel.

"Well, let's get you home, little gal," Alamo said. "I'll carry you to the wagon."


An hour after the Kanes had arrived back at the big ranch house, Daisy had a delicious Sunday dinner on the table in the dining room, and the whole family sat down to enjoy the meal.

Abram asked Abel to lead in prayer. After thanking the Lord for the food, Abel also thanked Him that Julia hadn't had a miscarriage, as some of them had feared.

Still a bit shaken, Julia didn't have much appetite, but she enjoyed being with the family.

Alamo kept his eyes on Julia during the meal, and after a while he noticed that her shoulders began to droop. When she laid her fork in the plate, he knew she would eat no more. He stood. "Julie, you're obviously very tired. It's time to take you up to your room."

The others watched as Alamo took her by the arm and escorted her through the dining room doorway into the hall.

When Alamo had guided Julia into the room that had been hers when she was staying in the big ranch house, he helped her lie down on the bed. Standing over her, he then squeezed her hand. "You take a nice nap now, Julie. I can tell that this little episode has taken its toll on you.

I'm sure Angela will be up to check on you shortly. If you have anymore pains or problems, just give a holler."

He gave her hand another squeeze, and she smiled up at him. "I'll be fine now. I'm relieved to know that the baby and I are all right."

"Me too." He smiled warmly at her.

Julia raised her arms. "I want to hug you for being so good to me."

Alamo bent down, and she put her arms around his neck and hugged him tight. As she released her hold on him, she kissed his cheek. "Thank you, Alamo, for everything."

"My pleasure," he said. "Now, you get some sleep."

She smiled and nodded.

Alamo headed for the door and pulled it shut behind him. As he walked down the hall toward the staircase, he gently rubbed his cheek where Julie had kissed him.

A week passed, and Julia Kane had no more false labor pains, for which she and the rest of the family were thankful.

On Sunday morning, July 10, the sanctuary of the church building in Washington-on-the-Brazos was almost full. The Kane family, as usual, was seated on the same pew, except for Angela, who was in the choir. The other Christians from the Diamond K Ranch occupied pews near the Kanes.

The church members in attendance that morning noted that as the pianist and organist began playing a familiar hymn to open the morning service, and as the pastor and the choir members came onto the platform from a side door, a young man was at the pastor's side. Pastor Merle Evans positioned himself at his chair, which was a few feet behind the pulpit, and the young man stood in front of the chair next to him.

The choir director stepped to the pulpit, announced the number in the hymnbook, and led the congregation as they stood and sang the hymn. After the pastor called on one of the men in the congregation to lead in prayer, there was more music. Then the pastor stepped up to the pulpit to make announcements and take the offering.

Many of the church members were quite curious about the unfamiliar young man on the platform and whispered to each other about him. Included among the curious whisperers were the members of the Kane family.

After the announcements had been made and the offering had been taken, Pastor Evans stepped back up to the pulpit, gestured to the young man to come and stand beside him, and introduced him to the congregation. His name was Patrick O'Fallon. Pastor Evans reminded them that many months ago he had told them that due to the church's steady growth, he needed help. He had asked them to pray that he would be able to find just the right man to become his assistant pastor. He smiled at the congregation. "Well, I found him."

The people in the pews and in the choir exchanged glances, smiling at each other.

Pastor Evans then reminded his people that he had made it clear back then that the church was in the financial position to hire an assistant pastor, pay him well, and provide a rented house for him and his family. Patrick O'Fallon was single, but the church would still provide him a rented house to live in.

The members of the Kane family exchanged happy glances, whispering that by his name, the young man had to be Irish.

Angela also noted that young Patrick O'Fallon was Irish. She whispered a comment to the women in the choir on both sides of her about how handsome he was. They both smiled and nodded.

Pastor Evans went on to explain that Patrick was twenty-five years of age. He and his parents had come to this country from Ireland when Patrick was eighteen and had settled in Beaumont, Texas. Recently, while preaching at a missions conference in the church at Beaumont, which the O'Fallons belonged to, Pastor Evans had met Patrick and was impressed with him. Patrick had explained to him that his pastor had been teaching him and four other young men in the church who felt called to the ministry in what he called the church's "Bible institute."

At that point, Patrick had shared with Pastor Evans that he was now ready to seek the Lord's will for a place to serve as an assistant pastor of a church of like faith, where he could prepare to one day pastor the church himself. When Patrick's pastor had Patrick preach during the missions conference, Pastor Evans had been even more impressed with him.

Pastor Evans smiled at his people. "After hearing Patrick preach and knowing that he was interested in becoming an assistant pastor, I felt that he was quite possibly the one the Lord had picked out for our church. I liked his attitude about serving the Lord and the way he expounded the Scriptures. I approached him, explained that I was look-ing for an assistant pastor, and asked if he was interested. He said he sure was."

Patrick O'Fallon smiled at Pastor Evans.

"So," the pastor said, "I told him I would pray about hiring him. Well, the Lord gave me absolute peace about it, and now he's here!"

The people cheered and applauded.

"Folks," Pastor Evans said. "I have asked Patrick to preach the ser-mon this morning. So after the choir sings a special song and takes their seats in the pews and Mrs. Elizabeth Harris and Miss Angela Kane from our choir sing a duet for us, Patrick will preach."

The choir director motioned for the choir to stand and led them in a rousing gospel song. When they had finished, he dismissed them to go sit with the congregation.

The piano and organ played as the choir descended the platform steps on both sides, and the two women who were to sing the duet made their way to a spot on the platform near where the pastor and his guest speaker sat.

When the choir members had been seated, the piano began play-ing the introduction to the song Elizabeth and Angela were to sing. As the two women stepped toward the pulpit, they both smiled at Patrick. He smiled back, and Angela said to herself, *He is indeed a handsome man. His smile is captivating too.*

When the two ladies finished their song, they made their way down the platform steps, and Patrick headed for the pulpit, Bible in hand. Speaking in his definite Irish accent, Patrick commented on the beautiful duet he had just heard, greeted the people, thanked Pastor Evans for what he had done for him, then announced his text, asking the people to turn there in their Bibles. He preached a tremendous sermon, encouraging Christians to live their lives centered on their Saviour and making the gospel and the plan of salvation plain and clear to those in attendance who were without Christ. He then gave the invitation.

Several visitors walked the aisle to receive Jesus as their Saviour, and a good number of Christians came to the altar to get things in their lives right with the Lord. The new converts were then baptized in the baptistry as a thrilled crowd looked on.

Just before closing the service, Pastor Evans called for a vote to receive Patrick O'Fallon into the membership of the church and got a one hundred percent agreement. He then announced that they would have a special service that evening to ordain Patrick into the ministry, and when that was done, he would officially be Pastor Evans's assistant pastor and could move into the furnished house the church provided just a block and a half away, at 1123 West Cimarron Street.

After the service, Patrick O'Fallon stood next to the pastor and his wife at the front door, and the members of the church came by and welcomed him warmly. When the Kane family approached him, they introduced themselves. Patrick flashed Angela a smile and told her she had a beautiful voice and that he had enjoyed the song very much. Angela blushed and thanked him.

Alamo then told Patrick of the Kane family's Irish background and that their name used to be O'Kane. Patrick was glad to hear it and was exceptionally warm to them. As Patrick visited with the other Kanes,

Angela found herself unable to take her eyes from him. When he turned and met her gaze, she felt her heart quicken its pace. She quickly told him how much she had liked his sermon. He again commented on her beautiful voice and told her that he hoped he could hear her sing again real soon. Her heart skipped a beat this time, and once more she blushed and thanked him. *I love that Irish brogue,* she told herself.

In his mind, Patrick told himself that he and lovely Angela had possibly just struck up a genuine friendship.

Libby and Vivian then invited Patrick to the Diamond K Ranch for a meal on Monday evening. He was quite pleased and told them he would love to come. Abram spoke up and said he would drive a wagon into town late tomorrow afternoon and pick him up.

The service that night was a blessing to all. Patrick gave his salvation testimony and his call to preach and correctly answered doctrinal questions the pastor asked him as he stood before the people. The pastor and deacons laid their hands on him, and Pastor Evans led in the ordination prayer.

The next day, when Abram drove up to the house at 1123 West Cimarron Street, Angela was with him. She had told her father that Patrick would probably be more comfortable riding to the ranch if two people came after him.

During the thirty-mile ride from Washington-on-the-Brazos, Angela sat on the wagon seat between her father and Patrick, and during a friendly three-way conversation, almost every time she turned to look at Patrick, she found his eyes on her. She enjoyed this, and each time an electric-like tingle ran down her spine.

As the conversation went on and the miles passed by, Angela so often found Patrick looking at her that his gaze seemed to devour her. She told herself that Patrick too must have felt the electric spark between them, for often after their eyes met, he lifted his hat and nervously ran his fingers through his thick brown hair. She was sure that she detected a slight tremor in his hand.

The dinner was held at Abel and Vivian Kane's home. Patrick enjoyed the fellowship of the Kane family immensely. During the evening, it was quite apparent to the others that Patrick was attracted to Angela and she to him, though no one said anything about it. Angela was two years younger than Patrick, they were both dedicated Christians, and they seemed quite compatible.

During the next two weeks, Patrick took Angela out to dinner several times at restaurants in town. He drove a rented horse and wagon to the Diamond K Ranch each time to pick her up.

At the end of the second week, Alamo invited Pastor Evans and his wife, Louella, Patrick, and the rest of the Kane family to a dinner in the big ranch house. During the meal, Patrick asked the pastor if he believed there was such a thing as love at first sight.

The pastor said he definitely did, because it happened to him and Louella when they were young.

Patrick smiled. "Well, good! Angela and I want to announce that we fell in love at first sight. We know without a doubt that the Lord has brought us together."

Abram smiled widely. "I know about love at first sight too! Kitty and I met when she and her family first visited our church in Pawtucket, Rhode Island. I was nineteen and she was eighteen. We both knew we had fallen in love the first time we saw each other. We got married within a few weeks. When I meet her again up in heaven, I'm sure we'll talk about our love at first sight!"

Angela thumbed a tear from her eye. "I have no doubt about that, Papa. I want you and all the family here to know that I have prayed for some time that the Lord would bring that special young man He had chosen for me when it was His time. Well, He did!"

Abram smiled. "Praise the Lord, honey."

Everyone noticed that Julia was dabbing at the tears in her eyes with her napkin. All this talk about love at first sight and weddings was surely making her think of Adam and of losing him. No one could think of anything to say, so all remained silent on the subject.

Abram sat quietly as the conversation at the table went to how God's wonderful hand works in Christians' lives. Abram's own thoughts went to his precious Angela. His little girl was now a young woman of marriageable age. Where had the years gone? One day she was in pig-tails, playing with her dolls, and the next thing he knew, she was a young woman.

In his thoughts, Abram spoke to his wife. *Kitty, my love, with God's help, I've finished raising our little Angela the best I knew how. She is a fine young lady and will make this young man a good and true wife.*

A silent tear trickled down his lined face, followed by more as he reminisced about the long ago day when he took the beautiful Irish Kitty Foyle as his own beloved wife.

After the meal was over, Patrick asked Abram in front of Angela if he could have a few minutes alone with him before riding back to town with the Pastor and Mrs. Evans. Angela told Patrick she would help Daisy with the dishes while the two men talked.

Abram took Patrick to his room, and when they sat down, Patrick asked Abram for permission to marry Angela if she was willing. Abram gladly gave permission, saying he would be proud to have Patrick as his son-in-law. When Patrick asked if he thought early September would be too soon for them to marry, Abram replied that these days, times were hard, and with the Mexican threat of war still hanging over their heads, the future was so uncertain. Plus, in Texas there weren't many long courtships. They should go ahead and get engaged and make their plans to marry in early September.

Moments later, Patrick spent a few minutes alone with Angela on the front porch. He held her in his arms, told her that he loved her with all his heart, and kissed her tenderly. She told him that she loved him too, and they kissed again. He said he'd be back the next evening to pick her up and take her to town for a meal together.

Angela stood on the porch with the rest of the family a few minutes later and waved at the man she loved as he rode away in the pastor's buggy.

The next evening, Patrick picked Angela up as scheduled and took her into town to her favorite restaurant. After the meal, they drove to the edge of Washington-on-the-Brazos, and in the soft moonlight, Patrick proposed, telling her that her father had approved of him marrying his daughter. Angela happily accepted his proposal, and he put on her finger an engagement ring that he had bought at the jewelry store that day.

Angela asked if her father felt this was too soon for them to be engaged and plan their wedding. Patrick told her what her father had said about times being hard and the future being so uncertain. He had approved of them getting engaged immediately and marrying in early September.

After a tender kiss, Patrick told her that he had looked at a calendar before leaving his house and thought Saturday, September 3, would be a perfect date for them to marry. Since he had the house the church had rented for him, they had a place to live. Angela agreed with him on the date. Smiling, Patrick said he would talk to Pastor Evans tomorrow and let him know they had set the date.

The next Sunday morning, when Pastor Evans announced to the congregation the engagement of his assistant pastor and Angela Kane and the date of the wedding, there was much applause and cheering.

## 14

That same Sunday night that Pastor Merle Evans had announced that Patrick O'Fallon and Angela Kane were engaged and would marry on September 3, Angela was at Julia's house to spend the night with her as usual.

Before Julia climbed into bed, she put her arms around Angela. "Oh, honey, I'm so glad for you! I know that you and Patrick will be very happy in your upcoming marriage."

Angela held her tight for a few seconds, then eased back and looked into her eyes. "I have no doubt of that, sweet girl. Thank you."

"And I have something to tell you," Julia said.

"Mm-hmm?"

"When Libby learned at church this morning that you and Patrick will be getting married on September 3, she told me that since I won't have had my baby by then, she'll stay nights with me like you're doing. She'll begin a week before the wedding so you'll have time to get everything ready."

Angela sighed. "Well, bless her heart. That indeed will be a help to me."

The very next Sunday, Patrick and Angela surprised the congregation and sang a duet together in the morning service, just before Pastor Evans preached.

As time moved on, Julia had no more false labor pains, and all was going well with her pregnancy. However, she still missed Adam and cried over him in private. She also thanked the Lord many times a day for how Alamo had provided for her in every way and asked Him to bless Alamo abundantly.

On the afternoon of Monday, July 25, Julia was sitting in the shade of her porch when she saw two Diamond K ranch hands ride their horses off the road and trot toward the houses, barns, and corrals.

She smiled at them as they drew up to her porch. One of them dismounted with an envelope in his hand. "We just got back from town, ma'am, and wanted to deliver this letter to you. I believe it's from your parents."

When he stepped up on the porch and placed the envelope in her hand, she looked at it. "It sure is. Thank you."

"Our pleasure, ma'am." The cowboy swung back into his saddle.

Julia watched as they rode away and noted that they went to the big ranch house, and the same cowboy dismounted, took some mail from a saddlebag, stepped up on the porch, and knocked on the door. Alamo opened the door, accepted the mail with a smile, and turned back into the house. As the two riders headed toward one of the barns, Julia opened the letter from her parents.

It had been just over an hour since Julia had seen Alamo receive his mail when she saw him come out of the big ranch house and head her direction.

As Alamo drew up to the porch, he smiled. "Hi, Julie. How are you doing?"

She chuckled. "I'm just fine, Alamo, except my girth is growing by the day." As she spoke, she patted her midsection.

"You look beautiful to me," Alamo blurted out, surprising both himself and Julia.

She noted the flush on his face as he realized that the words had left his mouth unguarded. She touched the chair next to her. "Come sit down."

"Okay." Alamo eased onto the chair. "You've asked me a couple of times lately if I had heard anything from Susanna Dickinson about she and little Angelina moving here. And I hadn't."

Julia nodded. "Uh-huh."

"Well, I just got a letter from her. She thanked me again for the offer, saying she still just might take me up on it later, but apparently Delia Washburn is having some health problems that are going to take some time for her to get over, and Susanna just can't leave her."

"Oh, I'm sorry for that," Julia said. "So Susanna will let you know if and when she'll take you up on it?"

"That's the way I understand it."

A smile spread over Julia's lovely features. "Well, I got a letter today myself. From my parents. Written by my mother."

"Yes?"

"They want to know if it would be all right with you if they come in early September since the baby is due late that month or early October."

"Absolutely! You write back and tell them that I said to come whenever they want and to stay as long as they want."

Julia's face lit up. "Oh, Alamo, you're such a generous man. I'll write the letter this evening. Thank you so very much."

Alamo gave her a lopsided grin. "My pleasure. I love having your parents here on the ranch. They can stay here with you, or they can stay in my house."

"Thank you," she said sweetly. In her mind, Julia thought, *When he grins like that, he looks so much like Adam. In fact, in many ways, Alamo is so much like Adam.*

Julia stood up, bent over, gave him a friendship-type hug, and kissed his cheek.

Once again, Alamo's heart felt like it was on fire.

Julia watched him walk back to the big ranch house. When he stepped up on the porch, he looked back to see her watching him. He smiled and waved. She waved back.

That night in his room, Alamo prayed again, asking the Lord to cause Julie to fall in love with him when the time was right in view of Adam's death, which had happened nearly five months ago.

~

On Thursday, July 28, Alamo was given his mail by another Diamond K ranch hand who had gone to Washington-on-the-Brazos on business and picked up the mail while in town.

Sitting down at his desk in the room he used as his office, Alamo sorted through the mail and found a letter that interested him very much. He quickly went outside and hailed the first ranch hand he saw, asking him to find Cort Whitney and tell him he needed to talk to him as soon as possible.

Some twenty minutes later, Alamo and his foreman sat down in his office, and Alamo said, "Cort, I received a letter in my mail today from the owner of the Sterritt Meat-Packing Plant in Nacogdoches. He has been made aware of the successful Diamond K Ranch and wants to purchase a hundred steers from us."

Cort's eyes widened. "Sterritt, eh? That's a big plant. I've heard a lot about it. Owner is Jack Sterritt, right?"

"Yep. He has offered us a fair price per pound for the steers. If the price is acceptable, he wants some of our ranch hands to drive the herd to his plant soon. I've never been to Nacogdoches, and I'd like to see it. So I'll take a dozen men, and we'll drive the steers to Sterritt's plant. Just wanted to fill you in."

Cort grinned. "Sounds good to me, boss. How soon you plan to leave?"

"Tomorrow morning, right after breakfast. I'll let you pick out the dozen men."

"Fine, boss. I'll do that."

"Okay. I'll write a letter to Jack Sterritt telling him I'm accepting his offer and get it in the mail today. He'll get the letter a couple of days before we arrive with the steers."

On Tuesday, August 2, Alamo and his dozen ranch hands arrived at Nacogdoches, Texas, with the herd. While the men stayed with the cattle just outside of town, Alamo rode into town, dismounted in front of the Sterritt Meat-Packing Plant, and entered the door marked Office.

When he stepped inside, he saw three desks across the room. Only one was occupied at the moment, and the man at the desk was talking to a man standing in front of him. Another man was seated on a wooden chair about halfway across the room and appeared to be waiting to talk to the man at the desk.

At that moment, Alamo was greeted by a silver-haired man who came from a small room to his right. "May I help you, sir?"

Alamo smiled. "My name is Kane. I own the Diamond K Ranch southwest of here. I need to see Mr. Jack Sterritt."

The elderly man's bushy white eyebrows arched. "Oh yes, Mr. Kane. Mr. Sterritt is expecting you." He pointed to the man seated at the desk across the room. "That's Mr. Sterritt sitting there at the desk. The gentleman he is talking to is a customer, and so is the one on that chair waiting to see him. Please go to one of those chairs and have a seat. I'm sure it won't be long before Mr. Sterritt can talk to you."

Alamo nodded and headed that way. He had only taken a few steps when the customer standing at the plant owner's desk said a word of thanks, turned, and headed in Alamo's direction.

Suddenly they focused on each other, and Alamo's scalp prickled. A crawling sensation crept up the nape of his neck.

A glint of puzzlement came into the man's eyes, and he stopped suddenly with some fifteen feet between them.

Alamo also stopped abruptly. "Louis!" The word fell from his open mouth like a stone.

Louis Rose's chest was tight, and he could only breathe shallowly.

Alamo's mind flashed back to the story Susanna Dickinson had told about the day before the Alamo was attacked by Santa Anna's sixty-five hundred troops. Colonel William Travis drew a line in the sand on the plaza, asking those men who would stay and fight to the death to step over the line. Louis Rose was the only man who had refused to cross Colonel Travis's line. He had run away in the night and escaped the battle.

Though Alamo Kane thought of Louis Rose as a coward, he subdued his feelings, walked up to him, and extended his hand. "Louis. I didn't think I would ever see you again."

Rose gripped Kane's hand weakly. "Alan Kane. It—it's good to see you. I don't suppose you ever knew that Nacogdoches is my hometown."

Alamo shook his head. "I guess that never came up in any of our discussions."

"I recall that you're a rancher."

"Yes. Some of my men and I just brought in a herd of steers to sell to Mr. Sterritt for beef."

Rose nodded. "Well, I now operate a meat shop here in town, and I just made a purchase of meat from him."

"I see."

Rose gave him a solemn look. "Alan, I recall that a few days before the big attack at the Alamo, Colonel Travis sent you to carry a message to General Houston."

"That's right."

"Since you're still alive, I know you didn't get back to the Alamo before the big attack."

"Right. I was on my way back later that very morning, and I ran into Captain Almeron Dickinson's wife, Susanna, a few miles east of San Antonio. She told me all about the battle, including the fact that every man in the Alamo had been killed."

"Oh." He looked at the ground uncomfortably. "Well, Alan, I'm glad you weren't there when all the other men were killed."

Alamo smiled thinly. "Thank you, Louis."

"Well, I must be going," said Louis. "Plenty of work to do at the meat shop. It's been nice seeing you."

"You too." Alamo watched him leave the office.

Alamo turned and saw that the other man who had been waiting to see the plant owner was just walking away from his desk.

Alamo approached Jack Sterritt and introduced himself. They got right down to business, and within a few minutes Alamo had the check in hand for the one hundred head of cattle. He and his men delivered the cattle to the corral behind the plant and soon were on their way back to the ranch.

When they arrived at the Diamond K, Alamo told his family about running into Louis Rose at Nacogdoches. They were surprised but were glad to hear that Rose was friendly toward Alamo.

On Thursday, August 4, at the Miller plantation just outside of New Orleans, Justin and Myra received the reply letter from Julia about their coming to the Diamond K Ranch in early September. They were happy that Alamo Kane was so kind to them, and both praised the Lord that they would be able to be present when their little grandchild was born.

Holding Julia's letter, Myra said, "Oh, darling, it will only be a few weeks, and we can head west! I'm so excited about seeing our precious daughter and returning to that beautiful part of Texas!"

Justin smiled and said in a teasing way, "I think you like Texas as much or maybe more than you like Louisiana."

She smiled at him. "Well, it is becoming quite dear to my heart since Julia lives there. And since that baby she's carrying does too!"

Justin chuckled. "I know just what you mean. Well, the first thing I need to do now is go down to the docks and get our reservations made for the trip. After that, I'll prepare my foreman to take care of the work at the place while we're gone."

Myra nodded. "All right. I'll make some detailed plans for the trip and arrange with our house servants to handle things while we're away. Ah, dear…"

"Yes?"

"How long do you want to stay at the Kane ranch?"

"Let's stay till after Christmas, okay?"

"That's all right with me!"

Justin drove his favorite buggy to the New Orleans docks and made reservations for Myra and himself on the ship to Galveston and on the boats necessary to get them to Groce's Landing so they could take a hired buggy to the Diamond K Ranch.

When he returned home with the information, he showed it to Myra. She immediately sat down and wrote a letter to Julia, telling her that they would arrive at the ranch around Wednesday, September 7. She added that since Alamo had told Julia they could stay as long as they want, they would stay till after Christmas.

Patrick O'Fallon and Angela Kane's courtship was a beautiful, Christ-filled one, and on Saturday, September 3, 1836, the sanctuary of the church in Washington-on-the-Brazos was filled for the wedding.

As the organ played, Pastor Evans and the groom stood on the platform and watched a beaming Abram Kane walk his only daughter down the aisle to be wed to the man she loved.

On the platform, Patrick was in awe as his bride proceeded toward him on her father's arm. *Thank You, dear Lord,* he said in his heart, *for bringing us together. She is so perfect for me, and I know she will be such a help to me in the ministry. You always do everything so well.*

When the bride and her father came to a halt at the base of the platform, Abram placed Angela's hand in Patrick's, kissed her cheek, and turned to take his seat among the family. A trickle of tears streamed down his aging face, and he quickly brushed them away. As he sat down, Abram could almost see his dear departed wife's face as he looked at his lovely daughter.

Although uncomfortable with child, Julia was at the wedding and sitting next to Abram. She saw the glistening tears on his cheeks, took his hand in hers, and squeezed it. Abram looked at her and smiled and squeezed her hand in return.

Patrick and Angela took their vows before the pastor, and there was much joy among the crowd when he pronounced them husband and wife.

After the bride and groom had been honored at the wedding reception in the church's dining hall, Patrick took his bride to the rented house, belonging to the church, where he had been living. It would now be her home too.

The very next day, in the evening service, Pastor Evans announced to his people that he was retiring. He was now in his seventies, and his body just couldn't function for the work of the ministry as it used to. He told them that he and Louella would be moving back to Memphis, Tennessee, where they were from originally. He then announced that there would be a business meeting after the preaching service.

At the business meeting, Pastor Evans strongly recommended that the church officially call Patrick O'Fallon as their pastor, which they did with a unanimous vote.

After the business meeting, Alamo had Julia at his side as he joked with Angela. "Sis, when we were kids, I never dreamed that one day you'd be the wife of my pastor."

Angela nudged him. "Well, little brother, for me, being the wife of your pastor is like a dream come true."

Julia hugged Angela. "Sweetie, it's been like a dream for me to have you as my sister-in-law. Now my dream is even sweeter since you are also my pastor's wife!"

Angela laughed as she hugged Julia and kissed her cheek.

Alamo smiled, dreaming that one day the Lord would make Julie his wife.

The following Wednesday, September 7, Julia's parents arrived at the Diamond K Ranch as scheduled, in early afternoon. The reunion between Julia and her parents was sweet, as was the meeting between the Millers and all the Kanes.

The Millers were pleased to meet Angela's husband at the Wednesday evening service in Washington-on-the-Brazos and thoroughly enjoyed his preaching.

In mid-September, Alamo and his brothers were in Washington-on-the-Brazos on a weekday. They stopped in to see Texas president David Burnet, and he welcomed them warmly.

They chatted for a while on a few different subjects, including what Mexico's dictator and military leader, Santa Anna, might be planning in regard to his country's relationship with the people of Texas. They all agreed that Santa Anna was not to be trusted, including David Burnet, who had definitely changed his mind about Santa Anna.

When it was time for the Kane brothers to head back to the ranch, President Burnet walked outside with them. As they were about to mount their horses, Burnet said, "Hey, fellas, it was good to spend some time with you. Feel free to drop by my office anytime you're in town."

"We'll be sure to do that, sir." Just as Alamo spoke, he caught sight of some Mexican soldiers riding horses on the street in their direction. Pointing at them, he said, "Look there, Mr. President. Mexican soldiers."

The eyes of Alex and Abel Kane, as well as those of President Burnet, swung to the oncoming Mexican soldiers.

"I count twelve," Alamo said. "And look! One of them is carrying a white flag on a pole."

"I wonder what this is all about," Burnet said, his voice showing the irritation he was feeling.

"We're about to find out," put in Alex as the dozen riders drew up in front of the Texas General Convention building, where the four of them stood.

The rider who was apparently the leader of the group looked down at the four men and said in perfect English, "We are here to see President David Burnet. Do you know if he is in his office?"

"I am President David Burnet."

"I am Captain Gaspar Gutierrez," said the leader from his saddle. "I have a letter here for you, President Burnet, from el presidente Antonio López de Santa Anna." As he spoke, he pulled an envelope from his uniform pocket and leaned down to hand it to Burnet.

Burnet eyed the Mexican warily. "I'll read the letter aloud so my friends here can hear what Santa Anna has to say."

Gutierrez shrugged his shoulders.

Burnet tore the envelope open, took out the single piece of stationery, and read it to the Kane brothers. In the letter, which was written in English, Santa Anna brought up that he had learned that the Texans were claiming that their border with Mexico was the Rio Grande. Santa Anna stated that this was wrong. He and the people of Mexico recognized the Texas border to be farther north, at the Nueces River.

When Burnet had finished reading the letter, the Kane brothers looked at each other, saying with their eyes that there was going to be more trouble with Mexico for sure.

Burnet looked up at the leader of the Mexican unit. "Captain Gutierrez, you wait right here. I'll go into my office and write a letter for you to take back to Santa Anna."

Gutierrez nodded. "We will wait."

The Kane brothers followed Burnet into his office and sat down as he went to his desk, took out a sheet of his official stationery, and began writing.

When Burnet was finished, he said, "Okay, gentlemen, let me read it to you."

Alamo, Alex, and Abel listened intently as Burnet read them his letter to Santa Anna. The letter stated clearly to the Mexican dictator that the Texas-Mexico border was positively at the Rio Grande and would remain so.

When Burnet had finished reading it to them, Alamo swung a fist. "Good for you, Mr. President! You made it plain enough!"

Alex and Abel patted Burnet on the back, saying that they were proud of him. The Texas president folded the sheet of paper, placed it inside the envelope, and sealed it.

The Kane brothers followed him back out to where the Mexican soldiers were waiting and observed as Burnet stepped up to where Captain Gutierrez sat on his horse and handed him the envelope. "This letter is for Santa Anna only."

Gutierrez nodded as he placed the envelope in his uniform pocket, swung the reins to turn his horse, and rode away with his eleven men following. The white flag was still flapping in the breeze.

Burnet said to the Kane brothers, "I guarantee you, the big bull isn't going to like my letter. I'm going to show Santa Anna's letter to General Houston and tell him how I answered. I'm sure the general will agree that trouble is coming about the border issue. I'm going to have him keep troops on our border at the Rio Grande."

"Excellent, sir," Alamo said. "The only thing you could do is what you did. Take the big bull by the horns!"

Alex and Abel both spoke their agreement.

# 15

At the Diamond K Ranch, the Millers were staying in Julia's house with her, since it had a large, comfortable guest room. This freed Libby Kane to be in her own house at night with her husband.

On Thursday evening, September 29, Julia's parents tucked her in her bed, kissed her good night, and went to their own room.

Julia sat up in bed in the middle of the night, not even sure what woke her up. She rolled over in the bed and looked out the window. The harvest moon was shining brightly, sending its silver beams into the room. She rolled onto her back, staring at the shadows the moon was forming on the ceiling.

Her hands were resting on the mound of her unborn baby when she suddenly felt a sharp twinge in her midsection, and her stomach muscles tightened. The pain soon passed, and she tried to find a more comfortable position on the bed.

Soon Julia was dozing again, but after a while, she began having more pains in her midsection. Rolling from one position to another alleviated the pains for a time, but not much later, she was hurting again.

For the rest of the night she was quite uncomfortable, and the hours seemed to drag on forever. She was awake when the moonlight faded, followed by the gray of dawn. Then brilliant sunlight began to cover the land. At that point, Julia sat up slowly and massaged her aching back.

When the back pain had subsided, she got up from the bed, went to the washstand, and splashed cold water on her face. As she was drying off, another twinge of pain gripped her midsection.

She shuffled to her rocking chair, sat down, and looked out the window at the small yard that surrounded the house. The golden sun was now lifting off the eastern horizon, and she marveled at its beauty. Grasping the hairbrush that lay on the small table next to the rocking chair, she brushed her hair and wove it into a long, single braid.

Suddenly there was another twinge of pain in her midsection, only this time it was much stronger. She bent over until the pain subsided, then rose from the rocking chair and slowly dressed while whispering to her yet unborn child, "Well, little one, it seems like September 30 just may be your birthday. I'm thankful your grandparents are here."

Moments later, Julia was walking toward the kitchen, where her mother was cooking breakfast. She could smell the fragrant aroma of brewing coffee and frying bacon.

When she stepped into the kitchen, her mother was at the stove. Myra smiled at her daughter and said cheerily, "Good morning, dear." Her brow instantly furrowed when she saw the uncomfortable look on Julia's features. "Honey, did you have a bad night?"

"You might say that, Mama," replied Julia as she pulled a chair from under the kitchen table and started to sit down. Just as she was lowering herself onto the chair, a strong pain hit her back and quickly clawed its way around to her stomach. She sat there rapidly taking short breaths.

Myra stepped up and laid a hand on her shoulder. "Julia, I think you're in labor!"

Julia flinched from a sharp pain in her midsection. "I—I think you're right, Mama. And this time it definitely isn't false labor."

"Honey, you sit there and rest. I'm going to send your father to the ranch house and have Alamo go to town for the doctor."

Julia nodded. "All right, Mama. I'll stay right here."

Myra was back in less than three minutes. As she walked toward her daughter, she said, "Your father is on his way to the ranch house. Any more pains?"

Julia was pressing her hands on her midsection. "Yes, Mama. They're getting harder and closer together."

Myra nodded. "Good girl. That's the way it should be. Let me help you to your feet, and let's get you back into your room, into a night gown, and into bed. Can you manage that?"

Once she was standing, Julia took hold of her mother's hand and nodded. "With your help, I can."

When they were in Julia's bedroom and she was settled in the bed, tears began spilling silently down her cheeks.

"What is it, dear?" asked Myra. "Why are you crying? This is a joyous occasion."

"I know, Mama, and I'm so glad I'll soon hold my baby in my arms, but—but I so wish that Adam was here with me to rejoice in the birth of his child."

Julia dried her eyes on a corner of the sheet and gave her mother a weak smile.

"Oh, honey, I know it's hard for you to go through this with Adam gone," Myra said, "but remember, the Lord is with you. And you have such good family support in the Kanes. Our precious little one will be just fine."

Julia nodded. "I'm so grateful that you and Papa are here, Mama."

At that instant, Justin entered the room. "Alamo's on his way to town. He'll be bringing the doctor as soon as possible. In the meantime, he told Daisy to come over here and be ready to act as a midwife if necessary. He assured me that she has a lot of experience delivering babies right here on the ranch."

Julia nodded. "That's right, Papa. She does."

Footsteps sounded outside the bedroom door. Then Daisy Haycock appeared, carrying towels. "Well, Julia dear," she approached the bed, "if Dr. Dewitt isn't here by the time the baby comes, I'm here to deliver it."

More than two hours had passed since Alamo had galloped away toward Washington-on-the-Brazos. Daisy was watching over Julia carefully. The pains were getting closer together, but as yet the baby had not been born.

Justin and Myra were standing on one side of the bed while Daisy was on the other side using a washcloth to wipe the perspiration from Julia's brow. At that moment, they heard the front door of the house open, followed by the sound of Alamo's voice.

Seconds later, Alamo led Dr. Dewitt into the bedroom. The doctor fixed his line of sight on Julia, and as he headed toward the bed, he smiled. "Baby's not come yet, I see."

"He or she is about to, Doctor," said Daisy.

Dr. Dewitt set his medical bag on the small table beside the bed and ran his gaze to the Millers. "You're Julia's parents, I assume?"

The Millers nodded.

"Well," said the doctor, "I'll ask you and Alamo to leave Daisy and me here for the delivery. We'll let you know when the baby is born."

Alamo closed the bedroom door and led the Millers down the hall to the parlor. He then told them he was going to go get the rest of the family.

Some twenty minutes after Alamo had returned to Julia's parlor with his father, his two brothers, and their wives, they heard a lusty wail come down the hall from Julia's bedroom. Everybody looked toward the door that led to the hall, and Libby said breathlessly, "The baby!"

Alamo stiffened but could not speak.

Abruptly, there were rapid footsteps in the hall, and Dr. Dewitt entered the room smiling. "Good news, folks! Julia just gave birth to a fine, healthy baby boy!"

"Whoopee!" shouted Abram.

A shiver of pure joy ran down Alamo's spine. "Hallelujah! Thank You, Lord, for this precious baby boy! Is Julia all right, Doctor?"

"She's fine," he replied.

The others joined in rejoicing.

Suddenly they heard another lusty wail come down the hall.

Alamo laughed. "Sounds like his lungs are in good shape! Praise God!"

The others laughed, including the doctor, who then said, "Daisy is preparing both mother and baby so all of you can see them. I need to get back to them now. Daisy will come and let you know when you can go in."

There was much joy among the family as they celebrated the baby's birth. A few minutes later, Daisy appeared with a smile on her face. "Okay, everybody, you can visit mother and child now!"

Justin said, "Daisy, has she given the baby a name yet? When we asked her about a name on the day we arrived here, she hadn't chosen a boy's name or a girl's name yet."

Every eye in the group fastened on Daisy. None of them had been able to learn what Julia would call her baby.

Daisy grinned. "I'll let Julia tell you what she named him."

"Let's go!" said Alamo.

When the family members entered the room, Julia was lying with her head on two pillows, holding her baby boy in her arms.

As they drew up to the bed and looked at the husky little boy, there were *oohs* and *aahs*.

Myra leaned down. "Honey, have you chosen a name for him?"

Julia smiled. "Yes. His name is Adam, after his father."

This pleased the whole family, especially Alamo.

Justin asked if he could hold his new grandson, and Julia allowed it. Myra was next to do so, and third was Grandpa Abram. While the baby was passed around to each member of the family, many tears were shed as they talked about Adam, wishing he could have seen his little son.

Alamo wiped tears from his eyes. "Adam *has* seen his son. Since Adam is part of that great cloud of witnesses in heaven spoken of in Hebrews 12:1, he is looking down at his little boy right now."

This brought a flood of tears, and as emotions settled down, the last family member to hold the baby was Alamo. Amazingly, the baby had not cried while being passed from person to person.

Before the group left to let Julia and the baby get some rest, Justin led them in prayer, giving praise to God that Julia and little Adam had come through the birth process just fine.

Dr. Dewitt set a time for Julia to bring the baby to his office for a checkup, climbed on his horse, and rode away.

⸻

As time slipped by, Alamo's love for Julia never weakened. It only grew stronger. He still prayed daily that one day the Lord would cause her to fall in love with him.

Not only was Alamo deeply in love with Julia, but little Adam had won a special place in his heart. Almost every evening Alamo found his feet taking him to Julia's house. He went there under the pretext of checking on the baby, but secretly he also wanted to be with Julia.

Julia's parents sometimes went to their own room soon after supper, but oftentimes they walked to the ranch house and kept Abram and Daisy company.

Periodically Justin got Abram aside and made inquiries about land prices in Texas and about ranching. He made it known that he was considering a change in his and Myra's lives, and asked that Abram keep their conversations to himself. From the things Justin told him, Abram understood that if such a move were to take place, it would be some years away.

Often while Aunt Libby or Aunt Vivian took care of the baby, Alamo let Julia choose from whatever spare horses on the ranch were available, and they went riding together. Alamo could see that she was so happy to be riding again.

The Diamond K Ranch continued to do well. With the passing of time, Alamo's fear that Santa Anna might start a war over the border dispute finally died out. No more had been heard from the Mexican dictator on the subject.

The church in Washington-on-the-Brazos was doing well under the leadership of Pastor Patrick O'Fallon. The visitation program was quite successful, and new people came to the church on a regular basis, many of them coming to know the Lord Jesus Christ as Saviour.

Pastor O'Fallon was working toward the church being able to erect a larger building. They needed an auditorium with more seating capacity, and they needed more Sunday school classrooms. The congregation agreed that they should begin construction on the new building in the spring. Angela was superbly happy to see her husband doing so well in his ministry.

Eventually the days grew cooler as autumn descended on southeast Texas.

One blustery, rainy evening, Alamo hurried along the well-worn path to Julia's house. Shaking the rain from his hat as he stepped up on the back porch, he tapped on the kitchen door with the rhythm that Julia knew well, and she called out, "Come on in, Alamo!"

When he opened the kitchen door, the sweet scent of warm apples and cinnamon greeted him. He took a deep breath and smiled at Julia while hanging his hat and jacket on pegs next to the door. "Whatever you're cooking sure smells delicious, little gal."

Julia's smile warmed his heart. "It's been a rather gloomy day, so I decided to stay busy. I've baked an array of goodies. Would you be interested in a warm piece of apple pie and a cup of coffee?"

"I'd like nothing better!" He walked over to the cradle that sat close to the stove and looked down at his adorable little nephew, who was sound asleep, a thumb in his mouth.

Julia smiled again as she observed Alamo eying little Adam.

Not wanting to disturb the sleeping infant, Alamo took a seat at the table and watched Julia as she busied herself cutting pie and pouring coffee. Soon Julia placed a large slice of aromatic apple pie and a steaming cup of coffee on the table in front of Alamo, then carried her own dessert and coffee and sat down across from him.

Alamo took a bite of the pie. "Mm-mmm! Wow, this pie is so good! It reminds me of my mother's apple pie."

Julia snickered. "Maybe that's because Angela gave me the recipe. It was your mother's."

"Well, no wonder it reminds me of Mama's apple pie!"

They laughed together, and as they ate pie and drank coffee, they talked quietly about their younger years and their respective homes, hers in New Orleans and his in Boston.

The warm fire and the cozy atmosphere began to take effect on both of them. Alamo became aware that Julia was feeling a bit sleepy, as was he, especially when she tried to discreetly cover a yawn.

The tall Irishman scooted his chair back and rose to his feet. "It's been a long day, Julie. I'm sure you're tired too. Thank you for that piece of pie and the coffee and for the trip down memory lane. I'll be going now."

Julia stood up and warmed him with another captivating smile. "It's always a pleasure to spend time with you, Alamo. Please come again real soon."

"Will do." Alamo went to the pegs by the door and put on his hat and jacket. "Good night."

"Good night," she echoed as she watched him step out into the cold night air and close the door. She smiled and wrapped her arms around herself then walked over and smiled down at her sleeping baby boy.

Outside, as Alamo made his way toward the big ranch house in the darkness, a smile broke across his rugged features. "Maybe. Just maybe," he whispered as he looked toward heaven.

⤝⤞

In the first week of November, David Burnet resigned as president of the Republic of Texas, and General Sam Houston was elected in his place.

⤝⤞

Christmas day fell on Sunday in 1836, and in Julia's house, baby Adam awakened early, as though anticipating the occasion.

The cradle was right next to Julia's bed, and when little Adam made waking sounds with his mouth, she slipped from her bed and quickly put a log on the red embers in the small fireplace, which had kept the room reasonably warm.

Lighting her lantern, Julia changed the baby's diaper, then carried him to the rocking chair, sat down, and sang to him while feeding him. By the firelight she could see him staring up at her, his big blue eyes shining.

Noting how much the baby resembled his father, she closed her eyes. "Oh, Adam darling, I miss you so very much. Your little son looks so much like you, and that makes my heart happy. I'm so thankful that I still have a part of you with me in him. I'll make this day a special one for little Adam as we celebrate Jesus's birth."

When the baby had been fed, Julia lifted him to her shoulder, rubbing her cheek against his. She whispered, "Little man, how very precious and special you are."

Then closing her eyes, she said, "Lord Jesus, thank You for this wonderful miracle You've blessed me with."

Soon little Adam was asleep again, and his mother placed him back in his bed. Covering him with warm blankets, she caressed his chubby cheek for a few seconds with a finger.

It was still very early, and dawn was barely a light gray streak on the eastern horizon, but Julia knew she was awake for the day. She picked up the lighted lantern, carried it to the small table next to her comfortable overstuffed chair, then sat down and picked up her Bible from the table. She opened it to Luke 2, and as she had done for years on Christmas, she read the old, old story in verses 1 through 20.

The Christmas morning and evening services at the church in Washington-on-the-Brazos were a real blessing to all. In the Sunday school classes, in Pastor Patrick O'Fallon's preaching, and in the music, the Lord Jesus was exalted as the virgin-born Son of God.

On Wednesday, December 28, Justin and Myra Miller made preparations to leave the Diamond K Ranch. Alamo and his brothers would take them by wagon to Groce's Landing, where they would board the boat that would take them to a ship at Galveston that would carry them to New Orleans.

As they packed their bags in their room in Julia's house, Justin and Myra knew that departing from their daughter and new little grandson would be very difficult, as well as leaving the Kane family and their friends who lived on the ranch. It would also be difficult leaving Texas, which they had come to love.

When the ranch wagon pulled up to Julia's house, and the Kane family, Daisy, and some of the ranch hands and their families were gathered there to see the Millers off, Myra wrapped her daughter and her grandson in her arms. Tears flowed down Myra's sad face, and Julia's tears started up as well.

"Oh, Mama," said Julia, "It's so hard to see you and Papa leave. It has been so wonderful having both of you here."

Myra dabbed at her own tears. "Now, dear, enough of these sad, long faces. We'll be back again. And I'm sure it won't be very long before we return."

"Oh yes, Mama!" A bright smile erased the sorrow on her face. "I'll pray that it will be *real* soon!"

Justin moved up and folded his wife, daughter, and grandson in his arms. This brought tears again to both mother and daughter, and Justin's own eyes were bubbling with excess moisture. Little Adam, who was nearly three months old, began crying when he saw his mother and grandparents crying.

The Millers then went to the wagon, where special seats had been put in the bed for the Millers to sit on. The Kane brothers told the Millers how glad they were that they could stay so long on this trip. Then all of them boarded, with Alamo gripping the reins, and Julia held her little son in one arm while waving with her free hand as the wagon drove away.

~

More than a year passed, and in February of 1838, Alamo received a letter from Susanna Dickinson, in which she told him that Delia Washburn's health was improving now, and she felt that she would be free to take little Angelina and move on within seven or eight months. She then explained that she was now engaged to marry a man named John Williams, who lived in Gonzales. They had known each other for several years. John was a widower. His wife had died almost three years ago. She and John planned to marry in the fall.

Susanna thanked Alamo once again for the offer he had made to give her and Angelina a home on the Diamond K and said she hoped she could see him and Julia again someday. If they ever came anywhere near Gonzales, she asked that they stop and see her.

When Alamo went to Julia's house and let her read the letter, she was touched, as he was, by Susanna's kind words. Alamo commented that he owed his nickname to Susanna, and he would never forget her, even if he never got to see her again. Julia batted her eyes at him playfully. "Alamo, if I married some man and moved away from the ranch, would you ever forget me?"

With his heart stirring, Alamo asked, "Do you have some particular man in mind to marry?"

She giggled playfully. "That's *my* secret."

Since Julia was obviously kidding, Alamo didn't let it upset him. That night in his room, he prayed earnestly that the Lord would work in her heart soon and cause her to fall in love with him.

As time continued to pass, Alamo and Julia often went horseback riding together. She still got to pick what horse she would ride each time.

## 16

On a bright, clear day in late April 1838, Julia Kane was sitting on the front porch of her house on the Diamond K Ranch, holding little Adam in her arms, when she caught sight of Alamo riding toward her from the front gate of the ranch. He was leading a superb stallion, which was also saddled and bridled.

Julia smiled at Alamo as he drew rein and dismounted. As he stepped up onto the porch, little Adam called out excitedly, "Unca Al'mo!" He raised his arms, wanting his uncle to take him.

Julia smiled and raised her son up toward Alamo. He smiled back and took his little nineteen-month-old nephew into his arms. Holding him close, Alamo said, "Julie, I want you to come and take a look at this stallion I bought in Washington-on-the-Brazos this morning."

She jumped up from her chair and followed Alamo down the steps. "He is magnificent!"

The stallion's coat was a sleek, fiery red with a touch of gold. His mane was pure gold, cresting from his majestic head along the imposing neck, rising, then falling low. The tail matched the mane in color. The horse was muscular, long of body, and long of leg, with the head of a war charger. His profile was graceful and suggested great speed.

Still holding his happy nephew, who was also looking the horse over, Alamo said, "You really like him, Julie?"

"Oh yes! You say you bought him in town. At one of the stables?"

"Mm-hmm. He's almost four years old now."

Julia moved up close to the big horse. There was a tenderness in the horse's eyes as the lovely lady stroked his long face and mane. He whinnied softly. Without taking her eyes off the stallion, she said, "You'll be mighty proud to ride him, Alamo."

Alamo cleared his throat gently. "Well, I'll have to get permission from his new owner first."

She turned and looked at him quizzically. "His new owner?"

"Yes. Her name is Julia Kane, but I call her Julie."

Julia's mouth fell open as wonderment filled her deep blue eyes. "Al—Alamo… Are you…are you telling me that you bought this magnificent animal for *me*?"

Grinning from ear to ear, Alamo nodded. "Uh-huh. He's yours."

Julia gasped, "Oh, Alamo!" She hugged the horse's neck, receiving another whinny. She then wheeled around and flung her arms around Alamo's neck, with a wide-eyed little Adam Kane in his arms looking on. "Oh, thank you!" she squealed, tears flowing. "I've never seen anything like him in all my life!"

Alamo shifted little Adam into one arm, then wrapped the other one around Julia as she embraced him. While she clung to his neck, fire surged through his veins. *If only she were mine,* he thought, *I would be the happiest man on earth.*

Julia raised up on her tiptoes and planted a warm kiss on her benefactor's cheek. Quickly brushing away her tears, she said. "How can I ever thank you?"

Alamo smiled. "Just seeing you this happy is thanks enough for me. You see, Julie, it has bothered me ever since you and Adam came to Texas after you were married that you had to give up your own special horse on your father's plantation. You've ridden many horses here on the ranch, but now you have your very own horse."

Julia turned back to the stallion, hugging his neck again. He bobbed his majestic head and whinnied softly.

Looking back at Alamo, she said, "Oh, I just love him!"

The stallion whinnied again, his eyes fixed on Julia.

Alamo grinned. "Looks like he feels the same about *you.*"

She giggled. "I don't know about him, but it was love at first sight for me!"

A numbness touched Alamo deep inside. *Yes,* he thought, *like the first time I saw you.*

Stroking the horse's long, graceful face, Julia asked, "What's his name, Alamo?"

"The owner of the stable told me the people he bought the horse from didn't say if he had a name."

Stepping back to admire her new possession, Julia looked at his fiery red-gold coat glistening in the Texas sun. "Then I'll call him Flame." She smiled broadly.

The horse whinnied again, bobbing his head.

"Guess he likes the name, Julie!"

She hugged Flame's neck once more, then went to Alamo and embraced him again. "Thank you! Thank you! Thank you!"

As usual, the tall Irishman's heart burned within his chest. He thought about the two years Julie had been on the ranch since Adam was killed at the Alamo. As much as every fiber of his being had yearned and longed for her to love him, Julia had been his brother's wife. Alamo's devotion to the memory of his brother was a living thing. It was almost as if Adam were still alive. There was an invisible line between Alamo and Julie. The only way he could ever cross that line would be by Julie's invitation.

Alamo took a deep breath to steady himself. "How soon do you want to ride him?"

Julia jumped up and down. "Oh, it has to be *today*! How about this afternoon? It's Vivian's turn to take care of little Adam if I need to leave him for a while."

"Then this afternoon it is. I'll take Flame to the barn where I keep my own horses, and I'll bring him back when it's time for you to ride him. What time should I be here?"

"How about three o'clock?"

At precisely three o'clock, Julia was standing on her front porch as Alamo rode up on his own horse, leading Flame by the reins. Alamo noticed that Julia was in her riding skirt, with a white blouse and a western-style vest over the blouse. She was also wearing riding boots and spurs. Julia bounded off the porch and hurried to her horse. Flame bobbed his head and whinnied, showing that he was glad to see her.

Alamo dismounted while Julia was petting Flame's neck and talking to him in sweet tones and swung the reins over Flame's head, placing them on the saddle horn. "Since Flame's so tall, I'll help you mount up," he said with a smile.

"Thank you," she said, "but that's not necessary. I can do it by myself."

Alamo watched as she raised her left foot, and though she had to rise on the tiptoes of her right foot to reach, she inserted her foot into the stirrup and swung into the saddle.

Alamo chuckled. "Well, you did it!"

"Wow!" she exclaimed, looking at Alamo. "He's the biggest horse I've ever ridden! Seems like I'm sitting on top of a two-story house!"

"You just hang on good whenever you gallop him, Julie. By the looks of him, I'd say he can outrun the wind."

"Should I take him for a good run before we ride together?"

Alamo eased back in the saddle. "Sure. I'll just sit here and watch."

"You do that!" She laughed. Then she reined Flame around and headed west toward open country, trotting him casually. She turned in the saddle and looked back at Alamo. He grinned and waved.

A few minutes later, Julia reached a broad, level stretch of pasture. Flame was warmed up now and was chomping at the bit to run. Julia could see it. She knew it was born in him to run. The big horse was obviously built for speed and had the heart to go with it.

Sensing the thoughts of his featherweight owner, Flame sniffed the breeze and snorted.

"Okay, big fella," said the beautiful young woman. "Let's see if you really can outrun the wind."

Julia tapped the horse's sides with her spurs. He was instantly in a gallop. She soon noticed that there was forest straight ahead and, wanting to stay where Alamo could see her, she turned Flame northward and gave him his head toward more open country. Mortal language could not describe the thrilling sensation Julia Kane experienced on Flame's back. This was the ride of her life. A wild roar, almost deafening, lanced into her ears. The wind! Flame was galloping so fast he was making his own wind!

She let him go until she knew they would soon pass from Alamo's view. Pulling rein, she slowed Flame down until it was safe to turn around, then gave him his head again and aimed him back toward Alamo.

Flame was once again making his own wind, and within a few minutes, she pulled up to the spot where Alamo was sitting on his horse, and said breathlessly, "You're right, Alamo! He *can* outrun the wind!"

Alamo grinned. "So you really like him, eh?"

"Oh, he's a dream! I think he could actually outrun a hurricane!"

"Think you can hold him to a normal trot while we ride together?"

"Oh yes! He knows I'm his owner."

Together Alamo and Julia headed in the direction of the forest that lay due west. When they hauled up in front of Julia's house over an hour and a half later, it was just past five o'clock.

Swinging from her saddle, Julia looked up at Alamo, who was still in his saddle. "Can I thank you for giving this marvelous horse to me by fixing you a special supper this evening?"

"Now that, young lady," he said smiling, "I'll let you do!"

"Good!"

"I'll put both horses in the corral, feed them some hay and oats, and be back shortly."

Little Adam had been brought back home when Alamo returned to Julia's house. After a delicious meal made up of Alamo's favorite foods, nephew and uncle played on the parlor floor until little Adam's bedtime. Uncle put nephew to bed and kissed him good night while Julia looked on, smiling. She then followed with a kiss of her own, and little Adam was tucked in for the night.

Eager for Julia's presence, Alamo asked if she wanted to go outside and sit on the front porch for a while. Pleased that he wanted to stay longer, Julia said she did. As they went out onto the porch in the silver moonlight, Julia once again told him how much she loved Flame and kissed his cheek, thanking him one more time. Then they sat down on the wicker chairs facing each other.

The power of the kiss on his cheek and the flame it ignited in his heart brought Alamo to a place where he could no longer hide his love for Julie. Somehow the dam that had held back a rushing river of love for so long broke loose inside him. The silver moonlight in her eyes, the loveliness of her face, the warmth of her presence—it was all too much. He felt like if he didn't tell her that he was in love with her, he would explode. In his heart, he said, *Dear Lord, I can't go on hiding my love for her. Please help me. You know I must do this.*

His heart pounding, Alamo leaned forward, took both of her hands in his, and looked into her puzzled, moonlit eyes. "Julie, there is something I must tell you. I've been hiding it for a long time, but I can't hide it any longer."

Her brow puckered. "Alamo, what is it?"

"Julie, I have been head over heels in love with you ever since the first time I saw you."

She swallowed hard. "You mean…you mean that you've been in love with me since—"

"Ever since you floated down the stairs of your parents' mansion the first time I saw you."

Julia was shocked. "But...but you never—"

"At first it was because of our social difference." Alamo fought a crack in his voice. "Then after I had inherited the ranch—"

"Adam," Julia said.

"Yes. I was planning to come to New Orleans and tell you of my love. Ask you to marry me."

Tears glistened in Julia's eyes, sparkling like diamonds in the moonlight. "And you never let on. You darling. You precious darling. You were so devoted to your brother that you smothered your own feelings to give Adam his happiness. Oh, Alamo!"

Julia's eyes filled with tears that spilled down her face as she broke into sobs.

Alamo squeezed her hands. "Oh, Julie, I'm sorry! I've upset you! I—I'm so sorry." He bent his head down and closed his eyes.

Julia's sobs stopped suddenly, and she squeezed his hands hard. "Alamo, don't punish yourself. Alamo. Look at me."

He raised his head, opened his eyes, and stared at the vision before him. Now it was his turn to be shocked.

"Alamo," she choked. "I am in love with *you*! I have been for better than six months. What I have felt for you ever since we met was a friendship love. After I married Adam, my love for you was also a sisterly love. But—but last fall... I—I began to feel that love change. I found myself *in* love with you. But I haven't known how to tell you. I've prayed so hard that the Lord would give me the time and place and—now He has!"

"Oh, Julie, I've prayed so hard too!"

She squeezed his hands again. "Isn't this something? We've both been afraid to declare our love for each other. But, praise the Lord, the time has come!"

Alamo smiled and nodded. "Yes! Yes!" He choked up a bit and then cleared his throat. "It's been so difficult for me since Adam was killed. When I felt my love for you growing, I—I felt disloyal to Adam. But somehow now I believe he is looking down from heaven and giving us his blessing."

Julia looked into his eyes. "I'm so thankful to hear you say this! Last fall, when I began to feel myself falling in love with you, I also had to deal with feeling disloyal to Adam. But God has given me peace now. I know that we are in His perfect will, and yes, I know Adam is indeed giving us his blessing."

"You know how much I love little Adam," Alamo said.

Julia smiled. "That is quite obvious."

"Then since we are in God's will to be in love and we both know that we have Adam's blessing, will you marry me?"

Without hesitation, Julia came back quickly with a yes!

Both of them were choked up as they rose to their feet and wrapped their arms around each other. As they clung tightly, Alamo bowed his head. "Dear Lord in heaven, Julie and I have peace in our hearts about our love for each other. Thank You for giving us this love and for allow-ing us now to plan our wedding. Please lead and guide us in our lives, and help me to be the stepfather to little Adam that You would have me be. In Jesus' precious name I ask this. Amen."

When they opened their eyes and looked up at each other, Alamo leaned forward and kissed her lips tenderly. She smiled up at him. "Oh, darling, I love you so much."

"And I love you so much," he replied. Then with his heart pound-ing for joy, Alamo told Julia he could hardly wait to break this good news to his father and the rest of the family, including Pastor Patrick and Angela. He quickly added that he wanted Julie to be with him when they were told. She replied that she most certainly wanted to be.

They discussed how they would do it and decided that when Alamo went home tonight, he would ask Daisy to cook up a nice lunch tomorrow at the big ranch house. He would go to the homes of Alex and Libby and Abel and Vivian when he left Julia in a few minutes and invite them to the lunch. In the morning, he would ride to town and invite Pastor Patrick and Angela to the lunch too. He added that, of course, Papa would be there. They would announce their engagement to the family and Daisy right after lunch. Then his father and his two brothers and their wives could help spread the word among the ranch hands and their families.

Alamo then said, "Sweetheart, I think it would be best if we allow at least a few weeks to pass before we marry."

Julia smiled. "How about a June wedding?"

"Hey, that would be great! June it is!"

With their plans in place for announcing their engagement the next day, Alamo kissed Julia good night.

As he started to leave, Alamo stopped and turned back. "Oh, Julie, I still can hardly believe this is happening. It's like a dream. Maybe you should pinch me so I'll know I'm not dreaming."

Julia grinned and playfully pinched his upper right arm.

"Ouch!" he said. "All right! I'm not dreaming! This is real!"

She giggled. "Indeed it is!"

Alamo kissed her again.

When he released her, Julia giggled again, her face alight with joy. "All right, now off with you, Alamo Kane! Go invite your brothers and their wives to lunch! Don't give anything away. I want to be with you when they hear the good news tomorrow."

He chuckled as he stepped off the porch. "Well, it'll be difficult not to show my happiness and enthusiasm, but I promise I'll do my best."

Julia watched him walk away in the moonlight and wiped happy tears from her eyes.

When Alamo was some distance away from Julie, he kept his voice low as he said, "Wow! Dear Lord, this is really happening! Julie loves *me* and wants to be *my* wife! Thank You, thank You, my heavenly Father! It is certainly true, what You said in Mark 10:27, Lord Jesus, '...*with God all things are possible.*'"

When Alamo had extended the invitation to both brothers and their wives, keeping the good news to himself, he went to the ranch house and in his father's presence asked Daisy to prepare the special meal the next day for the entire family. Though Daisy and Abram wanted to question him as to what the special lunch was all about, they refrained.

The next day, Daisy indeed prepared an excellent lunch, and while the family ate together with Daisy observing from close-by, the conversation was lively and animated around the large dining room table.

As the meal was ending, Abram looked across the table where Alamo was sitting beside Julia, and said, "Okay, Alamo, what is this lunch all about? If you've got something to tell us, let's hear it."

Everyone at the table was quite aware of the surreptitious look that passed between Julia and Alamo.

"Come on, Alamo," Abel said. "Our curiosity is about to get the best of us."

"Yeah," put in Alex. "Open up!"

Alamo stood up, took Julia by the hand, and raised her to her feet. Smiling at the group, he said, "We can tell you the story in detail some other time, but last evening Julie and I admitted to each other that we are in love. I fell for her the first time I saw her in Louisiana a long time ago, but I hadn't told her by the time she met Adam. She didn't know until I told her last night. She then told me that she started feeling the same for me about six months ago. Last night, when we had both admitted how we felt for each other, I asked her if she would marry me, and I got a quick yes." Alamo smiled at Julia. "So we are now engaged."

*See? I knew it! I knew it!* Angela thought.

After a moment of stunned silence, everyone began speaking at once. Hearty congratulations were given to the happy couple. The family was obviously overjoyed with this heart-touching news.

Angela finally spoke up loudly so she would be heard above the excited voices. "So when's the wedding?"

Alamo looked at her then shifted his eyes to Patrick. "Well, that really depends on our pastor's schedule."

Alamo had checked his desk calendar before going to bed the night before and had picked Saturday, June 16, as the date he wanted. He had told Julia about it privately before lunch, and she had agreed.

Patrick met Alamo's gaze. "What date do you have in mind?"

"Saturday, June 16," replied Alamo. "Are you free to perform the wedding ceremony that day?"

The pastor smiled. "I am, but even if I wasn't, I would change whatever engagement I had and perform the wedding."

Abram cheered and applauded. There was happy laughter as they all joined in and did the same thing.

Later, as the family members were preparing to leave the big ranch house, Angela took Julia aside. "Sweetie, I saw in Alamo quite some time ago that he was in love with you. I never said anything to him or anyone else though. And I must tell you that maybe even a little earlier than six months ago, I noticed that you were showing more and more tenderness toward my brother. I was not the least surprised when Alamo made this wonderful announcement after lunch today."

Julia hugged her and said with a giggle, "You're pretty smart, sister!"

~

Alamo and Julia's period of engagement was a precious one, with them falling deeper and deeper in love. They were wed at the church in Washington-on-the-Brazos on Saturday afternoon, June 16, 1838, with Patrick officiating.

The Kane family was ecstatic about the marriage, as were all the people in their church. Even the ranch hands and their families, who were not members of the church, were overjoyed.

On the following Monday, Alamo put Julie and little Adam in a ranch wagon and drove to Washington-on-the-Brazos, where they met with Judge Edgar Wilson, who was a member of the church there. Alamo had come to know him shortly after inheriting the ranch.

At the wedding reception, Alamo had told the judge that he wanted to legally adopt little Adam, and the judge had said to come and see him on Monday. He would take care of the matter.

When Alamo, Julia, and little Adam returned to the ranch and announced the adoption to the Kane family members, it brought them much joy.

The Diamond K Ranch continued to do well as time passed. Everyone on the ranch was pleased that so far there had been nothing in the news about trouble between the Texans and Mexico. Under orders from Texas president Sam Houston, the Texas army continued to keep troops along the Rio Grande, with the Texans still holding to the river being the border between Texas and Mexico.

Alamo and Julia were superbly happy in their marriage, and Alamo was delighted that little Adam now called him "Papa."


The Lord added to their happiness when baby Abram was born on October 7, 1840. He was named, of course, after his paternal grandfather, which made Grandpa Abram very proud.

Julia's parents had come to the Diamond K Ranch ten days earlier to be there when their little grandchild was born. When they left to return to Louisiana, they both spoke again of how much they loved Texas.

Time passed on, and Andrew Kane was born on January 16, 1842.

Alamo and Julia were happy to keep up the Kane tradition by giving their children names that began with an *A*. Andrew was affectionately called Andy. His maternal grandparents, Justin and Myra Miller, were there when he was born and again had a hard time leaving Texas, which they loved more each time they came.

The dimpled darling of the Diamond K was born on October 7, 1844. It greatly pleased little four-year-old Abram when he learned that his baby sister's birthday was on the same day of the month as his.

Little sister was named Amber, and she had the reddish blond hair to prove it. All three boys—Adam, Abram, and Andy—carried the male Kane characteristics, including light-colored hair and blue eyes. Amber was her beautiful mother all over again, except for the color of her hair. Julia's hair was dark brown. Amber did, however, have the exact same shade of her mother's blue eyes.

As each precious child was born to Julia and Alamo, a deep sense of contentment filled their hearts.

Once again, Justin and Myra Miller were present, desiring to be there when another grandchild was born. They stayed a little longer with each trip they made to Texas.

On the day of their departure, sometime after Amber's birth, Alamo talked in private with his father-in-law and asked if he and Myra had ever seriously discussed moving to Texas. Justin admitted that they had, especially since Andy was born. He then confessed that privately he had been thinking of it ever since they had come here the first time.

Justin then told Alamo that he would let him know how it was looking for them to move to Texas and be close to their grandchildren, daughter, and son-in-law. Alamo thanked him, saying that he and Julia would be praying that the Lord would make it happen.

When the Millers were about to depart from the ranch in a wagon driven by Alamo, Julia and her mother were saying tearful good-byes. Justin said quietly to Alamo, "This may well be the last time they have to part."

"Amen to that," said Alamo. "I'll tell Julie about our talk."

With that, Alamo gave his father-in-law a big hug.

## 17

In the spring of 1844, United States president John Tyler received a lengthy letter from well-known American inventor Samuel B. Morse of New York City telling him of his newest invention, which he called the electric telegraph.

Morse had invented a code of dots and dashes, which could be used to send messages wherever the telegraph had been wired and installed. He explained to President Tyler that this would make it possible for government authorities in Washington, D.C., to have steady contact with United States Army forts and outposts all across the country. He asked if he might come to Washington and present the invention to President Tyler and Congress.

The president was thrilled to learn of the invention and sent a letter back inviting Morse to come to Washington as soon as possible. Morse was there within a week and demonstrated his invention to the government leaders. Tyler and the members of Congress were amazed and pleased with the invention.

Under President Tyler's leadership, Congress drew up a government contract with Morse to produce the necessary equipment and to guide men hired by the government as they installed the marvelous invention in all U.S. forts and military outposts.

As word of this invention spread across the nation, private businesses working with Morse began installing telegraph lines in many parts of the country.

At Washington-on-the-Brazos, when Texas president Sam Houston learned of the invention and of the U.S. government contract with

Samuel Morse, he sent a letter to President Tyler saying he wanted to
have the telegraph installed at his office and be in connection with the
military authorities in Washington, D.C. Then, if the Mexican government started trouble with the Texans again, he could advise them
immediately.

⌒

In early 1845, in Mexico, el presidente Antonio López de Santa Anna
had a series of disputes with other Mexican men in political power.
Those men joined forces and, with the help of certain leaders in the military, arrested Santa Anna. They deposed him from his office as president of Mexico, and he was taken by force to Havana, Cuba, where he
was placed in exile.

When newly elected U.S. president James K. Polk learned of this,
he brought the news before Congress, and all rejoiced. Some of the congressmen spoke up and said they had continued to be on edge about
Santa Anna being the leader of Mexico because of his past record of
hatred toward Texans and other Americans. They were now relieved.
President Polk told them he was too.

As newspapers all across the country carried the story and told of
the attitude of the president and Congress toward the deposed Santa
Anna, the American people were also relieved...especially the people of
the Republic of Texas.

At the Diamond K Ranch, the Kane family discussed the story that
had been reported in the *Washington Post* as they sat together in the parlor of the big ranch house. Julia Kane showed the relief she felt, as did
Libby and Vivian. They knew their husbands had stood ready to fight
again for Texas ever since the Battle of San Jacinto.

As the Kanes discussed Santa Anna's deposition and exile, Alamo
said, "We can't relax too much, my dear ones. Because of things I've
heard Mexican Texans say, I still think that Santa Anna or no Santa
Anna, some political and military leaders in Mexico are going to rise up

one day and insist that the Texas-Mexico border be established officially at the Nueces River, a hundred miles north of the Rio Grande. They want that land between the two rivers. Those leaders, I am told, still hold a grudge against us Texans for even daring to stand against Santa Anna at the Alamo and for declaring that the Texas border is the Rio Grande."

"That's the way I see it, Alamo," said Alex.

"Me too," Abel said. "I just don't think we're through fighting Mexico yet."

"Me too," spoke up Abram. "I've had a feeling since the Battle of San Jacinto that one day the border between Texas and Mexico would become a real serious issue. Of course, I hope it can be settled without warfare. I don't want my sons having to fight the Mexican military forces again." He paused and blinked at the tears that were forming in his eyes. "The Mexicans already killed one of my sons."

The Kane women each softly spoke their agreement with what the men were saying.

Alamo sat quietly as his brothers, his father, his wife, and his sisters-in-law each verbalized their feelings about the Mexican American situation. He knew that the entire family had been praying for peace between the two governments.

When the last of the Kane women had spoken, Alamo ran his gaze over the faces of his family. "I hope President Houston, the people of Texas, the United States president, Congress, and the American people aren't being lulled into a false sense of security. We don't dare let down our guard. I don't mean to frighten any of you, but Alex, Abel, and I know from experience just what the Mexicans with political power are like. They very badly want total control of this territory. A full-scale war would be a bloody one. All of us Kanes must remain vigilant in our prayers for peace."

The others considered Alamo's words in hushed silence. Then Abram spoke up. "We will, Alamo, but we also must go on with our lives as usual. Enough of this gloom and doom. For sure we'll be very much in prayer, and we'll stay on our toes concerning the Mexicans, but this ranch won't run itself. We always have plenty of work to do."

Alamo nodded. "Amen to that, Papa. So let's get busy."

The men rose from their chairs, including Abram. The three younger men told their wives they would see them later, and all four filed out the door.

When the door had closed, Julia looked at Libby and Vivian, who were frowning, worry obvious on their faces. "Now this just won't do, my dear ones. Life must go on. We can't let this Mexican threat get us down. Let's keep our minds on our wonderful heavenly Father. Remember what He told us through Isaiah's pen in Isaiah 26:3: 'Thou wilt keep him in perfect peace, whose mind is stayed on thee: because he trusteth in thee.' We must keep our minds on our Lord and trust Him in the face of all this potential trouble with Mexico."

"You are so right, honey," said Vivian. "So let's get about doing the things that need to be done."

The three Kane women hugged each other, and Libby and Vivian departed the big ranch house, heading for their separate homes, while Julia went to work on her own chores, each with a prayer in her heart.

⌒

In late November 1845, the silver-haired fifty-year-old United States president James K. Polk stood before Congress in Washington, D.C., while snow was falling outside. "Gentlemen, the more I observe the border situation between the Texas Republic and Mexico, I feel that the days of peace are numbered. The things I hear coming from the Mexican leaders have led me to believe that the day will soon come when the political and military leaders of Mexico will start a war with Texas over the border dispute."

Polk noted the way the men of Congress looked at each other, nodding their agreement with what he was saying. Pleased at what he saw, the president went on. "I have a proposal to bring before you. I believe if Texas were made a state in this country, the Mexicans would realize that if they start trouble over the border issue, it would no longer just be with the Republic of Texas, but with the entire United States government, including the military."

Throughout the auditorium, heads were nodding, and hands were being waved to show agreement. President Polk took a congressional vote on the subject right then, and it passed one hundred percent by Congress to make Texas the twenty-eighth state of the United States.

A few days later, in Washington-on-the-Brazos, Sam Houston, the president of the Republic of Texas, received a telegram from President Polk saying that he and Congress wanted to make Texas the twenty-eighth state of the Union and giving Houston the basic reasons as related to Mexico's threat.

The next day, Houston called the Texas General Convention together for a meeting. Standing at the podium, he read the president's telegram to them.

When he had finished, Houston could tell that it had set well with the delegates. He smiled. "Gentlemen, I am all for Texas becoming a state. Please understand that it would not bother me at all to step aside as president of the Republic of Texas to see it happen. With the United States government at our side and the United States Army to protect us, all of Texas will be a great deal safer."

The delegates jumped to their feet, waving their arms and shouting out their agreement. A vote was taken, and it passed without controversy.

The next morning in Washington, D.C., President Polk was at his desk in conversation with Vice President George M. Dallas when there was a knock on the door. "Yes?" Polk called out.

The door opened, and his secretary, Carson Dupre, walked toward the desk. "Mr. President, a telegram just arrived from Texas president Sam Houston. I figured you'd want it immediately."

"You're right, Carson." The president rose to his feet. "Thanks for bringing it right away."

"You're welcome, sir." Dupre handed the envelope to the president.

When the secretary had left and closed the door behind him, Polk tore open the envelope.

Dallas said, "I have no doubt that President Houston will go for it, Mr. President."

Polk smiled at him as he unfolded the sheet of paper. "Let me read it, and I'll tell you what he says."

Dallas nodded and settled back on the wooden chair he occupied in front of the president's desk. He watched the expression on Polk's face as he read the message. Dallas knew Houston had agreed to the proposal.

When Polk finished, he smiled. "He likes the idea, George, and says he does not mind at all stepping aside from his position as president of the Republic of Texas to see it happen. He says there was a positive unanimous vote taken by the delegates of the Texas General Convention."

Dallas smiled. "I figured as much, sir. And I sure am glad."

"Me too. I'll call for a meeting of Congress tomorrow, and we'll soon have Texas in the Union."

At ten o'clock the next morning, President Polk stood before Congress and read them Houston's telegram. An official vote was taken to make Texas the twenty-eighth state of the United States, and of course, the vote was one hundred percent.

On December 29, 1845, with Sam Houston and a good number of the delegates of the Texas General Convention standing before President James K. Polk and Congress in Washington, D.C., Texas was officially granted statehood. Dozens of reporters from newspapers in many parts of the country attended.

President Polk then stood before Congress and the reporters and declared that all men of the Texas army at Washington-on-the-Brazos and outposts were now part of the United States Army. Explaining that he was leery of the Mexican government, he told them he would immediately send more troops to Texas, along with some of his top army officers.

Polk then boldly pointed out that, like the Texans, he and Congress absolutely considered the southern Texas border to extend to the Rio Grande, not just to the Nueces River, where the government of Mexico had stated.

There was much applause. Then the meeting was dismissed.

A short time later, when the news had reached all over Texas and to Mexico City, the uninhabited land between the Nueces and Rio Grande rivers was suddenly crawling with people from both Texas and Mexico, who were there to begin claiming sections of land as their own property.

When President Polk received a telegram from Texas authorities about this happening, he read it to his vice president.

Vice President Dallas rubbed his square jaw. "Mr. President, something's got to be done to protect those Texas citizens. With Mexico's history of shedding Texans' blood, this could turn into a real bloodbath."

Polk nodded. "We've got to protect that wave of Texas citizens who've moved into that disputed area. I'm going to send a telegraph message to General Zachary Taylor immediately."

Dallas nodded and smiled. He knew General Taylor was an excellent military leader. Only a few weeks ago, President Polk had stationed the general, along with some two thousand troops of the United States Army, in Washington-on-the-Brazos.

Sixty-year-old General Taylor had been in the United States Army since 1806 and had proven himself to be a brave and courageous soldier. Taylor had won the nickname "Old Rough and Ready" in the Black Hawk War of 1832 and in campaigns against the Seminole Indians in Florida shortly thereafter. George Dallas greatly admired Old Rough and Ready.

The vice president went with President Polk to Carson Dupre's office, where the telegraph machine was kept, and dictated the message he wanted sent to General Taylor at Washington-on-the-Brazos. In the telegraph, the president told Taylor to immediately take his two thousand troops to protect the Texans in the disputed area between the Nueces and Rio Grande.

⌒

At the Mexican army headquarters in Mexico City, Generalissimo Mariano Arista—who had replaced the deposed and exiled Santa Anna—was advised by his scouts that United States troops were moving into the disputed area. Soon news came to the United States that Arista was very angry over this.

Shortly thereafter, rumors came to President Polk and many other United States government authorities that Arista was about to declare war on the United States over the land in question.

Though war was not declared as had been expected, as time passed, it looked more and more like the Mexican army was going to attack the American troops who now occupied the disputed area.

By mid-April 1846, the smell of war was strong in the air.

⌒

On Wednesday, April 22, 1846, Diamond K Ranch foreman Cort Whitney and a ranch hand named Jess Kottman took a wagon to Washington-on-the-Brazos to purchase supplies from the hardware store for the ranch. Kottman was in the driver's seat.

When they pulled into town, they saw a large crowd of people standing on the boardwalk and in the street in front of the *Washington Post* office. The chief editor and some of his staff and reporters were in some kind of discussion with the crowd.

Cort elbowed Kottman. "Pull over, Jess. Let's see what's going on here."

As Jess veered to an open spot across the street from the newspaper office, Cort spotted Clarence Yates, the owner of the hardware store, standing near there. He hopped out and said, "What's going on, Clarence?"

Yates rubbed the back of his neck. "The newspaper people are talking with the crowd about the front page article of today's edition of the *Post*. It boldly declares that war is absolutely imminent between Mexico and the United States over that disputed land between the rivers and that President Polk knows it."

Cort sighed. "Oh boy."

"I'd say this makes it look for certain like there's going to be war," said Jess.

"Quite possibly," said Yates. "There is one tiny ray of hope, though."

"What's that?" Cort asked.

"The article states that President Polk is now asking for more Texans to join the U.S. Army quickly. The president has stated that he is hoping by a show of force that he can discourage Generalissimo Mariano Arista and the other Mexican government authorities so that they won't want to go to war."

Cort shook his head slowly. "Well, I hope the president can get enough new soldiers to do that, but if Arista is anything at all like Santa Anna, there will be war no matter how many new men the president can muster up."

Yates nodded. "I've read a little about Arista, and he definitely is a hothead."

Cort nodded. "Well, I guess I'll go across the street and buy a copy of today's paper. I've got to take it back to the ranch and let my boss read the article. Is one of your clerks at the store, Clarence?"

"Yes. You need to get something?"

"Uh-huh. That's why Jess and I came to town."

Clarence tipped his hat. "Well, I've heard all I need to hear from the newspaper folks. I'll see you at the store."

As Clarence Yates headed down the street toward his hardware store, Cort said, "I'll be right back, Jess."

After Cort had purchased a copy of the *Washington Post,* the two men climbed in the wagon and headed for Yates Hardware.

Midafternoon that same day, Alamo Kane was sitting on the front porch of the big ranch house with Julia and their four children. Nine-year-old Adam and his two half-brothers—Abram, who was five-and-a-half years old, and Andy, who was four—were sitting on the porch steps. Adam was showing them how to play dominoes.

Little one-and-a-half-year-old Amber, who was the apple of her papa's eye, was sitting on his lap.

Alamo and Julia were talking about how quickly their children seemed to be growing up when their attention was drawn to one of the Diamond K wagons as it left the road and headed down the tree-lined lane toward the ranch houses and buildings.

Alamo fixed his gaze on the wagon for a few seconds then chuckled and said to his wife, "It's Cort and Jess, Julie. They must have dilly-dallied awhile in town. Normally they'd have been back before now."

Julia echoed his chuckle. "As if you'd care if they did dillydally awhile!"

Alamo grinned down at Amber, lifted her up, and kissed her cheek. "Sweet stuff, you know your papa is a hard taskmaster, don't you?"

Not understanding his words, Amber squealed and giggled.

"See there, honey?" he said to Julia. "Amber knows how tough I am on my employees."

Julia snorted. "Yeah. *Real* tough."

Noticing that the wagon was heading directly toward the ranch house, Alamo rose to his feet and handed Amber to her mother. "Guess I'd better see what they want."

Julia hugged the baby girl close to her heart and watched her husband step off the porch as the wagon drew up.

"Welcome home, fellas. Get everything you needed?" Alamo said.

"We did," the foreman replied from the wagon seat. "We also got something else." He raised up a folded newspaper and extended it to his boss.

As Alamo took the newspaper, Cort said, "Big article on the front page."

"Oh?" Alamo opened it and read the bold headline:

WAR WITH MEXICO POSSIBLY IMMINENT

"I knew you'd want to read it, boss," Cort said.

With a frown on his brow, Alamo kept his eyes on the front page, and said, "I appreciate you bringing a copy, Cort. Let me read the article before you go, okay?"

"Of course."

Julia looked at her husband as he read the article, wondering what had happened to make war with Mexico possibly imminent.

Three minutes passed, and Alamo looked up from the page. "Cort, will you go over to corral number three and tell my father and brothers to come to me immediately, please?"

"Sure will, boss. See you later."

"And tell Alex and Abel to bring Libby and Vivian with them. I want to read this to them."

"Sure." Cort looked at Jess, who held the reins. "Let's go."

While they were waiting for the rest of the family to arrive, Alamo told Julia the gist of the article.

Her face turned pale. "This means you and your brothers will be joining the U.S. Army, doesn't it?"

He folded her in his arms, including little Amber, whom she was holding. "We have a duty to our country, sweetheart."

## 18

B y the time Alex and Abel Kane, their wives, and sixty-one-year-old Abram Kane had arrived at the front porch of the big ranch house, several ranch hands and a few wives of the married hands had gathered as well. Cort Whitney and Jess Kottman had told some of the ranch hands about the newspaper article, and word spread quickly. They and some of their wives wanted to hear it for themselves, so they immediately made their way to the ranch house. Alamo had told everyone they would have to wait till his father and his brothers and their wives arrived. Then he would read the article aloud so all could hear it.

With the small crowd standing in a half circle before the house, Alamo stepped up on the porch. "All right, everybody. My family members are here now. Listen closely as I read this article from today's edition of the *Washington Post.*"

Some of the crowd pressed a little nearer to him.

When Alamo had finished reading the article, he said, "When my sweet Julia asked what my brothers and I were going to do in the face of President Polk's plea for Texas men to join the U.S. Army and be prepared to fight the Mexicans, I told her that the three of us had agreed several times that if anything like this ever happened, we would join the army. We feel that we have a duty to our country."

"That's right," spoke up Abel, who was standing close to Vivian. Her features were pallid, but she nodded her assent to her husband's words.

"It sure is," said Alex. "If the Mexicans conquered Texas, they would take this ranch from us. If for no other reason than protecting the Diamond K, Alamo, Abel, and I must answer the president's call."

Libby, who was also a bit pale, nodded her agreement.

"As you heard in the article," Alamo said, "President Polk is hoping that a show of force—that is, our army being significantly enlarged immediately—will discourage the Mexican military and government leaders, and they'll decide not to start a war with us. This is why my brothers and I must join. We must do our part to ward off war with Mexico, and even if the war comes, we want to help bring it to a quick end."

One of the younger ranch hands spoke up. "Mr. Kane, what about some of us men joining up with you?"

Alamo shook his head. "No, Fred. Cort Whitney needs every man he's got to run the ranch smoothly. My brothers and I want the rest of you men to stay right here and keep the Diamond K in operation. I have no doubt that a great number of other Texans will join the army too. Since Alex, Abel, and I have already been in battle for Texas, we feel that we are the ones from the ranch who should go."

The people in the small crowd discussed it among themselves and agreed that it should be as their boss wanted. Soon the crowd had dispersed, leaving the Kanes alone in front of the big ranch house. Julia, Libby, and Vivian spoke up, saying that although the thought of their husbands joining the army frightened them, they were proud that the men were willing to fight for their country.

As their wives embraced Alamo, Alex, and Abel, Abram said, "I am very proud of you boys too. I lost one son to Mexican bullets at the Alamo, but I will trust the Lord to keep His mighty hand on all three of you and protect you."

Alamo kept an arm around Julia as he nodded and smiled at his father. "I appreciate your attitude, Papa. Thank you for your prayers."

The next morning, Alamo hugged Julia, Adam, Abram, and Andy, speaking encouraging words about his return home while Alex and Abel were doing the same with their wives. Each boy then hugged his father as Julia stood by with Amber in her arms. Alamo kissed the baby and then kissed Julia. He hugged his boys again and mounted his horse as his brothers were mounting theirs.

The Kane family and many of the ranch hands and their families watched the Kane brothers ride away, waving to them and shedding tears.

⌒

When Alamo, Alex, and Abel arrived at Washington-on-the-Brazos, they approached the recruiters and signed up in the United States Army.

Some of the army officers who observed them knew about Alan "Alamo" Kane's heroic deed just before the battle at the Alamo, and they also knew about all three of the Kane brothers having fought in the Battle of San Jacinto. When the officers shared this with the other soldiers and the new recruits, the Kanes were warmly welcomed.

The recruiters told the Kane brothers that they would be sent to boost up the forces under General Zachary Taylor in the disputed area between the Rio Grande and the Nueces rivers, along with a large number of men who had just joined the army in response to President Polk's request.

Privates Alamo, Alex, and Abel Kane put on the uniforms provided for them by the army and were told by the colonel in charge of the induction center that the new troops would be leaving to join General Taylor the next morning. He would allow them to quickly ride back to the ranch today and inform their wives where they would be going and that they would be serving under the famous General Zachary Taylor, who was known as Old Rough and Ready.

⌒

Some three hours after the Kane brothers had ridden away toward Washington-on-the-Brazos, Julia and her sisters-in-law were sitting in the parlor of the big ranch house, where they were trying to comfort each other. Little Amber was taking a nap in Julia's bedroom, and the three boys were playing out on the front porch.

Julia was telling Libby and Vivian about a verse of Scripture that had really been a help to her as she considered Alamo's going into the army. Suddenly they heard rapid footsteps in the hall, and nine-year-old Adam burst through the door, eyes wide. "Mama! Papa and Uncle Alex and Uncle Abel are back! They're ridin' their horses down the lane toward the house!"

All three women instantly followed the boy up the hall toward the front of the house. When they stepped out on the front porch, the three men in army uniforms were off their horses and were hugging the excited Abram and Andy.

There were hugs all around as the women and young Adam bounded off the porch, asking why they were back. At that instant, Grandpa Abram came from the backyard, having heard the excited voices, and hugged his sons.

When the excitement had settled down, Alamo told them why the colonel at the induction center had allowed them to ride back to the ranch, explaining quickly that they had to head back to Washington-on-the-Brazos in just a little while.

Grandpa Abram grinned. "So you're gonna be serving under General Zachary Taylor! One of the ranch hands just came back from town and gave me a copy of today's edition of the *Washington Post*. It has an article in it about General Taylor on the second page. It's in my room, but I can remember that the article said that Taylor enlisted in the U.S. Army in 1806 and was commissioned first lieutenant in the infantry by 1808. He advanced to captain, then major, then to colonel as time passed, and in January of 1846 he was promoted to the rank of major general."

"It's going to be an honor to serve under him, Papa," said Alamo.

"It sure is!" agreed Abel.

"Yes!" Alex said.

Alamo then turned and looked at Julia and their children with tears in his eyes, saying he would be back as soon as possible.

By this time, Cort Whitney and a few of the ranch hands had gathered around and had heard what was being said about General Taylor. They wished the Kane brothers the best, and Cort said to Alamo, "Boss, while you're gone, don't you worry about this ranch and your family. We'll protect it and all the women and children with our lives. We'll keep everything going as you expect us to until you return safely home."

Alamo smiled and put his arm around his foreman's shoulders. "Cort, I know I can count on you and every man on this ranch. My brothers and I will rejoin you as soon as possible."

"I'll be praying about that, boss. You can be sure of it."

Cort and the others turned and walked away, telling Alamo, Alex, and Abel that they would be looking forward to their return.

Alamo hugged his father, Libby, and Vivian, then hugged his children once more, telling them he loved them. Finally, he folded Julia in his arms. "Sweetheart, I wish there was a way I could stay in touch with you so I could keep you up on what's happening, but I doubt there is any mail service from that land between the two rivers."

"I understand, darling." She tried to smile.

He kissed her tenderly. "I'm trusting the Lord that this situation will be over soon and we can come home. Hopefully when the Mexicans find out the size of our army, they'll give up wanting to fight us. I'm glad you understand why my brothers and I have to do this."

Tears were now welling up in Julia's eyes. "You three brave men go and help General Taylor find peace and security for Texas and the rest of this country."

Alamo nodded. "Yes. And we go for Adam, who so bravely gave his life for this cause."

Tears spilled down Julia's cheeks. "Thank you, my love, for saying that."

Alamo made a smile. "I love his memory very much." He kissed her again. "We've got to get going. I love you so very, very much."

Wiping tears, she said, "And I love *you* so very, very much, my darling. May God go with you."

Each of the three husbands kissed their wives once more, then mounted up. Alamo told his father and his children that he loved them, and they galloped away. Looking back, all three waved at their loved ones, and the family waved back.

Alamo kept hearing his wife's voice in his mind, *May God go with you.*

That night, as Julia readied for bed, she recalled her last words to Alamo: *May God go with you.* She had uttered those same words once before, and suddenly a stab of fear pierced her heart. *Those are the exact same words I said to Adam just before he rode off to fight in the battle at the Alamo. He never returned from that battle...*

Tears filled Julia's eyes as she put out the lantern, crawled into bed, and laid her head on the pillow. She pulled the covers up to her chin and whispered, "Oh, dear Lord in heaven, please don't let that happen to Alamo! Please protect him, as well as Alex and Abel!"

Suddenly words filtered into her mind. She did not hear a voice with her ears, but in her mind the words rang clear: *Rest in Me, My child. Rest in Me.*

In the days that followed, the Diamond K Ranch and the church in Washington-on-the-Brazos offered much prayer for God's protection on the Kane brothers and the other men in the church who had joined the army.

The Kane brothers and a number of new recruits arrived in the disputed territory on April 26 at an area called Point Isabel. They were surprised to see that a fort had been built there. A sign at the front gate identified it as Fort Polk.

Alamo Kane was especially eager to meet General Zachary Taylor and was glad that his brothers wanted to meet him too.

When army officers led them inside the fort, the other soldiers welcomed them. Alamo asked if General Taylor was around, saying that he and his brothers would like to meet him. A lieutenant pointed to a tent some fifty feet away and told them the man standing in front of the tent brushing his horse was General Taylor.

The Kane brothers hurried to the spot, and when they drew up to the square-jawed, muscular, silver-haired man in the braided uniform, he smiled and said, "Hello, gentlemen."

"Hello, General Taylor," they said in unison.

Alamo introduced himself and his brothers.

The general laid aside his brush and shook hands with the three men. "I'm very glad to meet all of you. I've heard of the Kane brothers from some of the men who fought with you at San Jacinto. And, Private Alamo Kane, I know of your valorous ride from the Alamo to General Houston for help prior to the battle there. I know that your real name is Alan, but I think it's really good that you were given the nickname Alamo."

Alamo blushed and cleared his throat lightly.

"Gentlemen," Taylor said, "I am pleased to tell you that I now have some three thousand men here under my command. A thousand of them, all Texans like yourselves, have joined up in just the past few days."

The Kane brothers exchanged glances that implied how glad they were to learn that so many other Texans had joined General Taylor.

The general explained to the Kane brothers that he and his troops were occupying two positions on the upper side of the Rio Grande. Taylor was with half his troops occupying Point Isabel, where the Kane brothers now stood. Point Isabel had been selected as the spot to construct Fort Polk because of its defensive possibilities on the edge of the

Gulf of Mexico where the Rio Grande emptied into it. Taylor had named the fort after the United States president.

The Kane brothers smiled and told him they liked the name.

"I'm glad you approve. The fort was put up in a hurry, and there are no barracks. We have to sleep on the ground here inside the walls. We also keep our horses inside the walls, as you've probably noticed. You will note that there are platforms from which we can fire our rifles at the enemies if they attack the fort. The gates in each wall are quite sturdy and will be very difficult for our enemies to break through."

"Looks good," said Abel.

Taylor went on to explain that the other spot occupied by his troops was a short distance to the south, on the north bank of the Rio Grande. There a fort was now under construction that would be called Fort Brown. Just across the river, in Mexico, was a town called Matamoros.

"General Taylor," Alamo said, "I'm glad to hear another fort is being built on these grounds. That'll really give us an advantage if we have to do battle with the Mexicans."

Taylor nodded. "It sure will." Then he ran his gaze over the faces of the Kane brothers. "You three will be on duty here at Fort Polk."

"That's fine with us, sir." Alamo nodded to his brothers.

The general then explained that between the two fort positions, on Texas land, was a large grassy area with a huge watering hole. The area around the watering hole was called Palo Alto. A short distance to the south of Palo Alto was a rocky area with a dried-up old riverbed called Resaca de la Palma.

"I've heard of Palo Alto and also of Resaca de la Palma, sir," Alamo said. "Never thought I'd see them."

"Well, you will, my friend." As General Taylor spoke, he pulled out a pocket watch and glanced at the time. "I've got a meeting for my men here at Point Isabel in just ten minutes. I set the time with my officers this morning. Since you men are here now, you are to be in the meeting."

The Kane brothers followed the general to the area just outside the east gate of the fort, where the officers were gathered with the troops. General Taylor stood before them. "I need to explain to all of you that just prior to leaving Washington-on-the-Brazos as ordered by President Polk, I received a telegram from him. In it the president instructed me to follow a policy of leniency toward the common citizens of Mexico whenever we come in contact with them. The president said he is hoping that by doing so, it will ward off the impending war, and there can be peace between the United States and Mexico."

Taylor could tell he had the full attention of everyone. "You see, men, President Polk has the same feeling about war with Mexico that President Andrew Jackson had when he showed leniency and released the vicious Antonio López de Santa Anna from captivity after the San Jacinto battle and let him go back to Mexico. Along with President Polk, I am hoping that leniency toward the Mexican civilians will work and that it will cause the military and government leaders to back away from war with us."

Some of the men were nodding.

The general said, "I'd like to know your opinion of this approach, men."

As the vocal reaction came from the soldiers before him, Taylor learned that overall, the troops were in favor of President Polk's approach. However, the same men also declared that they had their doubts that this approach would stave off the impending war.

❧

Before dawn on the morning of Tuesday, April 28, several hundred Mexican troops quietly rowed across the Rio Grande with the intent of attacking both Fort Polk and Fort Brown and wiping out the U.S. troops there.

Half of the Mexican boats silently drew up to the bank of the river near the Fort Brown position and waited for the other boats to move north the short distance to the Fort Polk position. Those at the southern landing spot would not begin firing on the sleeping American soldiers until the first shots were fired at the northern one.

At Fort Polk, General Taylor had sentries posted along the platforms on the inside of the walls all night. So each sentry could get sufficient sleep, each was on duty one hour, then was replaced by others who would spend their hour on watch.

Dawn was just turning the sky a dull gray when one sentry spotted the Mexican boats with the soldiers climbing out and assembling on dry ground, ready to make their attack. He called in a hoarse whisper to another sentry and pointed at the Mexican troops. Word quickly spread along the walls as one of the sentries scrambled to the ground and dashed to where General Taylor was sleeping. He awakened the general, who quickly awakened officers nearby, telling them what was happening and prepare all their men for the attack.

The men, who slept in their uniforms with their rifles in reach, quickly made their way to the platforms of all four walls.

When the Mexicans drew near the fort, approaching from every side, they were shocked to hear a sudden commencement of rifle fire and see gun flashes along the walls. Many were hit and fell, while others began fighting back.

While firing their weapons, the men on the south wall at Fort Polk could see flashing gunfire at Fort Brown and knew that the Mexicans were also attacking down there. Word was taken to General Taylor about the battle going on at the Fort Brown position so he would know about it.

The Americans outnumbered the Mexicans by far and were also more accurate with their weapons. Taylor's men at both positions soon drove the Mexicans back to their boats. A great number of Mexican soldiers had been killed within minutes, and their bodies were lying on the ground; some were floating in the river. The retreating Mexicans carried their wounded, piled into the boats, and rowed downriver with all their might to get away. They had discovered that they were no match for the American soldiers, who not only vastly outnumbered them but were skilled fighters.

When the Mexicans who had lived through the battle were out of sight, General Taylor sent a couple of riders to Fort Brown to tell all the men there to come quickly to Fort Polk.

When all of his men were gathered before him just outside the walls of Fort Polk, General Taylor's first words were how proud he was of his men. They had put down a great number of the Mexican troops and sent the rest of them on the run. He was glad to be able to report that in the battle, not one American soldier had been killed and only one had been wounded at each position. Their wounds were not serious, and they had already been bandaged.

One of Taylor's officers spoke up and suggested that the soldiers from both forts should head to the riverbank on horseback and gun down the fleeing Mexican soldiers. Others shouted their agreement.

The general shook his head. "No. We will not go after them. I know for sure that this would be President Polk's order if he were here."

No one argued. Taylor then gave orders to his men at both positions to find a spot nearby and bury the dead Mexicans. It was done immediately.

## 19

That evening around the campfires at both forts, where the American soldiers were gathered in small groups, they were talking about this morning's battle with the Mexican troops and voiced their relief that only two American soldiers were wounded and only very slightly. They were thankful that not one American had been killed.

Inside the walls of Fort Polk, the Kane brothers and the other men from their church who had joined the army were sitting around a crackling fire and having a time of Bible reading and prayer. Alamo was leading. After reading their Bibles and praying together, they talked about the battle. "It sure is a blessing to know that if any of us in this group had been killed today, that man would be in heaven right now," Alamo said.

"Amen," said one of the men. "I'm so glad to know that if I had taken a bullet and it killed me, I'd be up there with my Saviour right now."

Others in the group were commenting in the same manner, praising God that they knew they were saved, that heaven was their eternal home, and that they would never burn in hell.

Some soldiers at a nearby fire were listening in. Finally one of them stood up, left his companions, and walked over to the Kane brothers and the other men. Standing over them, he said, "I'm Corporal Lance Brooks, and I heard what you fellas said about being in heaven now if you had been killed today."

"That's right," Alex said.

Brooks eyed Alex with disdain, swung his right hand in a circle, covering all the men in the fort, and said, "All of these men are true American soldiers. If any of them had been killed today, they'd all be in heaven."

"Not unless they'd been born again, Corporal," Alamo said. "The Lord Jesus said, 'Except a man be born again, he cannot see the kingdom of God.' That's heaven."

Brooks guffawed. "I've heard about the 'born-again' theory, and it's nothing but foolishness. I heard a minister say in a sermon one time how absurd the born-again theory is, and he emphatically said that only the very worst people, like murderers, robbers, and such go to hell. And I heard you guys say you would never burn in hell. That very wise minister also said that even the people in hell do not suffer in flames because hell has no fire. He also told his audience that the Bible backs up what he said."

Alamo stood up, shaking his head. "That minister was lying, Corporal, and he was a fool too. You quoted him as saying the born-again theory is absurd, right?"

"That's what he said."

"Well, he was not only a fool, but also an ignoramus. The new birth is not a theory. It is *fact,* straight from the mouth of the Lord Jesus Christ Himself."

Corporal Brooks appeared to sense the strength in Alamo's eyes and licked his lips.

Alamo continued. "And that minister was also dead wrong saying hell has no fire. The Bible plainly says that hell is real, literal fire and brimstone and that people who go there suffer forever. The Bible does *not* back up what he said."

The corporal started to speak, but Alamo beat him to it. "Will you let me show it to you in the Bible?"

The men in Alamo's group smiled knowingly when the corporal replied in a cocky manner, waggling his head, "Sure. Show it to me."

Alamo opened his Bible, and while the other two Kane brothers and the rest of the Christians in their group looked on, Alamo said, "Listen to this. In Revelation 14, it speaks of those who have refused to believe on Jesus Christ. 'The same shall drink of the wine of the wrath of God, which is poured out without mixture into the cup of his indignation; and he shall be tormented with fire and brimstone in the presence of the holy angels, and in the presence of the Lamb: and the smoke of their torment ascendeth up for ever and ever…' See? It does not back up what that minister said. He lied."

Brooks silently looked at Alamo, who turned his Bible around and extended it to Brooks. "Here, look at it for yourself."

The cockiness was gone. Brooks shook his head. "I don't want to look at it."

Alamo turned the Bible back to himself. "So you're willing to take my word that it's in here?"

The corporal swallowed with difficulty and nodded. "Yeah."

"Then will you listen while I read you some more Scripture?"

The corporal nodded again.

Alamo then read Corporal Brooks Matthew 5:22, where Jesus spoke of those who were in danger of hellfire. Next he read Mark 9:43–48, where Jesus said five times that the fire in hell will not be quenched. Brooks remained mute. Alamo then read Luke 16:19–24 to him, where Jesus told the story of a rich man who died and went to hell and cried out, "I am tormented in this flame."

Alamo looked him straight in the eye. "I could give you a whole lot more Scripture on this, Corporal Brooks, but isn't this enough for you to see that the minister you quoted was dead wrong?"

Brooks licked his lips nervously. "Uh…yeah."

"Will you let me read you some more Scripture? This time on the salvation that God has provided so sinners like you and me can escape hell and go to heaven?"

The corporal nodded slightly. "Go ahead."

So Alamo read him passages on Calvary, covering the suffering of

Jesus on the cross, His blood being shed, His death and burial, and His glorious resurrection three days later. He showed him what Jesus said about a person having to be born again in order to go to heaven…making sure Brooks understood that it was not a theory, but a fact…the *only* way to obtain salvation.

Alamo looked the corporal straight in the eye again. "That minister you quoted was indeed lying, wasn't he?"

Brooks nodded. "Yes."

"Well, what do you think now that you have heard it directly from the Word of God?"

The corporal drew a quivering breath. "I—I never heard it like this before, Private—what's your name?"

"Alamo Kane."

"Alamo?"

"It's a nickname. My real name is Alan. Long story. Maybe I can tell it to you sometime. Anyway, the reason you've never heard it this way before is because you have never heard a real Bible preacher and have never read the Bible yourself."

Brooks frowned, shook his head, turned around, and walked away without a word. He passed his group of friends silently and kept walking. They glanced at him, but no one called to him.

Alamo sat down beside the fire again, and one of the men in his group said, "The corporal was indeed shaken by what you just showed him from the Scriptures, Alamo."

Alamo nodded. "He was indeed. Let's pray for him."

As his brothers and friends bowed their heads, Alamo led in prayer, asking the Lord to convict Corporal Brooks of his lost condition with the Scriptures he had just heard and to draw the man unto Himself.

Three days later, Alamo happened to run into Brooks at the fort's main gate and took a few seconds to remind him that hell is real fire. He told him that he needed to repent of his sin and receive Jesus as his

Saviour before it was too late. He also offered to help him in calling on the Lord.

Brooks simply walked away, muttering to himself.

⌒

On Sunday morning, May 3, Abram Kane, his daughters-in-law, and his grandchildren were in the preaching service, listening to Abram's son-in-law, Pastor Patrick O'Fallon, preach a sermon on the power of prayer. His main purpose for the sermon was to tie it to the fact that several men from the church had joined the U.S. Army and were on the Texas-Mexico border at the Rio Grande, where there was probably going to be a big battle between the U.S. and Mexican armies any day.

The pastor showed from Scripture how God answers prayer for His born-again children in marvelous ways and asked the congregation to be praying daily for all the American soldiers there, especially those who were members of their church.

The pastor paused, then ran his serious eyes over the crowd. "Folks, I am told that our army is well-armed. They have the firepower with which to wage this seemingly unavoidable war. Our government has them well-supplied, but we, as God's people, have the greatest, most effective weapon of all. It is called *prayer.*"

There were some "amens" from the crowd.

Pastor O'Fallon smiled. "In Matthew 17:20, the Lord Jesus said, 'If ye have faith as a grain of mustard seed, ye shall say unto this mountain, Remove hence to yonder place; and it shall remove; and nothing shall be impossible unto you.' Faith and prayer are our most valuable weapons, the tools by which we, as born-again believers, should live and conduct our lives. Let's all grasp these marvelous tools and claim the victory as we trust our mighty God to protect our Christian loved ones and friends who will no doubt be facing the guns of the enemy."

From that point, the pastor also put the gospel of Jesus Christ in

the sermon, appealing to those who had never received Jesus as their
Saviour to do so today. When he gave the invitation at the end of the
sermon while the organ and piano were being played, a few came forward to be saved. While the counselors took them to the altar, many of
the church members were also coming to the altar, kneeling to pray for
the soldiers at the Rio Grande.

Nine-year-old Adam, five-and-a-half-year-old Abram, four-year-
old Andy, and little one-and-a-half-year-old Amber were on the same
pew with their mother, their grandfather, and their Aunt Libby and
Aunt Vivian. The invitation continued, and some of the church members were still moving down the aisles to the altar.

Young Adam Kane—who had been saved and baptized when he
was six years old—was beside his grandfather, seated on the aisle. When
Adam pressed past his grandfather to the aisle, Grandpa Abram took
hold of his hand, and asked, "Where are you going, Adam?"

Adam looked up at him with tears in his eyes. "I'm goin' to the altar
to pray for Papa, Uncle Alex, and Uncle Abel."

Grandpa Abram choked up and blinked at the tears in his own
eyes. "I'll go with you."

As the organist and pianist continued to play, Libby and Vivian
moved along the pew toward the aisle. When they reached Julia, Vivian
said, "Honey, if you want to go forward, I'll stay with Abram, Andy, and
Amber. I know your heart is heavy remembering how Adam was killed
fighting Mexicans and knowing the danger Alamo is in right now."

Julia's eyes were filled with tears. "Thank you, Vivian, but I'll stay
with the children and pray right here in the pew."

Vivian and Libby smiled at her through their own tears and made
their way down the aisle, where they knelt and prayed together at the
altar.

After a while, as people left the altar and returned to their pews, the
last to rise to their feet were Grandpa Abram and nine-year-old Adam.

The boy sniffed and wiped tears from his eyes. "Grandpa, my papa taught me how to use a .22-caliber a few months ago and took me hunting. Remember?"

Abram nodded. "Yes. I remember. Your papa told me that you're a real good shot with that rifle."

Adam grinned. "I've bagged lots of jack rabbits and wild turkeys for Mama to cook and feed the family."

Abram nodded. "I know. I was invited to come and help all of you eat one of those turkeys you shot. Remember?"

"Oh yeah! Now I remember!" Adam paused, then looked up at his grandfather. "Grandpa, since I'm a good shot with my rifle, would the army let me be a soldier so I could go and fight the Mexicans with Papa and Uncle Alex and Uncle Abel?"

The question touched Abram deeply, and he laid a hand on the boy's shoulder. "Adam, you have to be at least eighteen years old to join the army."

Adam nodded, disappointment showing in his eyes. "Oh. I figured if a fella was a good shot with a rifle, they'd let him fight no matter how old he is. The bullets would fly just as fast if I squeezed the trigger as if an eighteen-year-old did."

Abram patted his shoulder. "There's a lot more to it than that, son. It's a hard life being a soldier, and sometimes a soldier has to fight the enemy hand-to-hand. You're too small. A great deal of responsibility rests on each soldier's shoulders. A boy your age just couldn't handle it. Besides, Adam, you have a very important job right here at the ranch."

The boy's brow furrowed. "What do you mean, Grandpa?"

"Well, for one thing, you and I have been left here to help protect the womenfolk in our family. Sure, we've got lots of able-bodied cowboys here on the ranch, but they have their families and each other to look out for. They would pitch in and help us if Mexicans tried to take this ranch, but your gun and mine would be sorely needed."

"Oh." Adam nodded.

"Besides that, son," Abram said, "we need you to continue to bring in jack rabbits and wild turkeys so your aunts, your mother, and Daisy can keep cooking those tasty meals."

Adam grinned up at him. "Yeah, I guess that's true enough, but I'd still like to be a soldier and fight alongside my papa and my uncles. When it came to hand-to-hand fightin', of course, I'd have to find a place to hide."

Abram squeezed his grandson's shoulder once more. He looked down into the boy's serious face, a face so much like that of his real father, Adam, when he was nine. "Son, I deeply appreciate your willingness to go to war for this country, and someday you may be called upon to do that very thing, but right now I need you here with me. And your mama, brothers, little sister, and aunts need you as well. As the world goes on with wars and rumors of wars, like the Bible says it will, the day will come when you will more than likely be called upon to fight our enemies, but right now, you are nine years too young."

Young Adam Kane nodded. "Okay, Grandpa. Since I'm needed here and I'm too young to join the army, I'll stay on the ranch and do my job."

"Good boy, Adam. We'll watch and pray and work as we wait for your papa and your uncles to return."

Adam's face lighted up with a grin. "Okay, Grandpa. That's what we'll do!"

Abram glanced up to the platform. "Looks like Pastor O'Fallon is about to close the service. We'd better get back to our pew."

As they walked back up the aisle, Abram directed his silent thoughts to his son in heaven. *This is quite a boy you brought into the world, Adam. Quite a boy!*

After the church service was over and the Kanes were headed home in a Diamond K wagon, Grandpa Abram proudly told Julia, Libby, and Vivian about Adam asking if the army would let him be a soldier so he could fight the Mexicans with his papa and uncles.

This brought choked throats and tears to the women, and Julia, who was sitting next to Adam with Amber on her lap, put an arm around him, and said, "Son, I'm so proud that you are willing to do that, even though you're only nine years old."

"We all are, Adam," spoke up Libby.

"Yes, we are!" said Vivian.

Abram cleared his throat gently. "But your old grandpa here is proudest of all!"

On Tuesday, May 5, Privates Alamo, Alex, and Abel Kane were riding along the bank of the Texas side of the Rio Grande, as General Zachary Taylor had commanded, looking for any sign of Mexican troops coming from the south. As they were headed back toward Point Isabel and Fort Polk that afternoon, they heard hoofbeats behind them and turned in their saddles. A lone rider was trotting his horse the same direction they were going.

"I wonder who that is," Abel said. "Can't be a Mexican. He's as light-skinned as we are."

"We'll find out shortly," Alex replied. "He's moving faster than we are."

As they continued at the same pace, they looked back periodically, noting that the lone rider was getting closer.

The next time Alamo looked back, he said, "Oh! I know him! He's a reporter for the *Washington Post*. His name is Michael Stewart. I met him back when I ran into Susanna Dickinson in the camp of displaced San Antonio residents as I was riding toward the Alamo. You remember—that was when I learned that Santa Anna's army had killed every man in the Alamo that morning. Stewart was there with the San Antonio residents, trying to learn what he could so he could write it up in the *Post*."

"Well, he must be after some other information now," said Alex.

"I would say so," Alamo said. "He's getting close. Let's stop."

As the Kane brothers pulled rein and turned their horses toward the oncoming rider, Alamo raised a hand. "Howdy, Mr. Stewart."

A smile broke over the reporter's features as he pulled rein. "Well, howdy yourself, Mr. *Alamo* Kane! I see you're in uniform now."

"Yes." Alamo glanced down at his uniform. "I want you to meet my brothers."

As he introduced Michael Stewart to Alex and Abel, the reporter guided his horse up close and shook their hands. He then shook hands with Alamo. "It doesn't surprise me that you're in the army now."

Alamo grinned. "So what are you doing out here?"

"My chief editor sent me here to see what was happening between General Taylor's forces and the Mexican forces."

"I don't suppose you know about the brief battle we had with the Mexicans a week ago today."

Stewart shook his head. "No. Tell me about it."

Alamo gave him a brief summary of the battle on April 28, when the Mexicans showed up on the Rio Grande in their boats at dawn and attacked both Fort Brown and Fort Polk. Stewart was making notes on a pad of paper with a pencil as Alamo gave him the details, including the fact that a great number of Mexican soldiers had been killed and that the rest of them picked up their wounded, got back in their boats, and hurried away.

When Stewart had finished writing, he looked up. "So, how's it looking now?"

"Not good. General Taylor is expecting more attacks by the Mexicans soon."

"I see. I'd like to talk to General Taylor if possible."

"Sure," Alamo said. "We're headed back to Fort Polk. We'll take you with us and introduce you to him."

Some twenty minutes later, when the Kane brothers and Stewart arrived at Fort Polk and dismounted, Alamo noticed that General Taylor was in conversation in front of his office with a young army officer. He pointed them out to the reporter and his brothers.

"I guess I shouldn't interrupt General Taylor right now," Stewart said.

Alamo nodded. "Right. Whatever they're talking about must be important. General Taylor is talking to Lieutenant Ulysses Grant, who is stationed at the Fort Brown position on the Rio Grande. As soon as they're finished, I'll take you over and introduce you."

Alex and Abel told the reporter they were glad they'd had the privilege of meeting him and excused themselves to stable their horses.

While Taylor and Grant were talking, the general happened to notice Alamo and the reporter standing nearby. He smiled and nodded at Private Kane, who smiled back. A couple minutes later, Taylor motioned for Alamo to come over. Alamo led the reporter to the spot where the general and the lieutenant stood. "Hello, Private Kane." Grant smiled.

Alamo smiled back and saluted. "Hello, Lieutenant."

Alamo introduced the general and the lieutenant to Michael Stewart, explaining that he was a reporter for the *Washington Post* and had been sent to interview General Taylor concerning the situation he and his troops were now facing with Mexico. As General Taylor was shaking hands with Michael Stewart, Alamo explained how and where he had first met Stewart the very day all the men at the Alamo had been killed by Santa Anna's troops.

Taylor smiled at the reporter. "I've read many of your articles in the *Post,* Mr. Stewart. You are most welcome here, and I'll be glad to give you an interview. It will be good for your newspaper to report what is happening here on the banks of the Rio Grande."

Alamo then said to Stewart, "Lieutenant Grant is from Ohio and is a graduate of the West Point Military Academy in New York."

Grant and Stewart shook hands. Then the lieutenant said, "I agree with General Taylor, Mr. Stewart. It's good that such a newspaper as the *Washington Post* would send a reporter here so the people of Texas, as well as the adjoining states, can learn what is going on here between the U.S. Army and the Mexicans."

Suddenly they heard a loud artillery barrage coming from the direction of Fort Brown to the south. Soldiers all over the Fort Polk area were looking that direction, though the rolling land between the forts made it impossible to actually see what was happening.

General Taylor's brow was furrowed as he searched the landscape as well. "Sounds like the Mexicans are attacking Fort Brown! We've got to assemble our men and get down there!"

Lieutenant Grant said, "General Taylor, I'll get on my horse and ride to where I can see what's going on down there for sure. I'll be back shortly."

Taylor nodded. Grant dashed to his horse and swung into the saddle.

Michael Stewart took out his pencil and notepad as he watched Grant gallop away.

## 20

The loud, thundering sounds of the artillery barrage from Fort Brown continued to fill the air above the resonant pounding of hooves underneath him as Lieutenant Ulysses Grant galloped his horse southward.

When he entered the area known as Palo Alto, he ran his gaze over the rolling, grassy plains, dotted here and there with pools of water. He thought of the thousands of acres of thick, dry grass about two feet tall that was now turning from brown to green. If there was a battle here, it could get really bad if cannonballs exploded and set fire to the grass. The slight wind was making the grass sway to and fro like waves of the sea. He pictured in his mind how fast the flames would sweep over Palo Alto if indeed the grass caught fire.

Shaking his head as if to throw the thought out of his mind, he pressed on toward Fort Brown. Soon he would be able to see exactly what was going on between the Americans and the Mexicans at the fort.

At Fort Polk, General Zachary Taylor was standing before his troops. "Men, if Lieutenant Grant comes back and reports what I think is happening at Fort Brown, I'm going to have to take half of you down there to help in that battle. I don't dare leave this fort without the other half because those Mexicans just might show up here from another direction and launch an attack."

The soldiers knew the general was right. The sounds of a barrage to the south demanded that he lead a good number of troops down there to join in the battle, but he also dare not leave this fort undefended.

General Taylor then named off the units and their officers that he would take to Fort Brown.

In the crowd of uniformed men, the Kane brothers found themselves included among the troops that would be going south. Alamo turned to Alex and Abel and said in a half whisper, "I'm glad we're going down there. At least we'll be on the offensive rather than the defensive."

Both brothers nodded their agreement.

Some twenty minutes later, the men chosen to go to Fort Brown with their leader were making ready to depart. They were saddling their horses and sliding rifles into the saddle boots.

Seeing that they were almost ready to go, General Taylor swung into his saddle and was about to give the order for them to mount up when the sounds of the roaring cannons to the south came to a sudden stop. Every man's face turned that direction. The silence seemed almost surreal.

Taylor looked around and said to his troops, "I wonder what's happened."

One of the captains, puzzlement on his features, said, "General Taylor, this is strange. Why would all that gunfire stop so suddenly?"

Taylor shook his head. "I don't know, Captain. I expect Lieutenant Grant back real soon. We'll give him time to get here before we move out. He'll probably be able to tell us."

At that instant, one of the soldiers who was to stay at Fort Polk pointed southward and yelled, "General! Lieutenant Grant is coming right now!"

Every eye turned that direction, and they all saw the rider galloping toward them across the rolling fields.

General Taylor dismounted.

Minutes later, when Grant drew up on his panting horse, he spoke loudly so all could hear. "General Taylor! The Fort Brown cannons have repelled the Mexican artillery! They suddenly turned and fled, heading westward along the south bank of the Rio Grande!"

With the mystery explained, the Fort Polk men lifted a rousing cheer, their arms waving in the air.

When the cheering died down, General Taylor said, "This is good news, Lieutenant Grant, and I'm glad to hear it. By what you saw, could you get an idea of about how many Mexican soldiers were in this attack?"

"Yes sir. I would say there were about six, maybe seven hundred."

Taylor nodded. "We have more than twice as many men down there." He ran his gaze over the faces of the troops. "Men, we dare not assume it is all over. Not at all! Without a doubt, the Mexican forces will build up their numbers and come back. They must have miscalculated how many men and guns we have at Fort Brown. They will be back, only with many more men and many more cannons next time! They know we're here in Fort Polk too. So we'll be attacked too, sooner or later. And my guess is that it will be sooner. Both forts must get ready for an all-out assault."

The soldiers were looking at each other and nodding as General Taylor turned to Ulysses Grant. "Lieutenant, I want you to hurry back down to Fort Brown and tell all the officers to see to it that they fortify themselves the best they can, because those Mexicans will be coming back with more men and more cannons. I'm sure of it."

Grant nodded. "I totally agree with you, sir. I'll tell them to get ready."

With that, Grant ran to his horse, mounted, and galloped away.

Taylor then looked around at his officers. "I need all of you lieutenants, captains, majors, and colonels to lead your men in fortifying this place where we stand for a huge assault. As sure as anything, those Mexicans will be here, and I really believe it will be very soon."

As the officers called out for the men in their units to follow them and the crowd of soldiers spread out, reporter Michael Stewart stepped up to Taylor. "General, I'd like your permission to stay here so that when the Mexicans come, I can make an eyewitness report of the battle."

Taylor rubbed his angular chin solemnly. "Mr. Stewart, you're welcome to stay, as long as you understand the danger in which you're putting yourself."

Stewart nodded. "I assure you, sir, I clearly understand the risk I'm taking. But I'm a reporter, and sometimes there are risks involved for a man of my profession when he is desirous of putting the facts together for the articles he's writing." He paused, then said, "I won't say I'm not on edge about being here with guns blazing and men getting killed and wounded, sir, but I take my job seriously."

Taylor nodded. "You'd make a good soldier, Mr. Stewart. Want to join up?"

Stewart grinned and shook his head. "I'd rather stick to the newspaper business, sir."

"I understand. Just be careful to stay out of the line of fire during the battle, okay?"

"Will do, sir."


For the rest of Tuesday and Wednesday, May 5 and 6, the troops at both forts worked hard to fortify their positions in every possible way for the pending Mexican attack.

At Fort Polk on Wednesday evening, after the troops had eaten their supper, Alamo Kane, his brothers, and the other men from their church were sitting by a small fire reading their Bibles together. When they had read the Scriptures they had chosen for that particular time, they prayed together, asking the Lord for His protection in the coming battle.

When the last "amen" had been said, Abel Kane got up and tossed some wood on the fire. The group looked up to see Corporal Lance Brooks walking past them.

Alamo rose to his feet and quickly stepped in front of Brooks. "Hello, Corporal," he said warmly.

Brooks halted and nodded. "Hello, Private."

"I'd like to ask you something," Alamo said.

The corporal's shoulders stiffened. "What's that?"

"Have you thought any more about what we talked about?"

"You mean the Bible stuff?"

"Mm-hmm."

The men in Alamo's group tried not to look up at Brooks but were listening intently to the conversation.

Brooks pulled at an ear. "Yeah, I've thought about it some, but I'm in no hurry to make the move about salvation that you brought up. There's plenty of time to do that if I should decide to."

"Corporal," Alamo said, with concern evident in his voice, "you shouldn't put off salvation. God warns in Proverbs 27:1 about thinking you have plenty of time. He says, 'Boast not thyself of to morrow; for thou knowest not what a day may bring forth.' Any day can be your last, the same as it is for every human being."

A twisted grin crossed Brooks's lips. "I'm not worried about it." With that he turned and walked away.

Alamo shook his head back and forth solemnly as he watched Brooks go, then sat down with his group at the fire. "Lance Brooks is heavy on my heart, fellas." Alamo sighed. "Let's bow our heads and pray for him right now."

Heads were bowed, and Alamo led them in prayer, asking the Lord to draw the corporal unto Himself before it was too late.

Later, in his bedroll, when his brothers were already asleep, Alamo's heart was still heavy for Lance Brooks, and he prayed for him again.

Alamo then prayed for his precious wife and children at the Diamond K Ranch, asking God to take care of them and protect them.

The next morning, Thursday, May 7, the Fort Polk men worked some more, fortifying themselves even better for the attack they were sure was coming.

Later in the afternoon, two privates came riding into Fort Polk from Fort Brown, telling the first soldiers they saw that they needed to see General Taylor immediately. One of the soldiers hurried to the general's quarters and brought him to the two privates, who had dismounted and were standing beside their horses.

Other men gathered around—including the reporter, Michael Stewart—as the soldier who introduced himself as Private Ben Fillmore said, "General Taylor, we were sent out of Fort Brown early this morning to ride the north bank of the Rio Grande and keep an eye out for any sign of Mexicans. We spotted a huge number of Mexican forces crossing the river from Mexico about ten miles upstream to the west. They were too far away for us to make an accurate guess as to how many there were, but we figured we should come and tell you about them before we go back to Fort Brown and tell our officers."

Stewart was taking notes as General Taylor, his voice strained, said, "You did right, men. Thank you. Now go on back and tell your officers what you saw. Tell them that I have some specially trained scouts here with me. I'll send them out right now to ride the Texas side of the river and take a look. Tell your officers I said to stay alert."

The privates assured him they would, mounted up, and galloped southward.

Ten minutes later, after informing the five scouts what the privates had told him, General Taylor sent them to ride the Texas side of the river and take a look.

As word passed through the fort, there was much concern among the soldiers.

Less than an hour later, the scouts returned and told the general that there were indeed Mexican troops heading directly toward Fort Polk on the Texas side of the Rio Grande. They estimated that there were about five thousand.

"Five thousand!" said Taylor.

"At least, sir," replied one of the scouts.

The general rubbed his jaw. "We only have three thousand total in both of these forts. We sure can't face five thousand with just fifteen hundred here in this fort."

The general quickly sent two of his scouts to Fort Brown, telling them to bring all the troops and their cannons from Fort Brown to Fort Polk as quickly as possible.

In a short time, all the Fort Brown soldiers arrived at Fort Polk, cannons and rifles ready. Ammunition wagons had also been brought along. Two Fort Brown colonels informed General Taylor that they had seen the Mexican troops coming along the north bank of the Rio Grande. They agreed that there had to be at least five thousand of them.

Lieutenant Grant was standing close-by and heard the conversation between Taylor and the colonels.

General Taylor immediately began to give orders as to where the cannons should be placed to balance out with the cannons that were already there.

When the men knew exactly where to position the Fort Brown cannons, Lieutenant Grant stepped up to General Taylor. "General, I have to tell you who's leading the Mexican troops. While we were coming up here, I used my binoculars to focus on the Mexican military leader."

"Did you recognize him?"

"Yes sir. It was General Mariano Arista, one of the most vicious Mexican army leaders. Do you know of him?"

The general's eyes widened. "Arista, eh? Yes, I know of him. You're right. He is quite vicious. I know enough about him to say this—he is very much like Santa Anna. Just as vile, heartless, and cold-blooded."

Grant shook his head. "With Arista in charge and the Mexicans outnumbering us by some two thousand, we've got a real battle coming up."

Taylor nodded. "Since Arista's troops outnumber us like this, I guarantee you he's figuring to wipe out the entire American force here."

Grant swallowed hard. "It *will* be a big battle, sir, but we can whip 'em!"

The general patted Grant's shoulder, giving him a thin smile. "Lieutenant Grant, I like your attitude. I hope you live to become a general in the United States Army. You would make a good one!"

Grant blushed. "Thank you, sir."

Before the sun set that day, the men who had been stationed on the south wall of Fort Polk to keep their eyes peeled for any sign of the Mexican troops called out for someone to fetch General Taylor. When the general emerged from his office, he saw the bulk of his three thousand men filing out through the gates. One of the officers on the south wall cried out, "General! Go out there with the rest of the men! The Mexicans are in view right now!"

When Taylor made it outside the fort, he hurried to the front of the crowd and beheld the awesome sight of General Arista on his white horse, leading his five thousand troops as they spread out on the rolling, grassy plains of Palo Alto, just south of Fort Polk.

They observed the Mexicans until the sun had set. Then General Taylor assembled his three thousand troops before him inside the fort walls and told them he would have men on the walls keep watch during the night, of course, but he expected the Mexicans to wait until morning to attack.

"We'll be ready for them!" he added.

The soldiers waved their arms and shouted their agreement. They indeed would be ready for the enemy when they attacked.

After supper that evening, the Kane brothers and their Christian friends gathered for Bible reading and prayer once more. Just before prayer time, Alamo asked them to join him in praying for Corporal Brooks, saying that Brooks was heavy on his heart. The group earnestly prayed for Brooks as they asked the Lord to convict him from the Scriptures Alamo had read to him and bring him to the place where he would repent and receive Jesus as his Saviour.

That same Thursday evening, May 7, at the Diamond K Ranch, Julia Kane carried little nineteen-month-old Amber from the parlor, where her sons were playing hide-and-seek together among the large pieces of furniture. At the moment, young Abram was It. She hurried to the master bedroom a bit concerned over Amber, who had been quite fussy that day. She was running a slight fever, causing her chubby cheeks to be rosier than usual.

Upon entering the room, where a lantern was already lit, Julia sat in her rocking chair, cuddling her wee one close in her arms and humming a lullaby as she gently rocked. Amber was still fussy. As she hummed, Julia said to herself, *Maybe she misses her papa as much as I do.*

The fussing eased as Julia continued to hum and rock her baby. Soon Amber's thumb found its way into her mouth, and finally sleep seemed to claim her. The loving mother caressed Amber's downy head and continued to hum, waiting to be certain that she was indeed asleep.

When she was convinced that Amber was asleep, the weary mother slowly rose to her feet, carried little Amber to the crib next to her own bed, kissed her cheek lightly, and lowered her into the crib. At that moment, Amber rolled her head from side to side, whimpered, and wiggled her body. Julia picked her up, placed her against her chest, patted her little back, and hummed another lullaby.

In only a couple minutes, baby Amber went quiet again, and sleep fully claimed her.

Julia laid her back down in her crib and covered her up, whispering, "Please, dear Lord, help her to sleep through the night and to feel better by morning."

*Maybe it's because she's teething,* Julia thought as she leaned down and placed a soft kiss on top of Amber's head.

She then doused the lantern and tiptoed toward the door. Pausing to kiss her fingertips and throw her baby the kiss, the loving mother closed the door quietly and made her way down the hall to the parlor.

When she entered the room, Andy was asleep on a sofa, and Adam and Abram were sitting on another sofa wiping tears and sniffling.

Julia rushed to the sofa and touched their heads. "Boys, what are you crying about?"

They looked up through their tears, and Adam said, "We miss Papa, Mama. We want him to come home."

Sitting down between them, Julia put an arm around each one. "Boys, I miss Papa too, but we just have to wait until the Lord brings him home to us." She paused then turned her head to look into both pair of eyes. "How about I read to you from one of your storybooks Grandpa bought when he was in town last week?"

Both boys nodded and smiled.

Adam dashed to the bookshelf on the other side of the parlor, returned with one of the books, and handed it to his mother. Julia began reading to them, and within twenty minutes, both boys' eyelids were drooping. They were yawning and rubbing their sleepy eyes.

Julia laid the book down. "Okay, boys, it's bedtime for all of us." She went to the sofa where Andy was sleeping and picked him up and led the other two down the hall. When they reached the room that Abram and Andy shared, Julia said, "Adam, you go on to your room. I'll be there after I get your little brothers in bed."

Julia took off Andy's shoes and put him in his bed without changing him into his pajamas, then helped Abram get into his pajamas and into his bed. She listened while Abram prayed a short prayer, then kissed him and tucked him in for the night.

The devoted mother then walked down the hall a few steps to her oldest son's bedroom. When she stepped into the room, Adam was sitting up in the bed wide awake, waiting for her.

She smiled. "I thought you might be asleep by the time I got here."

"Oh no, Mama. I always want you here while I pray before I go to sleep."

Julia sat down on the bed and put an arm around Adam's shoulders while he prayed. In his prayer, he asked the Lord to protect his papa and his uncles and to bring them home safely.

Julia hugged him and kissed his cheek. "Good night, honey," she said. She then noticed the strained look on his face. "What's the matter, Adam?"

He frowned. "Mama, I wish I could take my .22 rifle and go join the army so I could fight the Mexicans with Papa, Uncle Alex, and Uncle Abel. I'd like to help them get this war thing with Mexico over with."

She smiled and patted his cheek. "Honey, you're not old enough to join the army. You know that."

Adam sighed. "Yeah, I know. But that doesn't stop me from wishin' I could do it. And you know what?"

"What?"

"If this Mexican problem is still goin' on when I do get old enough to join the army, I'm gonna do it. I'm gonna help protect this country from the Mexicans."

"Well, sweet boy," said his mother, "I certainly hope all this trouble between the United States and Mexico will be over by the time you turn eighteen."

Adam nodded. "Well, yeah. So do I."

Julia kissed her oldest son's cheek again, and he scooted down under the covers and lay his head on the pillow. She put out the lantern and headed for the door, saying, "I love you, son."

"I love you too, Mama. Good night."

Julia closed the door and walked down the hall to her own bedroom. She quickly got into her night gown and leaned down to the crib next to the bed, kissed the top of her sleeping baby girl's head, and then crawled into the bed. She picked up her Bible from the small nightstand and read from the psalms for a few minutes. As she closed the Bible and placed it back on the table, she suddenly had a strong feeling that Alamo and his brothers and the other soldiers were in trouble, wherever they were.

She put out the lantern and began praying for her husband and his brothers, asking the Lord to protect them by the power of His own hand. She felt that she should pray for them some more and did so. Julia finally fell asleep praying.

## 21

At the break of dawn the next morning, Friday, May 8, 1846, with a strong wind blowing, General Zachary Taylor and his troops had their big cannons in place on the fort's wall platforms and on the open land just outside of the fort's south wall. Cavalrymen and infantrymen were in place and ready for combat.

Alamo Kane and his brothers had a time of prayer together, asking the Lord to give the Americans victory and to spare their lives so they could go back to their families at the Diamond K Ranch soon.

Taylor's men, in their ready positions, watched as the Mexicans moved their cannons about on the grassy plains of Palo Alto, positioning them strategically. Their cavalry and infantry were spread out amid the long, dry grass, which was bending with the wind.

On the land adjacent to Fort Polk's south wall, General Taylor was riding his bay gelding, moving along the lines of his cavalry, infantry, and the big cannons. All of the American soldiers were watching the Mexican troops carefully.

As he rode past his men, General Taylor told them in a low tone to keep their cannons and rifles aimed at the Mexicans, but not to fire until the Mexicans did. He explained that he wanted it to be said that the Mexicans started the battle, not the Americans.

As Taylor rode along, he glanced toward the Mexican forces often, and at one point he caught a glimpse of Mexican General Mariano Arista on his white horse, riding along the lines of his soldiers and weapons.

Every American soldier's nerves were tight. They knew the battle was about to begin.

At the precise moment when the sun peeked over the eastern horizon and a flood of golden sunshine streamed across the land, the Mexicans opened fire.

Old Rough and Ready, General Taylor, gave the order for his men to fire back. The artillery cut loose, and the infantry followed suit. The thunderous roar of cannons and the piercing bark of rifles filled the air.

Mexican guns continued to blast away across the grassy fields of Palo Alto, but while Taylor's cavalry galloped toward the enemy and his infantry ran toward them, rifles barking and bayonets flashing in the early morning sun, the American cannonballs were taking a tremendous toll on the Mexican troops.

Surprisingly, the Mexican cannonballs were quite ineffective. They were missing their targets, falling great distances too short. The American cannonballs, however, struck their targets, blowing Mexicans in every direction. As the cannons on both sides fired, the stiff wind quickly grasped the smoke from the muzzles and carried it away.

At the same time, the cavalrymen on both sides were riding and firing at each other while the infantrymen on both sides ran toward each other through the long, dry grass, rifles spitting fire.

Great patches of grass on the rolling plains were blasted by both artilleries as the cannonballs struck ground and exploded. American cannonballs were throwing about the bodies of men and horses as the Mexicans scattered right and left, trying to escape them. On one large open area, which had small water pools around its perimeter, so many men and horses were killed that the field looked as if it had been struck by a storm of bloody hail.

American cannons and rifles belched their volleys with telling accuracy. Cannonballs hissed and exploded while bullets zipped and whistled.

During this exchange of cannonballs hitting the ground and

exploding, the extremely dry grass in one section suddenly caught fire. As the wind drove the flames and smoke, the battle raged on.

Stark disaster was on the way.

Soldiers on both sides were being engulfed in the wind-swept flames as the fire spread. Bloodcurdling screams filled the smoky air. As the fire continued to spread while artillery roared and rifles resounded, an angry crimson glow brightened the sky overhead, and fiery sparks fell. Periodically the wind increased in velocity, sending sparks soaring and small flaming balls of grass tumbling across the prairie. The wind was causing much of the smoke to whirl and spiral as it was lifted toward the sky. Other clouds of smoke stayed close to the ground, giving off an intense smell.

At one spot where several dozen Mexican infantrymen were charging after American infantrymen, the wind-driven flames engulfed an entire unit of Mexicans. The savage fire was not to be denied. The Mexicans were humans one second, a mass of flames a split-second later, and finally lay on the ground as charred corpses.

Where Mexican cannons had been spread out on the fields at dawn, the flames spread, and the boxes of gunpowder in their path caught fire and exploded, adding to the terror that men on both sides were experiencing. Agonizing cries could be heard above the gunfire and the roar of the flames.

Some men fell when shrapnel and bullets struck them, and as the flames reached them, their bodies were incinerated.

Being in the infantry, the Kane brothers were firing their rifles a fair amount when suddenly they saw Corporal Lance Brooks running through an open area of dry grass that had not yet caught fire off to their left some forty yards away. Brooks was running from two Mexican soldiers who were trying to avoid the fiery grass close-by as they chased after him.

One of the Mexicans raised his rifle and fired. The slug hit Brooks in his left thigh, and he fell in the dry grass, not far from flames the strong wind was blowing in his direction. As bullets were flying between the two armies, the two Mexican soldiers were hit and fell to the ground. Neither moved.

Gripping his wounded leg, Corporal Brooks gritted his teeth in pain and noted that both of his pursuers were now lying absolutely still, facedown on the ground. He could make out bullet holes in their upper bodies. Some of the Americans had taken them out as they were chasing him.

The wind was still blowing hard, and as Lance heard the constant firing of artillery and rifles, he saw that the red tide of flames was coming straight toward him.

Still gritting his teeth, he struggled to rise to his feet. Breathing hard, he finally made it to a standing position, but when he took the first step to attempt to escape the oncoming flames, pain shot through his wounded leg, and he fell flat on his back.

The wind seemed to change direction at that moment, and flaming cinders began falling on him. In panic, he sat up and slapped at his clothing to extinguish the sparks that threatened to set him afire.

Just as he put out the last spark, the wind switched back, and now a writhing wall of fire was closing in on him, no more than sixty or seventy feet away. Knowing he could not run to escape the flames, he began crawling away, using his good leg and both hands. However, after only a few seconds, he collapsed, facedown.

Sweat beaded on his face. He could feel the heat of the flames on his body. Suddenly he thought of what Alamo Kane had shown him in the Bible about hell being real fire. He knew that if he died in those flames not having Jesus Christ as his Saviour, he was going to drop into burning, everlasting hellfire. His eyes had a wild look as he rolled his head over to stare at the flames that were about to engulf him and burn him to death.

Amid flying cannonballs and bullets, Corporal Brooks lifted his head and let out a wild cry. "Oh-h-h, dear God! Hel-l-lp me! Hel-l-lp me!"

All of a sudden, the terrorized corporal saw an American soldier running toward him, zigzagging in an attempt to miss the patches of flames in the grass and to avoid the bullets and shrapnel that were flying.

*It was Private Alamo Kane!*

Still holding his face out of the dirt, Lance gulped and gasped, hardly able to believe his eyes.

With the roar of the wind and the thunder of the battle still going on, Alamo bent down and put his hands under the fallen corporal. Lance felt himself being lifted up and cradled in the private's strong arms.

Still dodging bullets, shrapnel, and wind-driven flames in the grass, Alamo carried the wounded corporal to a place of safety between two pools of water. The fire had not come near this spot, and they were between two mounds of dirt where no bullets or shrapnel were striking. Three American army medics were nearby working on wounded soldiers.

Alamo laid Lance down, knelt at his right side, and called to the medics, "Hey, fellas, I've got a wounded man here!"

One of the medics had just finished bandaging a captain. He picked up his medical bag and ran to where Private Kane was kneeling over Corporal Brooks. The medic dropped to his knees opposite Alamo and spotted the bloody left pant leg. He made a quick examination of the wounded leg. "Corporal, I'll have to dig that slug out of your leg right now!"

Corporal Brooks nodded and said through clenched teeth, "Go ahead, Doc."

The medic opened his bag and took out a bottle of clear liquid. "First I'll give you this, Corporal. It'll ease your pain. I know you're hurting bad enough now, but when I cut that slug out of your thigh and stitch up the wound, it'll hurt all the more. This medicine will dull the pain."

"What is it, Doc?" Lance asked.

"Laudanum," he replied. "Believe me, it'll make a big difference in what you feel."

Lance nodded. "You're the doctor."

The medic poured the laudanum into a small cup, measuring it carefully, and put it to Lance's lips. "Drink it all, Corporal."

When Lance had drained the cup, the medic took out his surgical knife. "I'll give the laudanum a couple minutes to get into your system."

Lance nodded then turned his head and looked at Alamo. His lips quivered as he said, "Private Kane, thank you for saving me from burning to death."

Alamo smiled. "I'm just glad I was able to get to you, Corporal."

Lance's voice shook as he said, "Y-you could have been killed while attempting to get to me." Tears then bubbled up in his eyes. "I want you to know that I deeply appreciate what you did. You risked your own life to save mine."

"Saving your life was worth the risk, Corporal."

Lance grinned. "Thank you for feeling that way, my friend."

At that moment, Alamo's attention was drawn to two American soldiers who were carrying a wounded comrade toward them, their eyes on the medic. "Looks like you've got another patient on the way, Doc," he said.

"I hope one of the other doctors is free to help him," said the medic. "Right now I've got to get this slug out of the corporal's leg."

Suddenly Alamo saw two Mexican soldiers emerge through the smoke some forty yards behind the two soldiers who were carrying their wounded comrade. The Mexicans' rifles were poised to plunge their bayonets into the backs of the Americans.

Alamo had left his rifle with his brothers when he ran to the wounded corporal. He remembered seeing that the wounded captain this medic had treated had a revolver in a holster on his waist. Alamo jumped up, dashed to where the bandaged captain lay, whipped the revolver out of its holster, and ran toward the two American soldiers. "Behind you! Behind you!"

As the soldiers carrying their wounded comrade paused to look behind them, Alamo met them and passed them in a dead-heat run. He raised the revolver as the wild-eyed Mexicans bore down on the two American soldiers with their bayonets ready and fired twice, hitting them both in the chest.

Panting as he stood over the Mexicans, Alamo saw instantly that both of them were dead. The slugs had pierced their hearts. Still panting, he turned to the soldiers. They both looked at him with surprise and thanked him for saving their lives.

"Th-that's wh-what being Americans is all ab-about," gasped Alamo.

At that moment, one of the other medics came running up. "I'll tend to this wounded man. Follow me. My medical bag is over there by those other wounded men."

As Alamo walked beside them, he said, "I've got a friend being tended to over here. See you later."

The two soldiers thanked him again for taking out the two Mexicans and followed the medic with their comrade in their arms.

Alamo drew up to where Brooks lay and saw that the medic was already digging into the corporal's bloody thigh. Kneeling beside the medic, Alamo asked, "How's it look, Doc?"

Lance set torpid eyes on Alamo as the medic replied, "The slug chewed into the meat of the thigh, but it didn't shatter any bone. He'll be a while healing up, but he'll be all right."

"Thanks to you, Private Kane," Lance said, his tongue slurring. The very tone of his voice showed how he now felt toward Alamo Kane.


The battle at Palo Alto was still going on as darkness fell, and it was evident to General Taylor that a large number of Mexicans had been killed.

What had been roaring fires in the grass of the rolling prairie were now only scattered small puffs of smoke lifting from the blackened ground.

Suddenly, in the fading light of day, the Mexican artillery and rifles stopped firing, and General Arista led his troops southward in the direction of the Rio Grande, as fast as they could go, carrying their wounded men with them. The American guns continued to blast away until the enemy had passed over some hills and vanished from view. In those few moments, more Mexicans went down dead.

General Taylor quickly assembled his troops inside the fort's walls. "Men, I'd like nothing more than to lead all of you after Arista and his troops right now and cut them into pieces, but we'll go after them in the morning. I doubt they'll try traveling in the dark. Right now we're all battle weary. I've got to check on our wounded men and also see if I can find out how many of our men have been killed. I'll need some of you officers to help me. I want the rest of you to eat some supper and get some sleep. The officers and I will eat a little later and then get some sleep ourselves."

The general then named the officers he wanted to help him count their dead. He called out the names of a few other officers, who were to assign men to guard duty for the night, switching them off hourly so every man could get the rest he needed.

While the assigned officers went out onto the blackened fields with lanterns to count the dead American soldiers, General Taylor went to the spot inside the fort where the medics were still tending to wounded Americans. Forty-seven of his men had been wounded, but he was glad to hear that the medics expected all of them to live.

Later the officers returned with their count of the dead and reported to the general that nine had been killed.

Nodding, the general removed his hat. "Of course, losing these men saddens me, but there is also gratification in my heart knowing that General Arista lost a much larger number of men than we did."

When the Kane brothers had been given their assignments for

guard duty during the night, they went to the spot where they planned on cooking their supper.

Alex looked around. "Well, the first thing we need to do is go get some firewood from the shed at the backside of the fort."

"Tell you what, boys," Alamo said. "If you don't mind, while you go get the firewood, I'd like to check on Corporal Brooks. I want to see how he's doing."

Alex and Abel agreed, and while they went toward the back gate, Alamo hurried to the area where the wounded men were being kept. Small fires were burning to give off light in the area, and it only took him a few seconds to spot the corporal, who was lying on the ground next to a fire. He was under a blanket one of the medics had given him.

Lance smiled when he saw Alamo, who knelt down beside him.

Patting his shoulder, Alamo asked, "Are you in pain?"

"I'm still feeling some pain in the wound," Lance replied, "but that's because the laudanum I was given wore off about a half hour ago. He came to check on me, and when I told him the pain was coming back, he gave me some more. The pain's fading fast now."

"Good," Alamo said. "I'm glad to hear it."

Lance looked at Alamo by the light of the fire. "Can I call you Alamo?"

Alamo grinned. "You sure can."

"Thanks. You call me Lance too, will you?"

"Sure."

Gratitude filled Lance's eyes. "Alamo, I want to thank you again for saving my life. If you hadn't risked your own life to enter that burning field, I would've burned to death, like three other American soldiers did today."

Alamo patted his shoulder again. "Lance, I'm glad I was able to get to you before the flames did."

"Me too, my friend! There's no way to describe the horror I felt when that fire was coming right at me."

Alamo squeezed Lance's shoulder. "Remember what I read to you from the Bible about hell's fire?"

Lance closed his eyes. "Yes."

"Well, hell's fire is a lot hotter than the fire you faced today. It's forever too."

The corporal's lips began to tremble, and tears misted his eyes. "I know, Alamo. When those flames were blowing toward me, I thought about what you had read to me from the Bible about hellfire."

Alamo felt his heart quicken. "You did?"

Tears were now bubbling from Lance's eyes and starting to flow down his cheeks. "Alamo," he said in a quivering voice, "I want to be saved."

Alamo was thrilled at this answer to prayer. "I'll go get my Bible, okay?"

"Yes!"

Lance put a shaky hand to his mouth as he watched Alamo hurry away.

As Alamo ran to where his rifle and other personal belongings lay, his brothers were in the process of starting a fire to cook supper. When they saw Alamo take his Bible out of its leather case, Abel asked, "What're you doing?"

Alamo smiled. "Dear brothers, I am about to have the joy and privilege of leading Corporal Lance Brooks to Jesus!"

"Really?" said Alex.

"Really!" Alamo replied.

"Praise the Lord!" said Abel.

"You boys go ahead and eat your supper," Alamo said, excitement evident in his voice. "I'll eat after Lance has become a child of God!"

Alex and Abel smiled as they watched their brother hasten back toward the area where the wounded men lay.

Lance was watching for Alamo to return, and when he saw him coming, he managed a smile in spite of the pain he was still feeling.

Alamo knelt down beside him and positioned himself so that Lance could read along with the Scriptures he would point out by the light of the fire.

Alamo smiled. "You ready?"

Once again, tears misted Lance's eyes. "Yes. I'm ready!"

While dealing with Lance on the subject of salvation, Alamo turned to several passages and had the wounded soldier read them aloud. In less than half an hour, with Alamo's help, Corporal Lance Brooks bowed his head and called on the Lord Jesus Christ to come into his heart, cleanse him from his sin, and save his hell-bound soul.

When it was done, Lance wept with relief and joy. Alamo then prayed aloud for Lance, asking the Lord to heal his leg wound and to help him grow in his Christian life.

When Alamo closed his prayer, Lance said with tears running down his cheeks, "I know you need to go eat your supper, but I just have to say thank you for leading me to the Lord. Now I know I'm going to heaven, and I'll never see or feel hellfire!"

Alamo patted his hand. "You sure are, and you sure won't!"

When Alamo returned to his brothers and told them that Lance was now a child of God, they rejoiced, shedding their own tears.

After Alamo had eaten his supper, the three of them went to their friends from their church and told them of Corporal Brooks's salvation. There was much rejoicing.

## 22

That night Alamo Kane could hardly sleep for the joy that was in his heart over Corporal Lance Brooks's salvation. Lying under his blankets on the ground next to his sleeping brothers inside the fort, he prayed in a low whisper, "Dear Lord, thank You so much for answering the prayers of my brothers and our friends from church...and for answering *my* prayers too. It is such a joy and a privilege as a child of God to have the honor of working with You in bringing precious souls to salvation. There is nothing on this earth like it, Lord. Thank You for letting me be a witness for You!"

Still unable to fall asleep, Alamo prayed for his family at home, even though he had prayed for them just after slipping into his bedroll. He thanked the Lord for the way He had worked in the lives of Julia and himself after Adam's death and brought them together as husband and wife. "Lord," he said, "I know Julie still carries love for Adam in her heart, and she should. But thank You, after all my praying, for causing Julie to fall in love with me. Thank You! Thank You! Thank You!"

With deep gratitude for God's blessings in his heart, Alamo finally fell asleep.

At dawn the next morning, Saturday, May 9, Mexican General Mariano Arista stood before his troops in the wooded area where they had spent the night. It was but a few miles from Palo Alto, where they had fought General Zachary Taylor's American troops the day before.

Arista's heart was heavy as he ran his gaze over his men. Over two hundred had been killed in the battle, and some seventy-three had been wounded. When he awakened that morning, he'd learned from his men who were caring for the wounded that six of those seventy-three had died during the night.

After breakfast, the sad-faced general gathered his men before him and said, "There is no question in my mind, men, that the American troops will be coming after us. We must find a stronger position from which to fight them. I know of a dried-up riverbed that offers excellent defensive possibilities. It is called Resaca de la Guerrero. It is not far away. It lies just a few miles north of the Rio Grande."

The dark eyes of the Mexican soldiers brightened as their leader encouraged them.

General Arista led his troops toward Resaca de la Guerrero. When they arrived there at midmorning, he placed his soldiers, along with their cannons and horse-drawn wagons bearing ammunition and wounded men, behind the natural fortifications of thick, heavy shrubs they found in the riverbed. Arista was convinced that his position was quite secure. He believed that this spot, in addition to his superior numbers, would give him the advantage over General Zachary Taylor's troops.

Standing before his men, Arista said in Spanish, "This time we will win the battle, and General Taylor will be our prisoner."

The huge crowd of Mexican soldiers cheered their leader and shouted out their hatred for the Americans.

○

After breakfast at Palo Alto, General Zachary Taylor left his wounded men with three medics to care for them and moved his troops southward in pursuit of the retreating Mexicans.

Just after ten o'clock, they arrived at Resaca de la Palma, which was a flat, rocky area, and General Taylor called a halt, telling his men that he wanted to let his weary foot soldiers rest. The cavalrymen and the soldiers who had driven the wagons carrying ammunition and pulling the cannons rested also, though they were not as tired as the infantrymen were.

While the troops rested, Taylor sent some of his mounted scouts ahead to see if they could locate the enemy.

Reporter Michael Stewart then approached the general, pencil and pad in hand, and asked pertinent questions concerning war and battles for his article. Taylor was glad to answer them.

Just before noon, Taylor's scouts came riding into Resaca de la Palma, and as they dismounted and approached the general, the rest of the troops gathered around, wanting to hear what the scouts had to say.

The leading scout was Sergeant Wilbur Cotten, who stepped up to Taylor. "General, we found 'em. Arista and his troops are fortified in the heavy chaparral of the old riverbed at Resaca de la Guerrero. You remember, we passed that area when we were coming to Point Isabel."

Taylor nodded. "I remember it well. That spot is definitely loaded with bushes. Arista probably feels quite secure there."

Sergeant Cotten grinned. "Yes sir. Let's go show him how wrong he is."

The general looked at the crowd of soldiers that surrounded him. "Did all of you hear what Sergeant Cotten just told me?"

Many heads nodded, and some called out to affirm that they had heard Cotten's report.

One of the colonels called out, "General, I'll gladly bypass lunch so we can go right now and attack them!"

A roar of voices stated their agreement with the colonel that they wanted to attack Arista and his troops *now.*

Within minutes, General Taylor had his men heading south toward the old riverbed. He and a few of his officers rode ahead of the troops. When they were within sight of Resaca de la Guerrero and could make out the Mexican cannons and wagons amid the heavy bushes, the general turned in his saddle, signaled silently for the troops to halt, and pulled rein. The other officers did the same, and the troops stopped instantly.

Taylor spoke quietly to his officers. "Even though we can't see them, the Mexicans are hiding in the chaparral."

Using his binoculars, Lieutenant Ulysses Grant focused on the scene, then turned to Taylor. "General, with these I can see a good number of their troops hiding in the bushes. They're ready to fight us."

Taylor nodded, studying the scene carefully. "Tell you what, men," he said to the officers. "The layout down there is going to make a flanking movement impossible. No way to come at them from every direction."

"You're right, sir," said Grant. "There is no choice but to make a frontal assault."

"That's right, Lieutenant Grant," another officer said.

The others spoke their agreement.

"Then we're going to make a frontal assault," the general said. "I'll go explain this to the troops." Wheeling his horse about, Old Rough and Ready trotted along the lines, telling the men what they were going to do, and why.

When Taylor had all the men ready, he sent the hard-riding cavalrymen galloping toward the right wing of the Mexican line with great force.

This took the Mexicans in that spot by surprise, and before the men at the cannons could fire, cavalry bullets were cutting them down. The Americans were capturing Mexican cannons.

At the same time, General Taylor's cannons were lined up, and they were blasting away at the rest of the Mexicans among the shrubs in the riverbed while Taylor had the remainder of his troops ready to attack on his command. The cannon fire went on steadily, sending cannonballs into the shrubs, striking with excellent accuracy. The cannonballs exploded on impact, sending shrapnel in every direction and instantly putting many Mexicans down.

After nearly forty minutes of the cannon barrage, Taylor's men ran out of cannonballs.

Taking advantage of the confusion the cavalrymen and cannons had caused, Taylor quickly sent his waiting infantrymen charging at the shrub-hidden Mexican troops, guns blazing.

Bullets were cutting through the shrubs, taking a serious toll on General Arista's men. Mexican bullets found a comparative few American soldiers. For the most part, the Mexicans were getting the brunt of the conflict.

Soon the Mexican right wing collapsed. Some of them had run to other positions, and the rest of them in that area lay dead on the ground.

While the battle raged, the American infantrymen kept on coming, sending hot lead into the chaparral. Before long, the infantrymen barged into the bush-laden riverbed, and the fighting transitioned to hand-to-hand combat, with bayonets, rifle butts, fists, and knives. Among those infantrymen were the Diamond K Ranch's Kane brothers.

At the same time, the cavalrymen were moving about on their horses, blasting away at every Mexican they could find.

As the brush fighting continued, wild disorder among the Mexicans prevailed. Officers and the men who were under their charge lost all contact with each other.

The battle went on, and by five o'clock that afternoon, General Arista's left wing had completely collapsed. His troops retreated hastily under the blazing guns of the Americans, and the retreat turned into a rout as General Arista's frightened and disorganized troops fled toward the Rio Grande, which they had crossed to get into Texas.

General Arista was with them, leading the retreat and leaving behind all of his wounded and dead.

General Taylor shouted out to his men as the Mexicans fled, "Fire away, men! Fire away!"

The Americans' guns spit fire, and hot lead continued to cut Mexicans down until they were out of range.

When the firing stopped, some of the soldiers agreed that they should pursue the Mexicans and wipe them out.

Hearing their words, General Taylor said, "No, men! We will not go after them! I say this because we have killed a great number of their men in this battle and in the battle at Palo Alto. We'll let the general and his remaining soldiers go on back to Mexico. I am sure President Polk would give that order if he were here."

Simmering down, the men who had wanted to go after the Mexicans agreed that the general was right. They would do as he said.

The general then sent some of the wagons back to Palo Alto to pick up their wounded men and the medics and bring them to this spot.

While the wagons moved northward, Taylor's men counted the dead soldiers on both sides. Nearly twelve hundred Mexicans had been killed in this battle, and some two hundred wounded lay on the ground. In comparison, only thirty-three Americans had been killed, and eighty-nine had been wounded. Taylor's men also reported that they had put the wounded Mexicans all in one place and had confiscated their weapons.

"That's good thinking, men." General Taylor rubbed his jaw with a solemn look in his eyes. "There's nothing we can do for all those wounded Mexicans. Our medics will be busy with our own wounded men, and besides, we don't have enough medicine to take care of that many wounded men in addition to ours."

One of the soldiers said, "General, I appreciate that you would see to it that those wounded Mexicans were taken care of if possible, but the Mexicans started this war, and that's just the way it goes in war. There's nothing we can do for them."

Reporter Michael Stewart was standing near the general. He stepped up at that moment and said, "General, I am amazed at the difference in casualties in these two battles between our soldiers and the Mexicans. They outnumbered us tremendously, yet so many more of their men were killed and wounded. Are our men that much better trained?"

"Yes, they are, Mr. Stewart," Taylor replied. "But there's a lot more to it than the fact that the Mexican soldiers are given very little training for combat."

Michael was writing rapidly as the general spoke. When he finished the sentence he was writing, he looked at Taylor. "Tell me what else made the Mexicans lose these battles even though they had the greater numbers."

"It's their weaponry."

Stewart's brow furrowed. "What do you mean, sir?"

"The Mexican army has substandard gunpowder and ancient guns. I'll tell you about the gunpowder first. It is of poor quality, thus doesn't have the power ours has, which shortens the range of both their cannon and rifle fire. Actually, I should say *musket* fire. I'll tell you about that in a minute. The poorly made gunpowder has a tendency to explode prematurely, which causes the soldiers to pour smaller amounts of it in their weapons, affecting their shooting range a great deal."

The general let the reporter get that piece of information written down and continued. "When it comes to their guns, they don't have rifles that are up to date. The type of musket Arista's men were using in these two battles is known as the British Brown Bess, B-E-S-S. It's the same weapon the British used during the Napoleonic and Revolutionary wars decades ago."

Stewart wrote speedily. "That really makes sense, General… Both the poorly made gunpowder and the ancient guns would create quite a disadvantage."

Taylor nodded. "They sure have paid a price in these two battles because of it."

"Yes sir. But they chose to come here and attack your troops anyway."

"Foolishly, I might add," Taylor said. "Yes, they managed to kill and wound some of our men, but they lost a lot more than we did."

Private Alamo Kane was standing close, listening to the conversation between Taylor and Stewart, as were several other men. Alamo said,

"A lot of prayer went up to the Lord during these two battles, General. That had a lot to do with the Mexicans paying a higher price than we did, I guarantee you."

Taylor smiled at him. "Yes, Private Kane. I'm sure you're right about that."

Even as the general was speaking, his attention was drawn to Lieutenant Grant, who was walking toward him swiftly, carrying a small leather case. A Mexican American sergeant named Carlos Mendez was beside him.

When Grant drew up to him, before he could speak, the general asked, "Where did you get that leather case, Lieutenant? And what's in it?"

"The answer to your first question, sir, is this. A few of us were looking over the spot where General Arista had planted himself when he and his troops moved onto the old riverbed. Some of his personal possessions were there. Apparently he was in such a hurry to get away, he left them behind. This leather case was among them. Let me show you something inside."

Taylor and the men who were close-by watched as Grant opened the leather case and took out some official-looking papers. "These are General Arista's private papers, General. They are written in Spanish, of course. Sergeant Mendez here was with us. I had him translate them into English for me."

The general shot a glance at Mendez, grinned at him, then looked back at Grant. "So what do they say?"

"Well sir, they're addressed to General Mariano Arista from Mexican government authorities in Mexico City, concerning his leading the attack on us here in this region."

Taylor nodded. "Okay."

"This first page, sir," Grant tapped the paper with a finger, "is an order to General Arista concerning *you*."

"Me?"

"Yes sir. You *personally.*"

The general blinked. "Well, tell me about it." He noticed a grim smile on Sergeant Mendez's lips.

Grant noticed the sergeant's smile also and met the General's gaze head-on. "General Arista is told here by the government authorities who signed this order, that when he and his troops meet General Zachary Taylor and his men in battle, General Taylor is to be captured and brought to Mexico City, where he will be put in prison for the rest of his life."

This brought a laugh from Taylor and all the men who were gathered around him.

When the laughter had faded, Lieutenant Grant said, "When General Arista gets back to Mexico City, he's going to face those Mexican authorities. I wish I could be a fly on the wall at that moment so I could hear what Arista is going to tell them when they ask why he didn't bring you with him, General!"

Taylor laughed again, and so did the men.

Michael Stewart was busily writing about the message of the Mexican authorities.

At that moment, the rattle of wagons was heard mingled with the sound of pounding hooves. Everyone looked in that direction and saw the wagons that were carrying the wounded men and the medics from Fort Polk.

When they drew up, the general greeted the wounded men and asked the medics if any of the wounded were in danger of losing their lives. He was pleased when he was told that all of them would recover with time.

Taylor then gave the medics the report on the thirty-three Americans who had been killed in that day's battle and the eighty-nine who had been wounded. The medics said they would make the wounded men from the earlier battle comfortable and would then get to work on the new ones.

Alamo made it a point to go to the wagon where Lance lay and greeted him warmly. Lance was just as warm to his friend who had led him to the Lord.

General Taylor spent some time with the newly wounded men, showing his concern for them and giving them the figures on the Mexican troops who were killed and wounded in today's battle.

When the afternoon had passed and the sun was setting, General Taylor called for a meeting of all his soldiers. They would gather on the same spot where all the wounded American soldiers lay so they could be a part of the meeting. Alamo Kane and his brothers stood over Lance Brooks.

When all the men were gathered together, reporter Michael Stewart looked on as General Taylor spoke of his men who were killed in the Palo Alto battle yesterday and in the battle today, saying what gallant and great men they were and how their memories would always be with him. He paid special tribute to all those who were killed by speaking of their love for their country and their willingness to die for it.

He then ran his tender gaze over the men before him, including the wounded, and said with a tightness in his voice, "I—I want to commend all of you for your gallant fighting in these two battles and for the love that *you* have displayed for your country. I am so very proud of every one of you."

"We're proud of *you* too, General!" came the voice of Lieutenant Grant from the crowd.

An instantaneous cheer for their leader rose from the soldiers.

Old Rough and Ready blushed and smiled. "I want to give every man here the proper totals of our dead and wounded in these two battles." He choked up for a moment, then told them that a total of forty-two men had been killed, and 136 had been wounded.

A hush fell over the crowd for a few seconds. Then the general said, "I want to publicly commend one of my men in a special way for an outstanding display of courage and love for a fellow soldier. I observed the act of courage and unselfishness he performed, but this soldier doesn't know I happened to see what he did."

The soldiers were looking around at each other, wondering of whom the general was speaking.

Taylor set his eyes on three men who were standing a short distance away, over the wounded Corporal Brooks. He focused particularly on one of them. "Private Alamo Kane, will you come here, please?"

Every eye was on the tall, muscular, handsome young man as he made his way to the general and stood before him.

Speaking loud enough for all to hear, General Taylor said, "Private Kane, as I said, I saw what you did. You risked your own life to rescue Corporal Brooks from being burned to death when he was wounded at Palo Alto and fell to the ground. The wind-driven grass around him was on fire, and he was unable to get up to escape it. However, *you* dashed to him, putting yourself in danger, picked him up, and carried him to safety."

The soldiers lifted a cheer for Private Alamo Kane, showing their appreciation of his courage and his willingness to risk his life to save a fellow soldier. Alex and Abel Kane were among those cheering, and tears filled their eyes.

When the cheering had died out, General Taylor surprised Alamo by commissioning him from the rank of private to the rank of first lieutenant for his brave and unselfish deed. He explained that as soon as possible, Alamo would get a new uniform with lieutenant's bars on its shoulders. He then took two shiny metal bars from his pocket and pinned them on Alamo's private's uniform. "With these bars, even on this uniform, Lieutenant Kane, you will receive due respect and will be saluted."

The soldiers cheered Alamo again, only longer this time.

The men were then dismissed. Immediately Lieutenant Alamo

Kane went to where Lance lay, knelt down, gave him a manly embrace, and stood up. Lance shed tears as a number of the soldiers cheered Alamo again. As this was happening, reporter Michael Stewart smiled at the newly commissioned officer.

# 23

The next morning, Sunday, May 10, after breakfast, Alamo Kane, his brothers, and their friends from church, along with the wounded Corporal Lance Brooks, gathered together to have a Bible-reading and prayer time. Together they praised the Lord for His protection over them in the two battles and that Lance was not killed at Palo Alto.

After Alamo had led in the Bible reading and one of their friends from church had led in prayer, Lance spoke to them about the peace he now had in his heart knowing that whenever it was his time to leave this world, he would go to heaven. The others rejoiced in his testimony and agreed that it was a wonderful thing to have Jesus in their hearts and know that heaven was their eternal home.

While this was going on, General Zachary Taylor was shaving his two-day growth of beard at the spot where he had his bedroll and personal belongings. Just as he was finishing and washing his face, he saw reporter Michael Stewart coming toward him.

Stewart rubbed his own cheeks as he drew up. "I did the same thing a few minutes ago, General. Felt good to get rid of my whiskers."

Taylor nodded and smiled.

"Sir," said the reporter, "I need a favor."

The general's brow furrowed. "What's that, Michael?"

"Could you give me the names of the forty-two men who were killed in the two battles?"

"Sure," Taylor replied, using a towel to dry his face. "Allow me a couple of minutes here, and I'll give the names to you."

As soon as his face was dry, the general dug into the leather pouch he had carried with him from Fort Polk, which held the records of all the men who were under his command. With the papers in hand, he said, "I'll read the names of the men who were killed, and you can write them down."

With pencil and paper at the ready, Michael Stewart nodded. "Yes sir. I'll need the correct spellings too, sir."

Taking it slowly, the general read off the names of the men who had been killed, spelling each one as requested to be sure the reporter got them right.

When Stewart had written the forty-second name down, he said, "I appreciate this, General. I'm going to list these names in the article I'm writing for the *Washington Post* about the two battles."

Taylor slipped the papers back into the pouch, then closed it. "Michael, I appreciate your doing this. The people out there need to know the names of the men who were killed fighting for their country."

Michael smiled. "They sure do, sir." He paused a few seconds then said, "General, is it all right with you if I stay a few more days, just in case there are any more developments linked to the two battles?"

"That's fine, Michael. I'm moving the troops back to Fort Polk today after I send Lieutenant Grant and a few other men on an errand."

Lance grinned. "Fort Polk's fine with me, sir."

"Good. Now, if you'll excuse me, I must talk to Lieutenant Grant." Stewart nodded. "Certainly, sir."

The general walked away, noting that Grant was in conversation with a group of soldiers who were standing near the spot where the wounded men had been positioned.

When Taylor drew near the group, Grant smiled at him. "Something I can do for you, General?"

"I need to talk to you," Taylor said. "I've got an errand for you."

"Of course, sir." Grant looked at the group. "See you later."

They nodded as the lieutenant walked away with the general.

When Taylor and Grant were alone, the general stopped. "I want you to take four men of your choice and ride to Washington-on-the-Brazos immediately."

"Yes sir," Grant said. "And what is this errand about?"

"When you get there, I want you to go to the telegraph office and send a telegram to President Polk in Washington, D.C. I'm sure the telegraph office is open on Sunday."

"All right, sir."

"By sending it today, the telegram will be there when the president arrives at his office tomorrow morning. I want you to inform him of the two battles we've had here with the Mexican troops under the command of General Mariano Arista. You are to further inform President Polk that even though a greater number of Mexican soldiers were killed and wounded in the battles than Americans, still 42 of our men were killed and 136 wounded. You might even give him some numbers on the Mexican casualties. Over 1,400 were killed in the two battles, and something over 300 were wounded. Explain that Arista took the remainder of his troops and fled like scared rabbits from Resaca de la Guerrero and headed south toward the Rio Grande, where they no doubt crossed the river and headed for Mexico City."

Grant nodded.

"Let me know which four men you choose."

"Yes sir. I already have them in mind. I'll take Sergeant Ed Burris, Sergeant Malcolm Henderson, Corporal Lionel Walker, and Private Billy Tomlin."

"Good men," Taylor said. "When you return, we'll all be back at Fort Polk."

"All right, sir." Grant saluted the general. "I'll send the telegram exactly as you have directed. I'll go find my men right now, and we'll ride out of here within a few minutes."

"Thank you, Lieutenant. And something else…"

"Yes sir?"

"While you're riding to Washington-on-the-Brazos, keep your eyes peeled for any stray Mexican soldiers along the way. They'd love to shoot you out of your saddles."

Grant nodded. "We'll do that, sir."

———

At seven o'clock on Monday morning, May 11, President James K. Polk was eating breakfast with his lovely wife, Sara, in their dining room at the White House.

Swallowing a mouthful of oatmeal, the president picked up his coffee cup, took a couple sips, then set the cup back in its saucer. He ran his hand over his balding head. "Old age is coming on me fast, honey."

Sara wiped her mouth with a napkin and set quizzical eyes on him. "What are you talking about?"

"Well, here I am, fifty years old, and I'm losing my hair. And what hair is left is totally white."

Sara smiled. "Don't think of it that way."

"How am I supposed to think of it?"

She crinkled her nose and smiled again. "Your receding hairline and what hair you still have, being white, only give you a distinguished look."

The president smiled back. "You are so kind, dear."

"What I just said isn't kindness." She reached for his hand. "It's *honesty.*"

James Polk chuckled hollowly, rose from his chair, and kissed his wife's cheek. "You're so sweet. And *that* isn't kindness either. It's honesty."

Sara giggled as her husband sat down again and continued eating his oatmeal. Then she asked, "Have you heard anything from General Taylor about the possible battle at the Rio Grande?"

He shook his head. "No, but I hope to hear soon." He took another sip of coffee, then returned the cup to its saucer. "I just can't believe there's going to be bloodshed at the Rio Grande."

"Why not?" she asked. "General Taylor sure seemed to think there would be."

The president sighed. "With all that President Andrew Jackson did to make relations between this country and Mexico good when he was in office and what President Martin Van Buren did to carry on in the same manner—and with what I've done along the same lines since I've been in office, certainly the Mexicans won't make war over such a minor thing as where the Texas-Mexico border should be."

Sara rubbed the back of her neck. "Well, dear, I sure hope you're right."

President Polk finished his breakfast, embraced his wife, and headed for the door that led to the hallway. As he opened the door, Sara said, "I hope your day goes well, dear."

"Thank you," he said as he stepped into the hallway. He closed the door behind him and headed for his office. A few minutes later, when the president turned the corner into the corridor that led there, he saw one of his aides standing at the office door with a yellow envelope in his hand.

Polk noted the time on the wall clock. It was ten minutes before eight. "Edgar, what are you doing here so early?"

The aide held up the yellow envelope. "I have a telegram for you that came in yesterday, Mr. President. It was on my desk when I arrived this morning. The telegrapher left a note saying it had come in at six thirty last evening. I knew you'd want to see it right away. I haven't read it, of course, but the telegrapher's note said it was sent by a Lieutenant Ulysses Grant from Washington-on-the-Brazos, Texas, as directed by General Zachary Taylor."

Polk's eyebrows arched as he reached for the envelope. "General Taylor?"

"Yes sir."

"Thanks, Edgar."

"You're welcome, sir." The aide headed back to his own office.

Polk quickly unlocked the door of the presidential offices, hurried to the inner office, closed the door, and sat down at his desk. Using a letter opener, he sliced open the envelope, took out the telegram, and started reading. He heard the door of the outer office open and close and knew that his secretary, Ralph Willis, had arrived for the workday.

By the time President Polk had finished digesting General Taylor's message, his facial features were a deep red color. He clenched his fists and bared his teeth like an angry wolf. Breathing heavily, Polk left his desk, entered the outer office, and said to his secretary, "Ralph, I want you to go to Vice President Dallas's office and tell him I need to see him immediately."

Willis rose from his desk chair. "Something wrong, Mr. President?"

"There is," Polk replied, heading back toward his office. "You'll hear about it later. Please hurry."

"Yes sir!" Willis hurried to the door.

Less than three minutes later, President Polk looked up from his desk as Vice President George Dallas entered, noting the harried look on the president's face.

Moving swiftly to the desk, Dallas asked, "What's wrong?"

Polk picked up the telegram and handed it to his vice president. "This was sent by one of General Zachary Taylor's lieutenants from Washington-on-the-Brazos yesterday. Read it."

As the vice president read the telegram, James Polk saw that its message was having the same effect on George Dallas as it had had on him. Dallas's face was beet red as he said, "This is awful! Those lowdown Mexicans!"

Polk wiped a palm over his eyes. "Well, at least they paid a heavy price for their attack."

Dallas nodded. "I should say so. Over 1,400 killed, compared to our 42. And over 300 wounded compared to our 136."

The president shook his head. "I'm still grieved that *any* of our men were killed and wounded."

A grimness distorted the vice president's face. "Yes sir. I am too."

Polk shook his head, took a deep breath, and let it out slowly.

"Well, so much for President Jackson's dream, President Van Buren's dream, and *my* dream that kindness shown to Mexico would keep us from war with that country!"

George Dallas moved around to the rear of the president's desk and laid a hand on his shoulder. "I had such high hopes, sir."

James Polk drew another deep breath and turned to look up at his vice president. "George, it seems that our country is caught in a web of destiny. No matter what we do to try to avoid war with Mexico, they still attack our troops."

Dallas rubbed his jaw thoughtfully, nodded, and echoed the words. "*Web of destiny.* Yes, Mr. President, that is exactly what it is. A web of destiny. We're caught in a seemingly unbreakable steel-like web with that country. There is nothing we can do with those Mexicans but fight them."

The president nodded as his vice president circled back to the front of the desk again. "That's exactly right, George. I thought when Santa Anna was deposed and exiled, things between us and Mexico would smooth out. But not so. The only way we can break this web of destiny and stop their bloody aggressiveness against us is to declare war on them and bring them to their knees."

Dallas swallowed hard. "You're right, Mr. President. We have no other choice."

Polk took another deep breath and let it out slowly as before. "I'm calling for an emergency meeting of Congress. We're going to declare war on Mexico!"

⌒

Having stayed the night at the army facility in Washington-on-the-Brazos, Lieutenant Grant and his four companions, Sergeant Burris, Sergeant Henderson, Corporal Walker, and Private Tomlin, were waiting Monday morning at the telegraph office for a return wire from President Polk. The five soldiers were seated near the desk where the telegraph key was operated by a friendly Texan named Kurt Ziglar. The amiable telegraph operator was listening to the soldiers as they talked about the battles at Palo Alto and Resaca de la Guerrero, when suddenly the telegraph device began clicking.

Ziglar picked up a pencil and quickly wrote down the message on a pad of paper. When the clicker stopped, it took him another ten seconds to finish writing it. He then looked at Grant. "Here's the message from President Polk you've been waiting for, Lieutenant!"

Ulysses Grant quickly read the telegram to his four companions.

A few minutes later, the five of them were galloping their horses northward as fast as they could go. Grant, Burris, Henderson, Walker, and Tomlin knew that the message in the telegram from the president was one that General Taylor would need to know about in a hurry.

It was late afternoon when they arrived at Fort Polk. Soldiers watched intently as they galloped through the south gate and made their way to General Taylor's small office. They dismounted, with soldiers hurrying in their direction. At the same moment, a major and a captain came out of the general's office.

Grant stepped up to them. "Is the general in his office?"

"Yes, he is," replied the major. "And he's been expecting you to show up any minute, Lieutenant. I'm glad you're back."

Grant looked at his four companions. "You explain about the telegram to them. I know as soon as the general reads it, he'll want every man in the fort to hear the contents. Let's gather where the wounded men are so they can hear it too."

"We'll do it, sir," said Sergeant Burris. "You go on in."

Grant quickly went to the office door and knocked on it, calling out, "General Taylor, it's Ulysses Grant!"

"Come in, Lieutenant!" came the loud reply.

As Grant was entering the general's office, the four men who had been to Washington-on-the-Brazos with him explained to the major and the captain about the telegram, and immediately, men who were gathering around were assigned to dash all over the fort and tell the rest of the troops to gather near the wounded so they could hear the president's message also.

Less than fifteen minutes after Ulysses Grant had entered the general's office, the two of them came out. General Taylor had the telegram in his hand.

They hurried to the place where the wounded men were lying on the ground and a few sitting up. Most of the fort's troops were there by then, but it took a few more minutes for all of the soldiers to gather before the general. When all were there, General Taylor showed them the telegram that Lieutenant Grant had carried from Washington-on-the-Brazos, explaining that it was addressed to him, as leader of the men at Fort Polk, from President James K. Polk.

The general then told them President Polk said that because of the Mexican attack at Palo Alto and the resultant battle at Resaca de la Guerrero, he was going to lead Congress to declare war on Mexico.

These words stirred the soldiers, and they sent up a cheer, waving their arms.

General Taylor then told his men that President Polk said for all of them to stay at Fort Polk until he sent orders for them to go elsewhere.

Alamo Kane and his brothers were standing over Corporal Brooks. The corporal looked up at the Kane brothers as Alamo said, "I wish we could go home to our families, but it can't happen right now."

"Right," said Alex. "Not at this point."

Abel nodded. "That's right."

Lance Brooks said, "I'd like to go home and tell my family about my salvation and try to lead them to the Lord, but it'll have to wait for a while."

"I'm afraid so, Lance," said Alamo. "But someday."

Lance smiled. "Yes! Someday!"

At that time, the Kane brothers observed as Michael Stewart told General Taylor he would now head back to Washington-on-the-Brazos, adding that he would not mind riding a good part of the night to get there. The general shook hands with Stewart, thanking him for getting the story of the two battles to his readers.

As Stewart walked toward his horse, the Kane brothers headed toward him. "Michael!" Alamo called out. "We'd like a minute with you before you go!"

The Kanes had their few minutes with the reporter; then he mounted his horse and rode away. They knew he was eager to get back to the chief editor of the *Washington Post* and give him the news about the battles and President Polk's determination to declare war against Mexico.

## 24

F riday, May 15, 1846, was a beautiful spring day in southeast Texas. At midmorning on the Diamond K Ranch, Julia Kane and her three boys came out of the big ranch house onto the front porch. Adam was carrying his baby sister's pallet of quilts. Julia pointed to the spot where she wanted the pallet, and Adam set it down there. Little Amber was in her mother's arms and was already showing signs of being drowsy.

Julia placed her baby on the pallet and sat down in the chair next to it.

Young Abram noted two women coming toward the big ranch house. "Here come Aunt Libby and Aunt Vivian, Mama!"

"Yeah, Mama!" called out little brother Andy. "Here they come!"

Since their husbands had been away, Libby and Vivian Kane had been spending several hours a day with Julia at the ranch house. It was now coffee time, and Libby and Vivian were arriving at the very moment Julia had invited them to come.

The three boys adored their aunts and ran to them, giving them hugs.

Julia rose to her feet as her sisters-in-law drew up to the porch. "Daisy will be here with the coffee shortly." She smiled. "Come, sit down."

Libby and Vivian smiled back and climbed the porch steps. Both noticed little Amber asleep on the pallet and commented on how cute she was. Then as the three women eased onto the porch chairs, the boys began their usual battle for the day. They were running around in front of the ranch house, carrying broken tree limbs they used as rifles and pretending to shoot imaginary Mexicans.

Their loud voices and the sounds they made with their mouths to simulate gunshots created quite a din amid the otherwise peaceful morning.

As the oldest, Adam was always the leader of his "band of soldiers," and the two little ones followed on his heels, yelling as loudly as they could.

"Yea!" shouted Abram. "I just got another one!"

Julia called out, "Boys! Quiet down, please."

"But, Mama," Adam said. "War is noisy!"

"I know that, son," Julia replied, "but maybe you could take your war somewhere else in the yard. Your aunts and I can't even talk with you making so much racket, and Amber is trying to have her nap."

"Okay, Mama," said Adam. "We'll go around to the side of the house."

Julia smiled at him. "That would be nice."

Quickly, Adam led his little brothers in that direction, and soon the noisy battle resumed.

Julia then looked down at Amber on her pallet. The "war" hadn't bothered her at all. Julia ran her hand gently over the baby's soft head just as Daisy Haycock came out the front door carrying a tray with cups, saucers, a steaming coffeepot, and a plate of cinnamon rolls. The delicious aroma of the cinnamon rolls instantly filled the warm spring air as she set the tray down on a small table.

Julia smiled at her faithful friend and cook. "Daisy, those rolls sure do smell good! I can hardly wait to bite into one of them."

"I hope you all enjoy them, Miss Julia." Daisy smiled in return. With that she turned and went back into the house.

The three women enjoyed the coffee and rolls, and as usual, their husbands being away in the army to fight Mexicans was the topic of conversation.

At one point in the conversation, Julia noticed that the "war" that had been going on at the side of the house had grown silent. Rising from her chair, she walked to the end of the porch on that side and put her hands on the railing.

"The battle over?" Vivian chuckled, looking at her.

Julia turned around and headed back toward her sisters-in-law. "Just a short break. Bless her heart, Daisy just took them some milk and cinnamon rolls. Right now their wooden guns are lying on the ground while they feast on the treats."

Libby giggled. "Well, even soldiers have to eat!"

A moment later, Grandpa Abram came out of the house onto the front porch. "I had my cinnamon rolls and coffee in my room," he told the women. As Abram sat down on his favorite porch chair, he looked around. "The boys are unusually quiet."

"Oh, that's just a lull between battles," Julia said. "As soon as their cinnamon rolls are gone, they'll be back at it again."

Abram chuckled. "Well, at least it's quiet for the moment."

"Yes, indeed." A grin broke over Julia's face. "As Libby said just a moment ago, even soldiers have to eat."

The boys' grandfather laughed. "Amen to that!"

At that moment, Diamond K foreman, Cort Whitney, was seen coming toward the porch from the corral and barn area.

Abram squinted. "Looks like he's got a newspaper in his hand."

The women focused on the foreman as he drew up, carrying the folded newspaper, and climbed the porch steps. "Got some news for you, folks," Cort said.

Abram frowned. "About the Mexican problem?"

Cort nodded. "Uh-huh. This is today's edition of the *Post*. Couple of the ranch hands went to town early this morning to buy supplies, and they brought back several copies of the paper to pass out."

Cort opened the newspaper and flashed the front page at them. The large headline stated that President Polk and Congress had officially declared war on Mexico yesterday, May 14.

The women gasped, and Abram shook his head sadly.

"I'll tell you what the article here on the front page says," Cort said. "And if you want to read it for yourselves later, you can."

Julia, Libby, Vivian, and Grandpa Abram listened intently as Cort told them what was in the article. Written by well-known *Washington Post* reporter Michael Stewart—who had been present when the two battles took place between American and Mexican forces near the Rio Grande—the story told of the battles of Palo Alto and Resaca de la Guerrero, with General Taylor leading the American forces and General Mariano Arista leading the Mexican forces. Stewart's article contained the numbers of American soldiers killed and wounded in the battles, as well as those Mexicans who had been killed and wounded.

Details were given about the president and Congress declaring war on May 14, which had been telegraphed to Stewart by the president himself. Before closing off the article, Stewart had listed the names of the forty-two American soldiers who had been killed. At that point, Cort told them that the names of Alamo, Alex, and Abel Kane were not in the list.

There were sighs of relief, and all four wiped tears.

Julia's voice cracked as she said, "I'm sorry for those forty-two American men who were killed, but I'm so thankful that Alamo, Alex, and Abel aren't on the list."

Abram wiped tears from his eyes. "But they might be among the hundred thirty-six who were wounded. I wish we could know."

Julia, Libby, and Vivian agreed.

Even as they talked, they saw a rider coming from the road, who stopped to speak to a small group of the ranch hands. They pointed him toward the big ranch house, and he rode that way.

"I wonder who this is," Cort said.

"We're about to find out," Abram said.

The rider drew up. "Good morning, folks. I was just told that you ladies are the wives of Alamo, Alex, and Abel Kane."

Abram rose to his feet. "They are, sir. I'm their father, and this gentleman is the ranch foreman, Cort Whitney. And who might you be?"

"I'm Michael Stewart, reporter for the *Washington Post.*"

Surprise showed on every face, and Cort lifted up the newspaper in his hand. "I have today's edition with your article on the front page, Mr. Stewart. We were just discussing it. Please join us here on the porch."

As Stewart was getting off his horse, Julia's three sons came running over, their eyes on the stranger.

"Come up here, boys," Julia said. "This gentleman is a reporter for the newspaper we always read. He was recently on the battlefield where your papa and uncles have fought the Mexicans. We don't know why yet, but he has come here to see us."

The boys looked at the reporter with wide eyes, then bounded up the steps, and Michael Stewart followed them.

Abram quickly pointed out which wife belonged to which husband and explained that the boys were the sons of Alamo and Julia.

Stewart nodded and set his eyes on Julia. "I met your husband, ma'am, on March 6, 1836, when he was riding toward the Alamo, unaware that the big battle had taken place early that very morning."

"Oh yes!" Julia said. "I remember now. He did tell me your name, saying he had met you where some of the San Antonio residents were camping outside of town."

The rest of the adults were now nodding.

Cort then said, "Mr. Stewart, these ladies and Mr. Abram Kane and I were just discussing with relief the fact that Alamo, Alex, and Abel were not listed among the forty-two American soldiers who were killed in those two battles."

Michael smiled. "Let me tell you why I have come here. Just before I left Fort Polk to return to Washington-on-the-Brazos a few days ago, Alamo, Alex, and Abel approached me and asked if I would come to the ranch as soon as possible and let their wives and their father know that none of them had even been wounded."

"Oh, praise the Lord!" Vivian shouted. Tears of relief flowed down all three women's cheeks, as well as down both Abram's and Cort's.

Adam went to his mother and hugged her as she wept. "Oh, Mama! Papa's all right!"

By that time, Abram and Andy were catching on to what the stranger had said and also dashed to their mother with open arms. Julia held all three of her boys close and wept, praising the Lord.

Grandpa Abram said, "Mr. Stewart, is there any news about how and when President Polk is going to actually have the army wage war on Mexico?"

Stewart shook his head. "No sir. I figure it will come very soon though. We'll just have to wait and see."

Abram nodded silently.

Michael Stewart then looked at Julia and, in front of the others, told her of Alamo's brave deed in the Palo Alto battle when he risked his life to save one of his wounded fellow soldiers from burning to death in a blazing field of grass.

Smiles crossed all five adult faces and the three boys' faces as well. Then Stewart said, "Now let me tell you what General Taylor did because of Alamo's brave deed."

Everyone stared at the reporter with wide eyes, waiting to hear this news.

Stewart smiled broadly. "General Taylor promoted Alamo from private all the way to first lieutenant!"

Julia's tear-filled eyes sparkled. "My darling husband just never ceases to amaze me. He is such a wonderful man! I'll be glad when this war is over and he can come home to his wife and children!"

# FAITH, LOVE, COURAGE AND STRENGTH...

In Texas, 1835, the Kane Family will need them all to follow God's will.

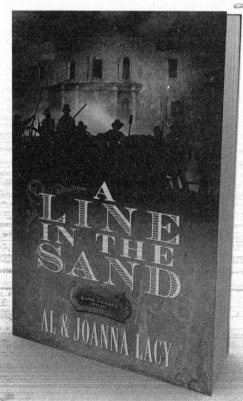

## The Kane Legacy, book one

In 1835, Alan Kane and his family come to the Circle C Ranch in Texas, little dreaming what the future holds in both blessing and danger. Beautiful Julia Miller has captured Alan's heart, but he hardly dares to hope for her hand. Then Colonel Travis calls for the men of Texas to rally against Mexico's General Santa Anna. What will the Kane family sacrifice to live freely?